RAW DEAL

DARK URBAN RISING BOOK 3

S M HENLEY

RAW DEAL

Good guys don't make deals with demons. Do they?

The world is approaching the Tipping Point—when the rising demons will outnumber humankind. Assassin for hire, Soren Huxford, needs to pick a side. It should be easy; he's human after all and so is Tazia, the girl he loves and his first priority. But when the only demon he respects calls in a favour, Hux faces an impossible choice: hold true to humanity or prove his loyalty by throwing-down alongside the demons.

Set against a backdrop of imminent disaster, where fighting the demons from his past are as real as those leaping from each dark corner, Soren needs to get a grip or he may become a monster too. And what about the girl? If he picks the wrong side, will he lose her forever?

Still with its gritty humour intact, *Raw Deal* is the darkest of the *Dark Urban Rising* trilogy. Though Hux leads the charge, this final book brings him back together with Tazia and Billy to face the day of reckoning. *Raw Deal* is a supernatural thriller set on the streets of modern-day Las Vegas, Detroit, and Turin. Blood is guaranteed.

To mum. Finally. (Ignore the cursing).

1

—————————————————————

TAKING CARE OF BUSINESS

THE DOG YAPPED up a storm trying to gain the attention of passing strangers. Through the rifle sights, Soren tracked the source. A handbag dog. A tiny white fur ball with a pink tongue and scrappy hair tied up over its paper-thin skull with a bow. Trapped in the car, it raced between the seats and desperately licked at the little fresh air that floated through the sliver of an open window. It would die in this heat.

Soren growled lightly in the back of his throat and caressed the trigger of his gun; he would do it a favour—

A movement in the car parked in front yanked him back. His target.

Although under cover, the sun was just at the right angle to bounce off the guy's bald head as he leaned forward and peered into the side mirror to check his teeth. He'd been eating a burrito packed with sloppy meat, chopped lettuce, and a nice thick layer of bright orange cheese. Soren's mouth watered for the food; his usual lean breakfast had been hours ago.

Balancing Oakleys above his eyebrows, the target continued to pick at his teeth without the distraction of a dark tint. Soren clocked the teeth: ebony black and sharpened to points, studded with little jagged diamond shards that flashed in the burning sun. A Bone Cruncher. A rich one—no one could afford that tooth job without great dental.

Despite the easy shot, he waited. If he fired now, Bald Guy would end up slumped out the window, blood spraying the perfectly white paintwork of his Dodge truck. Too messy. He wanted a clean job. Besides, it was a rental. Why should a low-paid high school kid have to clean up blood and brains? Not fair. He'd wait longer.

Still motionless, lying flat on his stomach, Soren eased out a breath. It tickled the feather, which had landed on his stretched out forearm thirty minutes ago, making it shimmy a fraction then settle again. It was down, a fluff feather used to keep the bird warm, not to help it fly. The magpie, the most probable owner, watched him from the stainless steel railing of the balcony with a beady look Soren sporadically returned. It eyed his wristwatch. Was it figuring out the time, or just attracted by the slight reflection on the black surface? Most probably the former. These days, birds weren't stupid.

He'd picked the apartment block on purpose. Only two stories high, but right in the centre of town, it was unusual for Las Vegas. It sheltered behind one of the huge, flashy hotel complexes right on the Strip. A holiday let. Cheap because of the mall car park he stared into. No view of a swimming pool or fountains moving in time to the *Star Wars* theme tune, just concrete, and row upon row of bland rental vehicles with the occasional celebrity dick-mobile thrown in for good measure. Even the rich and famous need mall stuff. Or else wanted their egos stroked for being seen out among Regular Joes.

Fame was pointless. Soren couldn't have told Miley Cyrus from Kim Kardashian. They were just faces, and fame just noise.

Bald Guy settled back in his seat, slurping a Coke directly

from the can—his fourth that day. The opportunity for the shot had passed.

Soren blinked and flexed his fingers. He'd wait all day if he had to.

Four jobs deep this month, Vegas crawled with demons. Some had always been here; others escaped the Risings elsewhere. It was a place where they could make some fast cash. Gambling, sex shops, gun sales. Everything in plain sight, the way the city had always done it. No change on the surface, but he knew better. He'd seen Detroit, the first city to fall. Five long, painful years from the first demon to the destruction of the last human. Stealthy. The underground taking control. And now, places were falling every day. The biggest surprise was Texas just last week; it had been all over the demon network. The decision-makers just handed over the keys. Done and dusted in a month.

Soren grunted. The whole damn state. How the hell does that happen? Resistance was strong in the South.

As though in response, the magpie hopped along the railing toward him, its head cocked, eyes staring. When its persistence forced brief eye-contact, it shook its wings to release a second feather. This one was for flight, a beautiful midnight blue. It floated down past the sights of the rifle. Still no wind to factor—

Movement pulled him back. Bald Guy was on his phone, getting pretty animated, too. Lots of hand-waving and shoulder-shrugs. His car was side-on to Soren's view, right by the walkway. People were passing by the demon all the time. Children dragged by the hand behind a parent or pushed in front in a buggy, everyone laden with bags and balloons, even now. Holiday towns! Another reason not to shoot yet; he didn't want to be responsible for some poor kid's PTSD.

The walkway emptied at the same time as Bald Guy put down his phone and stared out of the side window. *Perfect.*

Soren got ready. His breath continued to flow gently. No drama. This job had been textbook: a three-day stakeout, and now, the shot. Job done. Money in hand.

Just taking care of business like always.

Soren needed the work. The money was nice, but the distraction was better. Kept his mind off her. Mostly.

There was never any likelihood Anastasia would fall into his arms, not after Boston. But he'd thought she might at least throw him a small bone. Some kind word, or a promise to talk in the future. Just talk. Christ, was that too much to ask? But turning human hadn't sat well with her. She was having problems adjusting. And that vicious tongue!

Soren growled again, deeper this time. Long and low. That special sound he kept just for her. After Boston, she hadn't even given him a chance. But then, did he deserve one?

He'd tried to explain. The words had come out wrong, too clinical, he knew, but what else could he say? *We used you. Trapped you.* His apology—*so fucking sorry*—had met a wall of silence. Nothing. He could still see her face, the flicker of disgust in her eyes before they went blank.

He'd offered to go wherever she wanted. He would just run alongside, keeping her safe. No strings. But she wouldn't even give him that. He'd known she wouldn't let him; she could take care of herself. Still, her last words before she left to go walkabout were unnecessary: *I'll cut your fucking heart out if you follow me.*

Soren breathed out slightly more heavily, with a conscious effort this time.

Box it up, soldier!

Still, he struggled. She stalked his thoughts, sometimes dancing on the periphery, smiling and teasing him. At other times, she came clearly into view, glaring, and flipping that damn knife from hand to hand.

He didn't know this new Anastasia. Human now, was she

as capable a killer as the demon she'd once been? She hadn't even wanted Billy with her. That *was* a little satisfying, the fact she seemed to blame Billy as much as him, but only a little. Billy was the good guy in all this. He was flying with the angels, making plans to save the world, and would probably lead the charge against the demons when the time was right.

He'd told Soren to relax: *Give her a break, bruv. Let her twist her knickers for a while.*

Well, she'd been twisting them for six weeks, and the waiting was killing him.

Soren did the last checks and prepared to squeeze the trigger.

For now, he worked. He took the contracts and killed the targets in this sweatbox of a city that both intrigued and repelled him. It was as good a place as any to wait for Heaven to make its plans, and to tell him what his role would be in the coming battle.

And for his own avenging angel to return.

The musical fountain surged to its crescendo. He braced and fired.

The loud crack shocked the magpie up into the air, but it soon settled again a couple of feet away. They don't give up ground that easily, little bastards. In the parking garage, no one seemed to notice.

Bald Guy's head snapped back against the neck rest, bouncing once. His body went limp in the seat. His head tilted to the side. He blinked once, then his eyes stuck wide and staring. A dark blue trickle of blood flowed from the wound between his eyes and followed gravity over the bridge of his nose and across the top of his cheek. One drop fell from him into the darkness of the car and then stopped. Coagulation was quick for this sort of demon.

Soren nodded, clean enough.

A pathetic whimper drifted to the balcony. The dog. A

desperate plea for help. Still lying in the same position, Soren shot again, this time at the SUV where the dog sheltered. The front side window exploded.

Without checking the result, he broke up the rifle and put the pieces back into its padded carrier. He took a few photographs through the spotting-scope then packed that away too. As he stood up, he replaced his sunglasses and briefly bared his teeth at the magpie, who squawked in mild alarm, then turned its back.

Soren casually walked through the living room, leaving the balcony doors wide open. Behind him, the dog yapped loudly as it breathed cooler air at last. He smiled. No doubt it would soon be in the arms of a puppy-loving Good Samaritan.

As he left the apartment, he gave a satisfied grunt: it was time to collect his payment.

2

—————————————

FOUR-INCH HEELS

THE HOTEL HALLWAY stretched out for miles. Disgusting abstract artwork bisected the cream walls at regular intervals. Matching doors identified room numbers in cheap gold, and acres of multicoloured carpeting sported a repetitive cross-hatched design. Soren slid his sunglasses back on. Never look at *that* with a hangover.

He searched for the lift to take him up to the penthouse, but it was an upmarket place, the kind to hide it behind a phony double door—utility replaced by aesthetics. A familiar knot of tension twisted in his stomach. Aesthetics had its place, in Georgian townhouses back in London for instance, or in the great churches of Paris and Rome, but not here. This place was a testament to the fake lunacy of Vegas architecture. It was designed to deceive, to disguise, to—

Dammit!

He stomped up and down the hallway for a second time, his temper rising as high as the blast furnace outside. For once, it wasn't the Risings causing the heat; it was simply the Nevada sun doing its best to beat all patience and reason out of the occupants of this overheated city.

The lift pinged, and he chased down the sound to the far right of the corridor. The doors didn't open, but a tiny downward-pointing arrow had lit up green when it floated past the floor and onward to the lobby.

At least he knew where the damn thing was now.

His stomach relaxed a little, but he still smacked roughly at the call button with the side of his fist. The plaster around the button crumbled slightly, leaving white powder on his hand that he rubbed away with the other—

Destroy! That was it. Vegas architecture was designed to destroy all those who entered inside. To chip away at them until only dust was left.

He waited, breathing slowly, and trying not to stare at the gold painted frames around the horrendous artwork.

Cold breezes from the air conditioning blew across the top of his head, ruffling his hair until he pushed it firmly back behind his ears. Just washed, like now, it was too soft to stay put for long. He sighed. Maybe he should get a buzz cut, too. Billy would crack up. Soren smiled. No more jokes about him looking like Princess Elsa. The air flowed down into the open neck of his shirt and jacket. A welcome sensation. It was difficult to pull off a suit in the heat, and the skin of his neck and cheeks buzzed too warm. Important for the client, though.

Another ping, and the lift finally opened its doors with a welcoming *whoosh!*

Inside stood a woman. She wore a low-cut black evening dress, even though it was just after lunchtime, dagger-thin high heels that could skewer an eyeball, and black lace elbow-length gloves. He stared at her for a beat, taking in the ensemble, then nodded, and took his place beside her, turning to face the doors.

She smiled and asked with the raise of one impeccable eyebrow, "Going up?"

"Yes, the penthouse, thank you."

She nodded, and re-pressed the penthouse button although it was already lit, then cast the back of her hand under the sheet of jet black hair to lift it from her neck for a moment, as though his entrance had disturbed a few of the straight shiny strands. It hadn't. The perfect central parting stood out white against the smooth ebony locks. Once her hair was tamed to her satisfaction, she stood motionless once more, staring forward at the doors, barely breathing.

Her movement had disrupted the flow of air in the small space, and he caught the smell of her perfume—fresh spring rain on a warm summer's day. Within seconds it transformed to the tang of ripe peaches just picked from the tree, juicy and soft. All of his favourite scents. Eyes forward, the hairs on his arms rose.

The energy in the lift oscillated, a pressure change that prickled his skin. He instinctively widened his stance, planting his feet. Just the ascent. The speed... It had to be.

Soren risked another side glance at her. That hair was incredible: thick and shiny, with just a hint of midnight blue. The magpie he'd seen earlier flashed again into his mind. No. That did her a disservice. Her hair reached to the middle of her back in one long, heavy curtain. Sweltering, but she didn't look hot. Not in that sense anyway. *Christ, am I turning into Billy?* He could practically hear the man's lecherous chuckle.

They travelled together up the remaining forty floors while Dolly Parton crooned about the femme fatale "Jolene" via the piped background music. It was one his mother used to sing to him when he was a young child. He frowned. Thinking about it now, it seemed an odd choice.

The woman moved again, playing with the long twist of cream-coloured pearls around her neck, lifting each one to her lips and sucking on it slightly. As the seal between each solid bead and her wet lips broke, there was a tiny smacking sound, and she moved onto the next like she was performing some fetishistic rosary. Before long, Soren was counting both the regularity of the smacks with the beats of the song.

He dwarfed her, filling almost half the lift space, while her slight frame only reached his chin, even with the four-inch heels. Curious, he tried to catch a good view of her face, but couldn't get a proper look. So, instead, he peered at her reflection in the dull mirroring of the lift's interior. The metal appeared to undulate under his gaze, blurring her features into just a smear of red, no, pink, no… red lips.

With a slight lurch, the lift stopped, and the doors opened. He wrenched his attention away from his companion and stared directly into the penthouse suite at the very top of the hotel.

The woman quickly stepped out. She turned slightly to look at him over her shoulder as she went. "Nice to meet you, Soren Huxford." The accent was English with a twang of something else. French?

With a flash of azure eyes, she was gone, and for a moment, he felt… lost.

The sound of the gun cocked level with his head broke the daze.

HOT CHOCOLATE AND TEDDY BEARS

SOREN LOOKED from the huge shiny revolver to the face of the man who pointed it at him. Billy would say the magnum was overcompensating for something. He wore dark Ray-Bans and an evening jacket that strained across mountainous shoulders. His finger fondled the trigger in a way that promised a quick climax if he had cause.

Stifling a sigh, Soren rubbed the blond stubble on his cheek with the flat of his fingers. They itched to grab the weapon and smash the guy's face with it. *Restraint, Huxford.* This job was easy, and a chance for more of the same. He forced his hand down. "Here for Dr. Drayden."

The man-mountain stepped back, dropped the revolver to chest height, and jerked the long barrel toward the left side of the corridor. Soren strode out of the lift and lifted his jacket to have his own, more modest, gun checked—he knew the drill. But the bodyguard made no move to remove the weapon. He just gave a smirk that said: "Mine's bigger than yours."

Motioning with the gun toward the corridor again, he moved further to one side to allow Soren to pass.

The hallway opened out into a large living space which wouldn't have looked out of place in a Warhol home movie: huge picture windows faced the Vegas city scape with low leather sofas, white shag-pile rugs, and huge swirls of purple paint on the wall.

He stopped dead. That shade of violet... the pattern... the lounge wall of Anastasia's apartment in Turin. That same image of distorted foliage like some psychedelic album cover from the seventies. She'd loved it. He'd spent two years wanting to paint it over. Compared to this huge scale monstrosity, he'd been making a fuss about nothing.

The woman from the elevator sat on one of the sofas, her legs curled to one side with sharp heels dangerously dragging on the black leather, and the split in her long skirt revealing shapely legs. She seemed taller somehow and now wore dark shades with little gold wing tips at the corners, viciously sharp.

Beside her was a small man, maybe five-foot-four, an Italian with tanned skin, slick steel-grey hair, and a black designer suit. The jacket hung open over a white dress shirt, its folded collar sitting high and snug against his neck. Jewellery dripped from his wrists to his throat—more mob boss than rap star.

His right hand was nestled between the woman's thighs, just above her knees, his thumb rubbing back and forth over the same spot, leaving a little trail of white in the olive skin. They both looked at Soren and smiled.

All at once, Drayden became animated. Still smiling, he stood, raised his hands wide in a welcoming gesture, and then clapped them sharply together. He left them there in the prayer position before bowing slightly. "Mr. Huxford—you good man —thank you for coming! Thank you. Thank you." He may have looked Italian, but his accent drilled New York, an odd match with the over-effusive greeting.

"You're welcome." Soren kept one eye on the man-mountain, who was still fingering his gun with a little too much affection.

"The job went well?"

"You got the photographs I—"

"Yes, beautiful!" Drayden's grin was wide.

"Then, sir, it went well." Soren still hadn't taken a step into the room.

"Come sit with us for a moment, Mr. Huxford, while Deke prepares your payment." He glanced at his bodyguard, who bowed his head, though his lips pursed disapprovingly, then walked along the corridor and out of sight.

"You met Ms. Skye, I understand?" Drayden continued, and glanced at the woman on the sofa, looking for her confirmation, not his.

She nodded at him, uncurled her legs and slid her body to one side, then patted the seat beside her. "Come sit, Soren." Strangely, her voice now had an Eastern European edge.

He glanced at Drayden. Should he? She didn't look like his wife, but he'd crossed lines before. It ended badly.

Drayden stepped to one side and gesticulated for him to sit exactly where she had motioned.

Soren moved to the spot and sat, instantly hating the lowness of the sofa, which left him with his knees higher than the seat. Trying to gain space, he pushed his butt back, but there was still no room for his long legs to stretch as a coffee table blocked them.

The woman curled her legs up again, momentarily rubbing her shoulder against his arm. Static shot up and down his limb, buzzing long after she'd moved away. Now her scent was sweet hot chocolate, and his mind flashed to a teddy bear he'd been given when he was five.

He jerked slightly at the oddly inappropriate image and

turned to look at her. Was that her? Her covered eyes gazed directly into his.

"Are you taller now?" he asked her.

"Possibly." The word pushed from her mouth, her red painted lips holding onto the pucker of the "p" a little longer than was natural.

Soren stared at them, feeling a very real urge to lean forward and—

"Here's your drink, Mr. Huxford." Drayden sat down on his other side, putting a glass tumbler into his hand.

"Did I ask for one?"

"Yes, whiskey. Just now." Ms. Skye replied.

Soren flicked his eyes from one to the other. He had no recollection of having asked for a drink. Bookended by the couple, with the coffee table in front of him, he had nowhere to go. He took a sip from the whiskey, and sucked a half-melted ice cube into his mouth, sticking it against a delicate side tooth. The freeze knifed into his jaw for a split second before fading. He winced, but felt more grounded.

"Better?" Ms. Skye asked.

"Yes." This time he did not look at her. But he could still sense her eyes, lips, hair—dammit, all of her. He felt unsteady.

The sound of heavy footsteps announced the return of Deke, who placed an open holdall on the coffee table in front of Soren. He seemed to have left his attitude, as well as the large gun, in the bedroom and grimaced a smile. "Your payment, sir."

"Count it, Mr. Huxford. It's all there, but I'd rather you were sure." Drayden shrugged, and circled his own whiskey, clinking the remaining ice against the edges of the glass. "This little demon issue we all have to suffer right now at least keeps us honest. Prevents the banks from taking their cuts on online transactions."

Leaning forward, Soren cast a practiced eye over the

mound of cash in the bag. He took in the denomination and the number of bundles before nodding. "It's all here."

"Good." Drayden stood. "I believe our business is done, for now, Mr. Huxford, but I would like the option to call upon you again, if I may?"

"Of course."

"Good. Yes, very good." Drayden offered his hand.

Soren stood to shake it, towering over the small man.

"Sowilo, would you please see Mr. Huxford out?"

Without demur, the woman uncurled, stood and swept her way around the far side of the coffee table and over to the hallway. "This way please, Soren."

Is her hair turning red? Soren knocked back the last of the whiskey and replaced the tumbler on the table. He picked up the holdall and walked toward her. Drayden had already disappeared down the corridor, and Deke was nowhere in sight.

They stood beside the elevator, her hand hovering over the call button, but she didn't press it. Instead, she raked a red nail down his arm gently, puckering the fine grey fabric of his suit. "The demons aren't done with you yet, Soren. And yet you must still trust them. Well, one anyway."

"What?" He twisted his head to look at her.

"Things aren't always what they seem," she whispered, then shrugged. "But then you know that. Just remember, it is the beginning, not the end." She gazed past him, staring into a middle distance, before finishing her commentary with, "Compassion is the key to humanity. Let her see it."

As soon as she'd said the last word, she pressed the button, and the lift opened. He stepped inside, but the doors didn't close after him; she had shifted her feet to straddle the door and block them. She reached into the bodice of her dress for a business card and offered it to him.

Soren took it automatically, the cardboard warm in his

fingers. She stepped away without a backward glance as the doors closed.

Dragging his eyes to the card, he read: Sowilo Skye—Escort Of Extraordinary Talent. Call 0666 From Anywhere.

4

DEAD MEN DON'T SPEAK

SOREN STOOD in the hallway beside his hotel room door. It shifted a creaky inch to and fro in the breeze from the window. He'd left neither the door nor the window open. He peered through the crack between the hinges. Nothing. But the hair on the back of his neck prickled. Someone was inside.

He reviewed possible intruders. Apart from Drayden's man and Sowilo Skye, no one knew he was in Vegas. He hadn't even told Billy where he was going, though, no doubt with his angelic superpowers, as he loved to call them, he could find him easily enough. But Billy wouldn't hide out in his room; he'd be more likely to slap a kiss on his lips.

Maybe someone had got wind of the job he'd just completed and thought he'd be returning with a pile of cash. If that was the case, they'd be disappointed; it was already safely stashed elsewhere.

He pushed the door with his foot and waited. If whoever was inside was innocently changing his sheets, cleaning his bathroom, or even casually rooting in his underwear drawer, they'd soon make themselves known.

When the voice came, Soren wasn't prepared.

"Hux? Come in now, won't yer. You can't be standing there all day, man."

Soren heard the softness of the accent and the familiar turn of phrase. His heart seized in his chest. A violent lurch. No, it couldn't be. Dead men don't speak.

Trembling, Soren's weapon lowered to his side. If this was a trap, or some sort of magickal trickery by the Advocate, he didn't care; he'd happily die at the hands of this man.

Stepping inside, and around the door, he faced the easy chair that stood in the opposite corner to the window. It was darkest there. What he took to be a shadow shifted just as lightning shot through the sky outside and lit up the room, the drapes billowing in the accompanying gust of wind.

Briefly illuminated, Conn O'Cuinn took a step forward, then faded again into shadow. *Don't be my imagination. Please.* Soren's hand slapped blindly at the wall, found the switch, and flicked on the weak overhead light.

The Irish demon looked the same: tall and broad, with a messy crew cut doing its best to control the thick brown hair, and eyes oscillating between aquamarine and light blue. His clothes were the usual dark blue jeans and a button-down shirt that matched the shade of his eyes for as long as they flashed green.

As the curtain fell back, the tremors in Soren's limbs intensified. He dropped to his knees, and his gun, suddenly a dead weight, gave a dull thump as it hit the linoleum covered floor.

"Wha...?" His voice failed him.

Cuinn took another step forward and offered his hand. "For sure, get up, man."

Mute, Soren opened and closed his mouth, the forefinger of his leaden right hand still hooked around his weapon. He couldn't move, his eyes stuck wide, drilling into Cuinn's. If he blinked, would he disappear?

As the pounding of blood in his head retreated, he found his voice. "Are you a… ghost?" Of course not, but what else? No one came back. Not ever. Not from the demon or the heavenly dimensions. Everyone knew the notion of an afterlife was bullshit. So how could he be here?

"Nah, man." Cuinn grinned. "What would a feckin' ghost be needing to come back to this hell hole for? Though I've heard Vegas is good for the shows." He laughed loudly at his own joke.

While Soren grasped for sense in the response, the thunder came, slow on the heels of the lightning. It was the ear-splitting kind, a deafening crack that splinters the sky like an ax cleaving a log. Both men instinctively ducked until the vibration in the walls and floor petered out.

Triggered by the thunder-clap, Soren at last found some strength. Leaving his weapon where it was, he leaped to his feet and seized Cuinn's shoulders. Driven by the momentum, he slammed the demon hard against the wall. Pieces of old plaster came loose and dropped onto them as they both slid to the floor.

Cuinn lifted his hands to the sides of Soren's neck, as if he was completing a circuit. His eyes zipped to ice blue, even lighter than Soren's own. But there they both stopped. Just large hands gripping each other, both collapsed in a heap at the bottom of the wall.

"You're… solid," Soren said.

"Yes."

"Flesh and—"

"Yes!"

"Not dead?"

"No!"

"And not… her?"

"Jegudiel?"

Soren nodded.

Cuinn squeezed out a laugh through the constriction of Soren's hands, his eyes gently deepening once more. "No recruit, I'm no feckin' psycho angel." He shifted his grip to pull at Soren's wrists. "Easy, Hux. Let me go, now."

"It's really you!" Soren let his arms flop to his sides, took a breath, and then grabbed at Cuinn again, this time scooping him into a hug that knocked the breath from them both.

His body. His scent.

Soren had lost his heart the day Cuinn died. Stone replaced it.

Now, here, this man brought it back to him.

Pain cut through his chest. Wet scoured his cheeks. He smothered his face against Cuinn's shoulder, trying to muffle the sound ripping from his throat. "Sorry," he choked out the word, and repeated it over and over. "Sorry."

For a short while, Cuinn allowed it, then pushed Soren away. He gripped his face and stared into his eyes. "You're forgiven, right? I understand why you did it. You had to. I know what Jegudiel did. She tricked you into it. It wasn't your fault, lad."

Soren pulled away, cheeks burning. He couldn't meet his eyes. Not forgiveness. "HIT ME!"

"I'll not do that, lad. Look at me!"

Soren jerked up his head.

Cuinn's eyes were gentle, fully green, and didn't match the sternness of his voice. "I forgive you. Do you understand, soldier?"

With his mind still spinning, Soren rubbed his wet eyes roughly with the heels of his hands, and took a deep breath to steady himself. Collapsing in a heap like this was unacceptable.

He nodded.

Hux stood and offered his hand to Cuinn, who took it and pulled himself up. He did it stiffly, like he was carrying an old injury.

"You got whiskey in this shit-hole?"

Soren nodded, still not able to speak.

"Good. Make it a feckin' double."

Another flash of lightning lit up the room, thunder closer on its tail now.

Cuinn settled in the easy chair while Soren fetched a couple of plastic cups from the sink in the bathroom.

While there, he splashed cold water on his face, then gripped the edges of the basin, and stared into the mirror, collecting himself, trying to stop trembling. He watched as the water built against the stubble on his cheeks, and dropped with a splash onto his shirt, chilling his chest too.

He shook his head roughly, throwing off the water like a dog, and clearing the last of the confusion. He allowed himself a brief smile into the mirror. Alive! My brother is back.

"Jaysus, this place gets some storms. Thought I'd left that behind in Hell." Cuinn's words floated through the bathroom door.

Soren flinched at his reflection, eyes narrowing. *Hell?*

5

STAND WITH ME, BROTHER

BACK IN THE BEDROOM, Soren filled the cups. He gave one to Cuinn then sat opposite him on the edge of the bed, waiting for him to say more.

The sky split again. This time, marble-sized hailstones accompanied the lightning flash. They bounced off the window ledge and hammered against the glass. A few shot through the gap at the bottom, scattering across the floor. The ice melted slowly, dotting the floor with dark pools. He couldn't look away, and neither, it seemed, could Cuinn.

The temperature plummeted with the storm. Cold air, finally. Soren's lungs unclenched.

Don't ask about Hell.

If he did, the dam would break again. He needed time. He needed words. *Any words.* "You think this place is a shit-hole?"

Cuinn grinned and nodded. "I'm thinking the only reason there are no cockroaches is cos they packed up and moved." He smiled wider. "You always did like 'character,' Hux."

Soren almost smiled. Of course, Cuinn would hate it. This old thirties mansion was miles from the Strip, back in the old mob district. Soren's gaze swept over the water-stained ceiling. He'd picked this place for its history. Every rattle of the windowpane and crack in the floor was a story.

Gingerly, the Irishman stretched both arms above his head, like he was testing his limits. Deep wounds marked his wrists and around his jawline. It looked like someone had dug into him with the sharp end of a potato peeler. They were still fresh: deep purple, some crusted yellow, or with blackened scabs. One place, around his right ear, oozed fresh blue blood. A fresh wave of guilt washed over Soren. *I did that.* When he'd slammed him against the wall.

He dampened a towel at the bathroom sink before giving it to the demon. "You're bleeding."

Cuinn took it and dabbed at the wound. "Sure, I cut myself shaving this morning, so I did." He winked.

"What happened?"

"Well, I can tell you, Hux, but don't you be getting all guilty on me again."

"I said, I understood. But I'll be guilty til my dying day." Soren refilled their cups. An additional bottle stood ready in the cupboard. They'd need it. "Tell me, man. What happened? Where have you been?"

"Hell. In the red zone. Cells of Permanent feckin' Incarceration, to give them their proper title." Cuinn knocked back the whiskey too fast, and an amber bead splashed onto his chin. He gathered it onto his finger and sucked. "Was hauled out of the Red River and shoved in a cell. Shackled—neck, wrists, ankles—just waiting for a chance to get out. I got it, finally, but had to wrench myself free from the metal." He showed the wounds around his neck and pulled up the legs of his jeans to show deep gouges in his ankles. "Made my way topside."

"You got out of Hell?" Soren looked at him sideways.

"It wasn't easy, man. I can tell you. But I couldn't do

nothin' could I? I fought my way out, so I did." Cuinn's eyes glittered ice blue against the green.

Something wasn't right with this explanation. In fact, it stank. Fight or not, no one simply *left* Hell. Not even Conn O'Cuinn. Was he being played?

But the man sitting opposite was solid, warm. *Alive.* And offering forgiveness.

Soren shoved down the suspicion. *Don't ask. Leave it alone.* If he did, the dream might crack, and he'd be nothing but a murderer standing in a cheap hotel room with a ghost. He had no right to the truth.

He threw back the rest of the whiskey, swallowing the doubt with the burn. "Then what?" He topped up their drinks for a second time, shaking the last drops into his, and crossed to the cupboard for the second bottle.

"Then, nothing. Decided to track you down. Get back to Detroit. Take a stand against these feckin' Risings. Tipping Point's nearly on us."

"Tipping Point?"

"When the number of demons up here outnumber humankind. Most of them scum-demons, Leeches and the like. Crawling up and out of their disgusting underground pits." Cuinn's face screwed up as he spoke.

"How do you know? So many cities are still not taken."

"I know. Ear to the ground." He blinked at Soren, light blue eyes holding his gaze.

They both took big gulps of whiskey. "Give us another, there, Hux. Been a long time since I had a good gargle."

As Soren refilled the cup, he said, "Not business as usual then, back in Detroit?"

Cuinn leaned forward in his chair. "I'm heading that way, but nah. There's a bigger plan brewing. That's why I came to find you. Get you on board."

"What plan?" Soren's stomach clenched.

"It's easy, Hux. I want you to stand with us. Stand with your Unit, man. Stand with the Soldiers."

6

———————————

SNAPPING JAWS

THE SILENCE in the room stretched, broken only by the continued rumbling of the storm outside. Each lightning flash lit Cuinn's face watching him. Waiting. The demon's eyes now burned a steady green, but the flecks of ice blue were still there, showing his thoughts ticking through.

Soren knew this man, had fought alongside him many times. Cuinn had trained him. Brought him back after Bali, for Godsakes! He'd taught him how to respect himself—and the enemy. At a time when all Soren wanted to do was taste blood, when he was on the verge of touching the monster inside, Cuinn had stepped in. He'd made it his mission to find the man again.

Soren owed him.

And yet, something wasn't right.

Cuinn's face had the same expression now as it did the first time they'd met. He was trying to figure him out. To anticipate his response. This would be an all-or-nothing deal, a chance to pay his debt.

"You just asking me to follow you? No questions?" Soren asked.

"Nah, man. I'll tell you what I can. You'll be on the right side. But you'll need to use your head, Hux—not your heart."

The lightning flashed again, and thunder exploded above their heads. This time Soren didn't flinch. Cuinn's eyes stayed steady, too, peering into his. The central light pendant swayed from the vibration, tracing a weak elliptical path across the room.

"Then explain it to my head, Cuinn." Soren pushed himself back on the bed. The heavy muscles across his back and shoulders hunched him over a little.

Forcing himself up from the chair, Cuinn crossed to the bedside table, wincing as he shuffled injured feet over the high pile of the floral rug that ran alongside the bed. He picked up the bottle of whiskey and topped up Soren's proffered cup.

If they kept this up, they'd both be sleeping it off well into tomorrow morning.

After refilling his own, Cuinn returned to the chair. Another battering of hail began hitting the windowsill.

Wait. The curtains. Cuinn hadn't just pulled them. A towel was draped over the wardrobe mirror. The bedside clock, face down. Pictures on the wall, reversed. Not a single shiny surface anywhere. "You're keeping Jegudiel out?" Now that the shock of seeing Cuinn was wearing off, Soren woke up.

"Yep."

"Have you seen her?"

"Yeah, I've seen the bitch."

"In Hell?"

Cuinn nodded. "She looked like she'd had seven bells knocked out of her. Alive, though, and recovering when I left."

Soren wondered why he said "left" and not "escaped," but he just said, "It was Billy. Nearly killed her. Damn hard to kill an angel—even if you are one."

"Billy? Tazia's friend from London?"

At the mention of Anastasia, Soren flicked his eyes away. Cuinn did the same.

"Yeah." Soren took a big swig. "Billy's an angel now, and Anastasia is… human." He waited. Would it change anything for him or did he already know?

"Where is she?" Cuinn said steadily.

"Dunno. She's gone walkabout. Finding the whole human thing… difficult." Soren wanted to ask more. Find out why Cuinn didn't seem surprised. Wanted to know what he still felt for his ex-lover, if anything.

"You back with her now?" Cuinn's eyes bored into his, and the silence stretched.

The last time they'd had a conversation about Anastasia, it had ended with violence. In fact, it had ended only when Cuinn's Core demon had emerged and tried to kill her. It was at least something to be grateful to Jegudiel for; she'd stopped her being ripped limb from limb.

"No." He shoved the subject back in its box.

Cuinn wanted to do the same. He gave a short nod, a gesture that said he'd already guessed. "So, this Billy, is he your contact? Some sort of angelic resistance to the Risings?"

"Yeah. We're in a holding pattern. Waiting for orders."

"How many?"

"There's a… few of us." He glanced away.

"Doesn't sound like a big army—"

"We're doing our best, Cuinn! Angels are on our side. Surely…" He heard his own tone; like an angry dog snapping its jaws and ending in a whine. *Control it.*

Cuinn blew out a noisy breath, and his tongue moistened cracked lips before replying. "Surely, what? When are they going to act? Angels know feck all about what's going on down here—"

"Not Billy. He knows." Soren heaved a sigh. Convincing Cuinn about something he didn't want to hear had always been an uphill struggle. "They'll act. Before the… What did you call it?"

"The Tipping Point."

"Yeah. They'll act before then."

"Okay. Let's just say they do, man. Do you think they can defeat all the demons in Hell before the humans are dead?"

"I—"

"When have you seen them swoop into action before?" Cuinn pulled his chair closer. It dragged on the thick pile of the rug and jolted his wrists, breaking the scabs on the right one, oozing blood. He didn't flinch. The pain must be second nature now.

For a moment, Soren was gripped with guilt again. *This was his fault.* Cuinn had been in Hell because of him. He'd caused all those wounds the moment he jumped at him with the dagger. "I'm not—"

"Well, recruit, when? When Vesuvius erupted? When water flooded the world? When feckin' Hitler rose to power? Or was it when the Black Plague killed millions—or AIDS?"

"Okay, okay. I get it. You don't think the angels will act." Soren checked for his gun. It still lay where he'd left it on the floor. He picked it up and replaced it in his chest holster.

"I don't know, man. But I'm past waiting on them and I'm not letting the feckin' Leeches win this one."

Soren focused. "So the plan is to take out the vampires? Are they behind the Risings? Not the Advocate or this demon we heard about?"

"What demon?"

"We worked with some witches back in Boston—"

"Pah! Feckin' witches. What do they know?" Cuinn threw back his whiskey.

"I'm not a fan either, but they helped us. Told us there was a demon involved."

Cuinn shrugged, wiping his mouth with the back of his hand. "I don't know about a demon, but the plan's bigger than me, so it is."

"What the fuck does that mean?" Soren gave up his pretence at neutrality, and his voice rose.

Cuinn stood up and took a pace forward. "It means: need to fuckin' know. It means: you gotta trust me. It means... it'll probably get worse before it gets fuckin' better..." His voice trailed away along with his anger, and he sat back down. "One thing I do know for sure, though. The angels won't save anything. The Tipping Point will come. And instead of wasting time trying to stop the inevitable, we've got to set it up right."

"Let it happen? Let all those people die?" Soren's eyes widened. This wasn't Cuinn. He'd never known him to allow violence for the sake of it.

"If necessary." Cuinn's face was a mask. Even his eyes maintained a steady deep blue hue.

Needing air, Soren got up and crossed to the window. The storm had petered out, though the darkness outside hadn't lifted even slightly. He pushed the curtain aside. The traffic lights on the corner cycled from green to amber to red without a single vehicle passing. A river of water rushed down the street; Vegas drainage wasn't equipped for the big rains.

Birds squawked from the rooftop of the building opposite, some sort of old-style community hall with fake red brick and a flat roof. There must have been fifty of them, bluejays, hopping up and down arguing over each inch of space. Had the storm carried them in, or had they brought the storm with them?

He faced Cuinn. "I... can't stand with you, man. I'm human. Anastasia's human now too. Up here it's our world. I can't just hand it over."

Cuinn shook his head slowly. "My world too, Hux. Soldiers live above ground. Or did you forget that?"

"You know what I meant…"

When Cuinn spoke again, his voice was level, but he gripped the plastic cup a little too tight in his hand, opposite sides bending toward each other. "Tell me, man, do you remember that recruit that came to me, all fucked up? Wanting to kill everyone, not stop till he'd wrung their necks and bathed in their blood? The one I helped be better than that—to be a man with integrity and honour and belief in a code. You remember him, Hux?"

Soren focused on the ground. A small black beetle circled the rug, getting caught in the fringe.

"I need *him*. I need him by my side right now. I need him to believe in me and do this because he trusts that I would never lead him wrong."

Inside, silence walled. Outside, the birds screamed.

Soren clenched his fists, setting his jaw as strong as Cuinn's, and returned the glare. He had no answer.

With barely a foot between them now, Cuinn's voice was icy. The plastic cup collapsed in his fist, sending a shower of whiskey over the floor. "Okay. How's this then? You know that guy who stuck a fuckin' blade in my brain, and sent me to Hell over some fuckin'… woman?" He spat out the word, threw the cup to the ground, and dropped his voice to a barely whispered growl. "I need him to make amends to me."

He'd pulled the ace.

Soren hung his head, his hands loosened. Defiance evaporated.

Cuinn relented. He took another step, squashing the beetle underfoot, and bent level with Soren's face. He gripped his shoulders gently. Warm whiskey breath kissed his skin, and Cuinn's voice caressed him, "Just get me to Detroit. I'm too feckin' weak, Hux. I need your help. I want you by my side, man, but if you can't give me that. Fine. Just get me to Detroit. You owe me that, surely?"

That he could do. Soren squeezed his agreement into the demon's forearms. "I'll get you there, brother."

The birds outside fell silent.

7

CLEAN SWEAT AND SALIVA

BILLY SPED OVER THE BRIDGE, the Thames wind a cool slap against his face. Gulls screamed their disapproval from perches on the decaying wooden markers, which stuck out of the river like stained teeth. The race was desperate. And he was loving it.

Twenty feet ahead, Tom stretched out with that long, infuriating stride of his, like a big cat that could run forever. His fair hair, usually brushing his collar, whipped back, disguising its length. A beautiful sight, even if he was winning.

Ahead, he lost ground on the turn. His stride shortened, and a hand dipped to the pavement to keep his balance before he took off again. As Tom glanced over his shoulder, Billy met his look with a grin and dug in. The space between them shrank with every pump of his arms.

The brief panic on Tom's face was delicious. He put his head down and almost plowed into a moped. He swerved at the last moment, just as the rider screeched to a halt and was still hurling abuse as Billy steamed past.

He panted a quick, "Sorry, mate," to the fuming rider and focused again at closing the gap. He felt himself snake the curve, bending low as if the breeze itself blew him into position.

Now he sprinted, teeth clenched, head down. He was gaining. *No bloody way he gets away this time!* His sweat felt like a second skin, coursing down his forehead.

The old tea warehouse loomed. They flew at the entrance. Tom pushed the door open first, sailing past George, the security officer, a fraction of a moment before Billy. The *thwack* of Tom's hand slamming the lift button echoed down the corridor. He slid down the wall, gulping huge, triumphant breaths.

Billy hit the wall on the other side of the lift with his palms out to stop his momentum. He bent over double, raking air into his lungs, his gaze fixed on Tom. "I'll bloody… have you… tomorrow, Tom!"

"If… you're lucky… you'll have me… before then!" Tom smirked, then coughed as the laugh caught in his throat.

"What about now?" Billy grinned and leaned in for a kiss.

A loud, deliberate cough came from the security desk. George. A gaggle of pre-teen girls spilled in from outside, hunched over their phones and laughing, sharing a joke.

Just as the doors to the lift opened, the two men separated, and tumbled inside, their legs still recovering from the sprint that always finished their daily run. The girls followed them, crowding the small space. Billy couldn't tell how many there were; just a sweet mess of cheap perfume, over-applied makeup, and excitement.

One sidled up. "Hi, Billy!" The little redhead with spiky hair and a face marked with almost orange freckles searched his face for a sign he remembered her. *Shit, what was her name? Jackie? Jess?*

"Hey… erm… Jess. How are you?" He flashed sparkling white teeth at her and motioned toward her cell phone. "What you got there, girl?"

"A puppy." She giggled. "It's sliding across the floor on top of one of those vacuum robot thingies. Then it hits the cupboard and falls off. So adorable."

"Adorable." The other girls echoed.

"As adorable as me, Jess?" He nudged her arm, and grinned even wider.

"Course not. You're the cutest, Billy." She giggled again, and her freckles now bloomed behind a beet red complexion.

The lift dinged to let them know they'd reached the girls' floor. They stepped out into the hallway where the flats stretched off each side, with a chorus of "Bye, Billy!"

"S'later, girls," he said, and gave them a big wink.

He held his smile until the lift doors hissed shut and the giggles receded from down the lift shaft. The muscles in his shoulders unclenched, and he slumped against the cool metal wall.

"You just love it, don't you?" Tom said.

"What?" The word came out flat.

"Being so fucking adorable."

Billy closed his eyes, too tired for words. The freedom of the run was already fading and his mind spun with thoughts of Tazia, as usual.

"You're thinking about her." The teasing note left Tom's voice, replaced by something quieter. His warm palm found Billy's hand and squeezed.

He gave a small nod, safe in the admission.

"Come here," Tom murmured, and pulled him forward.

The kiss continued until the doors opened into the short hallway that led to the penthouse, and then it lasted longer. The scent of clean sweat and saliva replacing the leftover perfume.

———

Billy eased out of bed an hour later and made his way to the kitchen to grab the menu. Time to call for pizza. Friday night meant their cheesy, messy reward for a week of running.

Thomas was showering and rapping at the top of his lungs as he always did. It was something by Eminem. He did it well, not missing a word of the homage to Detroit.

Billy wished he wouldn't, Detroit was not a place he needed to be reminded about. Tazia had suffered there. Been used as a pawn in a fight that had nothing to do with her. Abused by all, even the people she'd trusted. People like Soren Huxford.

People like him.

He could still smell the stink of her burning skin. The scorched handprint on her back would remain forever now that she was human. *Jesus, the shame.*

Billy took the menu over to the laptop to enter his order online. It distracted him for a couple of minutes. And then, another image: Tazia held in Hux's arms on a cold, damp basement floor in Boston, newly human and struggling with every sensation, thought, and feeling.

Now she was gone. He'd heard she was in Europe. Back to Turin?

He'd respected her request not to track her for a whole twenty-four hours. Then tuned in his angel mojo to just "check" on her.

Thomas had pointed out that spying on the girl he'd given his solemn word to leave alone was not cool. Billy had shrugged: *It's important angel business, babe. You wouldn't understand.* But they'd both known it was an excuse. He could still hear Tom muttering *control freak* under his breath.

It was pointless anyway; he couldn't locate her. She knew him too well, had covered her tracks with a charm she'd cajoled from Aideen and the other witches. It had made her untraceable to even the most magickal eyes. Not even technomancy could find her. The one thing that comforted him was that if he couldn't find her, neither could Jegudiel, so he had to believe she was safe.

He lay in bed every night sending out a message into the ether, telling her he loved her, that he hadn't forgotten, that he was sorry. Then he would turn over and find comfort in the curves of Thomas's back.

Billy was pretty sure that Joshua would have been able to find Tazia. *Where the bloody hell is he?* The necromancer's soul had disappeared at some point during the events in Las Vegas.

Initially, Billy had just thought he'd gone to have some fun, enjoy freedom; whizzing around the world, taking the body of this person or that. Maybe even persuading a living person to shift his soul for a while and let him party. Getting laid a few times! He deserved it. Apart from online porn, he'd been living like a monk in the computer for nearly two years now. But as the weeks ticked by, Billy had become more and more worried. All his location spells failed. Something was wrong.

The front door buzzed. Pizza.

"Tom! Food!" he shouted into the bedroom before he crossed to the door. From the shower, there was no reply, but Eminem had given way to "Wuthering Heights." Thomas was doing his best to hit the top notes. He had eclectic tastes, to say the least. It was just one of the things Billy loved about him. *Yes, loved!*

Smiling, Billy hit the button to the intercom. "Send them up, George."

The security man's efficient voice echoed up to him. "Will do Mr. Nadig, Sir." The "sir" was emphasized like George was talking to an army officer.

When the lift announced its arrival, Billy had already walked the few steps down the corridor and was waiting at the doors, cash in hand. Thoughts of Tazia and Joshua had generated a hankering for comfort food, exacerbated further when the doors opened and sausage aroma wafted toward him.

He flashed a glance at the delivery kid, but his fixed smile was more directed at the pizza. "How much?"

The boy wiped something off the front of his jacket with one hand while balancing the box on the other. "Have it for free, mate."

"Why? It's on time." He saw the smear on the boy's palm, and his stomach flipped. "Is that… blood?"

The kid looked at his hand and rubbed the palm on his pants. "Oh, yeah, vampire. S'okay. All good. Dead." He gave a big proud grin. "Can I come in, Billy, and put this box down? It's burning a hole in my fuckin' arm!"

"Ju?"

Julie, Billy's angelic superior, took a step out of the lift. "Course it's me, arsehole."

"Nice attitude! I've never seen you be a boy before."

She smiled again. "I think I look cute."

Billy stuck out his lower lip, taking in the shaved afro and long lashes, and nodded appreciatively. "Yep. You do. How old?"

"Illegal!"

"Shame. Like the kicks by the way. Why the hell are you delivering me pizza?"

"For fun! Had a message for you so thought I'd come visit." She thrust the food into Billy's hands and wandered through the flat to settle on the black leather sofa that straddled the midsection of the big warehouse space.

Billy followed. "You not heard of a phone? Texting's popular with the cool kids, I heard."

Julie stuck out her tongue. "I don't like speaking into bits of metal, computer chips, and wiring. Radiation fries brains you know. There are studies."

"You don't have a brain."

"True, but cruel. Do you want to photograph my shoes?" She gestured to the photographs on the wall. Artistically arranged pictures of women's boots and shoes were hung on the wall, mostly above the fifty-inch television. Some were small; others were vast canvases, stacked dramatically, stretching into the rafters of the open ceiling.

Billy assessed the boy's runners again. Solid black with a silver line separating the sole and emblazoned with a cool logo. Some basketball player's promotional line. "No thanks."

"What's wrong with them?"

"Just not my thing."

"But you're not exclusively female." She nodded toward a smaller picture, which featured a pair of heavy men's work boots. Old and cracked, the frayed laces were threaded through holes that shone.

"They're different. Memories, innit." Billy looked away, killing the conversation. After a moment, he asked, "So what did you want to tell me?"

"In a minute. I want some answers from you first." She slouched onto the sofa and patted the seat next to her.

Billy sat and put his feet up on the central coffee table beside hers. A weird, high-pitched siren sounded. In his head or outside? He rubbed his right ear. "S'up?"

"We haven't seen you upstairs for a while. Since a week after Boston. Are you okay?"

Before responding, Billy shuffled in his seat and blinked several times in quick succession. "Hmm."

She frowned. "Is that 'hmm'—affirmative—or more 'hmm,' like 'I don't know'?"

"The first one. I think. Yeah. Probably."

"That's not much more convincing than the 'hmm.' Come on. Dish. Wassup?"

"It's just that… I didn't really like it upstairs. It didn't feel natural to me. All that silence. Angels don't really have a laugh, do they? They were all… staring at me."

"Billy! You practically killed Jegudiel. You gave us the

advantage for the first time since Detroit fell. Of course they were staring at you—most of them don't even get to visit the Earth plane, let alone influence it the way you did. It's called admiration, mate." She gave him a pat on the back as she reverted back to pizza-boy chat.

He shrugged. "I prefer it here. Heaven's too… intense. I think I'll stick to London for now thanks. Not a problem is it?"

"Not to me. But you should really pop in now and again. You know, for appearances' sake. Will you?"

"Maybe…"

She smirked. "So how's it going with lover boy?"

"Good. Nice. Actually, it's fan-fuckin-tastic, love." Billy turned to face her. "So what are you here for? Is there news about the plan?"

She sat up straighter too, and leaned into him, lowering her voice like they were being overheard. "We know who's masterminding the whole thing. Who the demon is."

The words hit him. Boston. Tazia confronting him in the street, sticking a knife into him, leaving him to die. She was under the control of the Advocate at the time, but had managed to shake it off enough to whisper: *It's a demon, pulling the strings. Not Jegudiel.*

Since then, they, as well as Heaven, had been trying to figure out who that demon was, but Hell had become tight as a drum. Informants were silent, and spells blocked. None of them. Not the angels, or the Precog, Jacob. Not even the witches in Dublin had managed to get any information. *This was big.* "Who?" he asked.

"The Abbot of Savoy—Tazia's father." She leaned back again.

Billy froze. Of all those they'd suspected, not once had his name been raised. Jegudiel had claimed she'd freed him when Conn O'Cuinn had died. Even if that was true, he'd still be languishing in a Hell dimension somewhere. Dead. Gone. Surely?

But if he did have power again and was in control of the Risings, Tazia would be at risk. She would be the first soul he'd come for. That was unthinkable. He couldn't allow that bastard to get his hands on her. Not again.

A white-hot flash rushed up Billy's body, setting each cell alight. As it surged into his cheeks, he stood, then briskly paced to the windows. *This would be bad.*

He swivelled, looking desperately for the angel. "Ju, I—"

Another surge rose. It built low in his belly, rose up and sank claws into his heart. The next wave drove him to the verge of panic. "Julie!"

She reached for him, but as he made contact with her outstretched hand, her image turned to ice and shattered. It broke into a million shards that spun away from him into space.

Get control, Billy! Her voice echoed in his mind.

Fear continued to flood him. It layered over him like ice forming on a lake at top speed. He stopped pacing, his mind wiped clean.

In the room, the windows rattled. The glass panes pulsed violently in their frames. And for a moment, the shrill alarm filled his head again, deafening him. He pounded on his temples with the heels of his hands, trying to shake the sound loose.

Billy, easy.

He dropped his hands, and a stream of strong blue light emanated from each palm. The beams burned two small flames into the rug at his feet, and smoke rose around them.

"Billy!"

The beams of light switched off. "Yeah. I hear you," he panted.

While she stamped on the flames, Billy yanked open the

sliding door to the terrace and took a step outside. Taking a breath, he gathered all the remaining fear and anger into his chest and blew it out into the air. It formed a chill mist in front of him, heavy with burning ice, twisting and turning like some frozen blue whirlpool.

As it dissipated, little flakes of snow frosted the tail feathers of the magpies that had been sitting on the railing watching the angels' conversation. They squawked loud objections and shot up into the sky, leaving just little puffs of smoke behind.

Billy's shoulders heaved as he finally regained control and went back inside. Julie continued to stamp on the rug.

"Still having the fall out then?" She shook her head. "I knew I shouldn't have accelerated your change in Boston."

"If you hadn't, we wouldn't be here now, Ju. The Advocate would have won. Don't beat yourself up. I'm getting better."

"Looks like it!" She pointed to the two burned spots on the floor.

Billy shrugged, "Last week I would have blown the window out." He crossed to the kitchen to pour a large glass of water from the faucet. Then he joined her, splashing water onto the burned spots to stop them smouldering. "Are you sure it's the Abbot?"

"Yes." Julie sat heavily on the sofa facing away from the windows. "Unfortunately."

"Then Tazia is in danger…"

"Yep."

With all the water gone, Billy sat beside her, cradling the glass in his hands. "Tell me…"

"When Tazia regained full use of her soul in Turin, the agreement was that her father would rise from the Red River. Jegudiel saw to that. She pulled him free. At the time, we didn't know why she did it. We thought their… alliance was over. But it seems not. The balance of power between the two of them is unclear though."

"How did you find out?"

"Ezequiel. I don't know how. He says he has… contacts." She sniffed and cuffed her nose with the back of her hand.

Billy got back up and raised the corner of the rug to check the wood underneath. It hadn't burned through. Momentarily relieved, he swapped the glass for a kitchen towel and used it to sop up the water. "What happens now? How do we get to him?"

"Well, we don't. For now." She returned her feet to the coffee table, watching his movements. "Don't look at me like that! Until we know more, we can't act. We know he's waiting for the Tipping Point, but beyond that, we don't know what his plan is or how to get to him. He certainly hasn't taken a step outside of Hell since Turin, and Jegudiel hasn't left since Boston. We'd know. We have eyes where we can, and traps set where we can't see."

Billy stopped what he was doing and perched on the coffee table facing her. "He's waiting for what?"

"The Tipping Point. That moment when the number of souls walking the Earth is less than the number of demons. Humankind will be weakest then and—"

"And, the demons will make it like Hell on Earth, I get it." Billy finished. "Okay. So we just wait? Seems risky!"

"No. We know our enemy now, Billy. We can prepare. Get ready for the moment—prevent it if we can. We tell the Resistance. "

"Ireland?"

"Ireland… and Tazia. Find her. She should know her father's back. If he can get to her, he will. That's a real danger." She got up from the seat and headed toward the door. "Enjoy the pizza. And Billy…"

"Yeah?"

"I'm really pleased for you. Thomas, I mean. You deserve him, mate."

The tension left Billy's shoulders for a moment, and he smiled as he glanced back to the bedroom. The sound of the "Wuthering Heights" top note suddenly ended, and Thomas walked out of the bedroom wrapped in a towel, his hair damp and fluffy.

Julie had gone, freeing him from the stasis as she went.

Thomas grinned. "Is that the pizza? I'm starving."

8

____

ON THE ROAD

"GET IN!" Cuinn shouted at Soren above the growl of the Camaro. It looked like he'd just driven it straight off the showroom floor: matte black paint job, a pair of gleaming silver racing stripes, and blacked out wheels. The souped-up engine purred, but it would roar like a lion on the open road.

Cuinn had been in a fine mood all morning, shouting about a "road trip!" and loudly whistling in the shower, the sound pulling Soren slowly into consciousness. He stayed in bed a while longer, listening for the sounds of the birds outside, and trying to get a handle on why his gut churned, besides the effects of his hangover.

The birds had remained silent.

Going to Detroit with Cuinn was a mistake. He knew it, but the actual logic remained stubbornly hidden, scratching away in the back of his mind. The guilt was more tangible. It clung so tight he felt it curl around his neck and slumped over his shoulders, heavy and unrelenting.

As he lay there, battling to blink himself awake. The memory of the escort in the elevator flashed back to him. Her cut glass accent, the nail running over his cheek. He shot up to sitting. She'd told him to trust a demon! Cuinn?

But so what? Who the hell was she to know his business? Magick certainly. A witch? That didn't feel right.

Regardless, he couldn't let Cuinn make the trip alone; the man was injured. Getting through demon-infested cities, and around resistance enclaves and army blockades, would be tough.

It was the least he could do.

So Soren had let Cuinn's excitement for the trip infect him, and now here he was.

He got into the car's passenger seat, reached over the back to squeeze his belongings beside Cuinn's pack, and smirked. "Muscle car? Not an SUV or something a bit more… bulletproof?"

"Nah, I liked the look of this one." Cuinn ran his hands around the smooth steering wheel lovingly, grinned wide, and shoved the car into gear.

As Cuinn pushed his way across two of the four lanes at a speedy angle, traffic screeched to a halt.

"Where did you get it?" With the windows all the way down, Soren shouted over the engine and honking horns.

"Casino," he yelled back. "Some celebrity charity thing. TV crews everywhere. Gobshite with a man bun and beard mouthing off to the valet about his paint job, so I thought we'd test it out for him." He grinned again. "Listen to that roar, man!"

Soren laughed; it was good to see him happy, and for a little while his concern about the trip melted. "Put some music on, eh? And put your foot down."

Cuinn didn't have to be told twice, and soon they were out of Vegas and heading north-east along the interstate, both of them singing loudly to whatever came on the radio, Beyoncé to Black Sabbath.

The four-lane highway quickly became a graveyard of abandoned haulage trucks, their trailers shoved to the shoulders to form makeshift steel walls. Crude spray paint on the rusty metal warned: NO STOPPING. THEY ARE WATCHING.

They didn't stop—just kept singing.

———

By the time they crossed into Utah, the engine no longer sounded like an angry lion; more like a squeaking kitten. Cuinn's lead foot had overheated something, and lights flashed dangerously on the dashboard.

He eased the shuddering Camaro into a dilapidated rest stop, where it came to a grinding halt and then went silent. They'd pulled up behind an old Dodge Caravan. It had more rust than paintwork and would have looked abandoned if it wasn't for the piles of brightly coloured kids' luggage in the back.

The two men sat side by side in the vehicle in silence. Soren glared at the dash that was no longer lit up like a frenetic disco display. The sun beat through the windows, and the skin on his face and arms began to prickle and tighten. He glanced at Cuinn. His knuckles were white on the steering wheel, his expression fixed straight ahead, his skin flushing a blotchy pink. Annoyance radiated off him in waves.

Soren got out of the passenger side and kicked a tire before crossing to one of the old concrete piles that marked the edge of the stop, and sat fiddling with his watch. The trip had distracted him, but now he wondered what Anastasia was doing right at that moment. Sometimes, if he thought about her really hard, it felt like she was beside him. *Stupid.*

An old transformer shed cast a little shade over him, cooling the temperature by a degree or two. Danger signs warning of electrocution still hung from the walls, but the shelter stood empty. Overgrown weeds had wrapped around the concrete supports to the roof and dug their sticky roots into the wooden boards nailed across the windows and doorway. The lowest planks were missing, and lizards scurried back and forth, pushing through gritty sand.

Beyond the shed, the highway fencing had been trampled flat by something massive, allowing the red desert sand to drift across the tarmac and bury the lane markers.

Soren scuffed his feet, watching a couple of scorpions scuttle out of his way before he ground the sole of his boot onto them. He scraped the splat of guts onto the desert grass and watched Cuinn battle with the engine, his arm holding up the car's hood, while a cloud of steam enveloped him.

"Fucked?" Soren called. The stink of burned oil drifted over to him.

Cuinn peered out from behind the hood for a moment. His skin had turned an even deeper shade of pink in the heat of the beast's breath. He muttered something about "gaskets" and "injection nozzles" then gazed once more into the depths of the engine, before adding in a pleasant enough tone, "American feckin' bollocks shite."

Soren laughed. "You drove it like a demon, man. You would've killed anything at that rate."

Cuinn looked back at him and shrugged. "How else did yer expect me to drive it…" and flicked his eyes to red. He let the hood close, wiped his hands on his jeans, and reached into the back seat for his pack. "Nice while it lasted though, huh? Grab your bag, recruit. Let's start walking." Turning his back, he hobbled off toward the highway.

With a final regretful glance at the beauty that had once been the Camaro, Soren pulled out his bag and rifle carrier from the back seat and headed after Cuinn. As he crossed the verge to climb the little incline to the road, he heard a whimper. A tiny kitten-like mew came from the minivan they'd parked behind.

For the first time, Soren noticed the windows on the passenger side were smashed. Scatterings of broken glass glittered on the ground, disguised by the shimmering grit and sand the wind had blown into place. The whimper came again, and his thoughts flew back to the dog locked in the car in Vegas. *Not again.* Why the hell couldn't people take proper care of their pets?

"Cuinn! Hold up!"

Cuinn stopped short and looked back, waiting.

Soren pulled his gun, not really sure why he felt an injured puppy might be a threat, but the sight of the broken glass had unnerved him. Something was up. Something more than an uncaring pet owner.

He scanned the side of the van. Large sticky drips of blood marked the doorway of the front passenger seat, and the palm of a bloody handprint stood out starkly against the light paintwork just below the bottom of the broken window. More black-red blood stained the shards. It looked like someone had been dragged through the window, struggling hard, and had grabbed at the remains of the pane to stop themselves from being carried away.

It didn't look like they'd won the fight.

"Human." Cuinn crossed back to stand beside him. He inhaled deeply. "Fresh too. Just missed them."

The cry came again, a more drawn-out whimper this time; it seemed to be gathering force. Perhaps whatever it was could hear them talking. Still expecting a puppy, Soren slid the side door of the vehicle open, putting his body in front of the gap so that nothing could bolt away.

It took a moment for his eyes to adjust to the darkness inside. He made out a pile of clothing and towels stuffed between the middle seats, and little else apart from the luggage on the back bench. There was nothing on the front seats. The whimper sounded again, but this time it dissolved into a gulp and a long, thready cry. Weak, but most definitely human.

All at once, it clicked. "Christ, it's a baby!" Soren crawled onto the back seat closest to him, and started lifting off the clothing and towels layer by layer, super cautious. He glanced back to find Cuinn standing with his back to him, ready for trouble. The nose of his short shotgun bobbed occasionally from behind his broad frame.

The remaining pile of fabric moved slightly under Soren's touch. The cries had gotten louder as he'd removed the layers, the sound of an infant crying drawn-out mewls.

Another movement, what looked like a kick this time, as he dislodged the final piece of clothing, a brand new white t-shirt with "A gift from Vegas!" printed on the front. Underneath was a tiny baby, he guessed around one or two months, bright red and squirming, dressed just in a onesie and diaper. It lay on its side on top of another layer of towels, which had been placed between the two back seats, facing away from him. An empty carrier was still strapped onto the back passenger seat.

A cry gurgled in the baby's throat. The sound seemed to brew in its chest for a moment and was then released. The scream hit Soren at the same time as the perfume of white-hot baby poop. Sticky yellow mush eased its way out the top of the diaper with a squelch and soaked through the onesie.

"Oh, God!" Soren yanked his head back, letting the smell float past him.

It reached Cuinn. "Jaysus, what's that feckin' stink?"

"Baby shit." Soren gingerly fished the baby out from between the seats, his big hands fumbling a little to ensure it was well-secured before raising it up and toward him. With liquid fecal matter now also smearing his forearm, he turned the child around so he was looking into its eyes for the first time. The scream abruptly subsided. Bright blue eyes gazed into his.

Soren looked the child over for injuries. Overheating and crying had taken its toll, giving it a deep red complexion, and there was a small cut on the forehead, but that was all. The baby was no worse for wear.

Easing backward out of the vehicle, Soren stood beside Cuinn, who had dropped the gun and was staring with equal amazement at the baby, who had closed its eyes away from the sun and turned into Soren's chest. It grabbed at the strapping of his gun holster and started sucking on it loudly.

"It's hungry." Soren said.

"Does 'it' have a gender?" Cuinn looked at the child with a smile hovering on his lips.

For a moment, Soren thought his question was genuine. "I'm sure, I just don't want to touch..." He pulled a little at the leg hole of the vest, but stopped, feeling unsure. Dazed, he peered back into the blue eyes that now stared up at him again. The baby burbled, but little unhappy hiccups were building as it found no nourishment in the leather of the holster.

Soren was out of his depth. He'd never been this close to a baby before, let alone held one. It was simultaneously exhilarating and terrifying.

"Looks like the wee mite's family were taken." Cuinn motioned his gun toward the blood and glass.

"Can you pick up their scent?"

Without waiting for an answer, Soren again leaned into the vehicle, and rooted around with one hand while holding the baby to him with the other, poop liberally soaking into his tee. "There must be a new diaper for this one—and some food."

"Milk."

"What?"

"The bairn needs milk, Hux. He'll be dehydrated after that

heat and he's too young to be eating anything other than liquid, man."

"Course." Soren felt stupid. "That's what I meant."

"Right. You'd be feeding him spaghetti or hot dogs, so you would!" Cuinn laughed. "While you sort him out, I'll go have a scout around. See if I can pick up the trail of his folks. If you can't find milk, give him a spot of whiskey—he'll at least sleep then."

Assuming this was bad advice, and after searching the vehicle, Soren came up with a bag of baby items including a fresh diaper and vest, and a small cool box full of pre-mixed bottles of formula. The ice packs were semi-solid, so it looked like the baby hadn't been on its own for too long.

Changing the diaper confirmed two things: the child was male and baby poop was stickier than semi-dried blood. Once the boy was clean and fed—and changed again—Soren piled him into the baby seat and placed him in the shade of the old transformer shed, draping a light towel over him to keep the bugs out.

As he finished up, Cuinn returned. "Found some tracks in the sand. More blood too. Three lots of heavy boots. Smells like Leech—" his lips curled "—and three lighter tracks. At least one more kid. One female. One male. Looks like the rest of his family." He nodded at the baby.

"Dead?" Soren asked.

"No, not enough blood scent. Bleeding for sure though. That peashooter all you have?" he asked, nodding his shotgun toward the Glock on Soren's chest.

Soren frowned. The "peashooter's" body count was close to fifty: he hadn't had it long.

Cuinn blew him a kiss, then grinned. "Let's go!"

Soren hesitated. "Thought demons lived and humans died. For that Tipping Point?"

"Don't you be quoting my own words back at me now.

There's a bairn involved. We do what's right. Besides—" he grinned again "—killing a few vamps will make my day even better."

He winked and set off around the building and back to the trail. "You smell of shite by the way," he threw back over his shoulder.

Soren looked down and sniffed. The scent was already becoming somewhat familiar.

Before leaving, he tucked the baby further back against the wall of the shed, out of sight of the busy highway and in even deeper shade, and set off after Cuinn.

———

Jegudiel willed herself to appear in the van's rear window. She projected her outline first. Then began to paint with intent. Purple for the dress. Red for the lips, her favourite shade of scarlet. Next, she threaded her hair with strands of grey, the authority of age. Finally, she polished her skin to a luminescent white, a beacon in the grimy reflection.

She brought the image to life, licking a forefinger and smoothing an already perfect eyebrow, her thin lips curving into a serpentine smile.

Her angle allowed her to see Soren's retreating form and the bottom of the baby carrier cocooned in its towel. *Interesting.*

"Kitchy-kitchy-koo, pet!" Her voice, sharp and English, sang out from the car. She watched with satisfaction. The sound seemed to tickle the child's feet, making his toes wiggle and drawing out a happy coo.

She looked away and tracked the path the men had just taken. "Who's a clever boy? Conn O'Cuinn, you are a genius." Her high, tight laugh burst from her lips. As the sound hung in the air, she dissolved her image, letting the grimy reflection of the empty desert reclaim the glass.

9

LET'S PLAY PRETEND

SOREN AND CUINN followed the blood trail to a jagged outcrop where someone had tried to build a sanctuary; coils of razor wire glinted on the top of the rocks, and plastic water drums lay slashed and empty in the dust. Once safe, it had become a trap to the occupants of the van.

A woman crouched beside a large boulder. Probably younger than she looked, fear had etched lines onto her face. They were highlighted by the sweat flowing from her forehead, and the blood dribbling from a small deep wound in her hairline. Lacerations zigzagged over her naked arms, with more across her stomach revealed through the rip in her vest top.

Gripped to her side was a young boy. Wide-eyed, he returned her hug like a baby gorilla, clutching his body to hers. He was doing his best to hide his face under her long brown hair, but still the whites of his eyes shone brightly between the blood-soaked strands.

To the right, a man stood flanked by two stocky vampires. They gripped his arms tight behind his back while another stroked the sharp tip of a feeding dagger over his face and down onto his neck. The dagger and the man's lips were the only things moving in the tableau, as he repeated one phrase over and over: "Please… kill me, but let them go!"

Tears streamed down the man's cheeks, but Soren saw fury in his trembling. He'd seen that mix of rage and terror many times. Humans bargained when they had something to protect, clinging to hope. To demons, it just looked like weakness.

The vampire with the dagger bent forward and licked the tear in the man's neck—as yet nothing more than a deep shaving nick. He slowly collected the blood on his tongue before twisting toward his comrades to give an exaggerated wide-eyed swallow. "Tasty!"

When he turned, Soren got a clear view of the swelling in his trousers. His stomach churned. He'd never get used to seeing vampires get that excited about their food. He whispered to Cuinn, "You ready?"

"I'm ready, man. Let's play pretend." He gave Soren a grin, grabbed his arm, and pushed him aggressively forward, shouting, "Get down there you miserable fecker!"

All eyes turned toward them.

"Fellas, you missed one!" Cuinn pushed Soren, who was doing his best to look weak, forward again. He held his hands behind his back as though they were tied, but where he actually clutched his gun.

Soren stumbled to a stop about ten feet away from them. Cuinn walked up beside him with his shotgun pointed down at his side. The middle vampire eyed the metal spike on Cuinn's gun suspiciously.

The other vampires shifted uneasily, but still held the man tight.

"You missed the bairn too, guys. All that sweet baby blood. Now that was really tasty." Cuinn sucked on his fingers.

There was a whimper from the rock. The mother hugged

her son even closer, pushing his head into her neck to hide his view.

Seeing her pain, Soren's stomach flipped again. *Really, Cuinn?*

"So Soldier, you giving him to us or what?" The leader was a tall guy, thin and willowy. He had a shock of bright red hair and a beard of practically the same colour.

"Nah, he's mine. I just want to see you kill that one, so I do. Us Irish stand together, right?"

"The only Irish thing about me is the whiskey I'll drink to wash his blood down, eh, boys?" The vampire laughed and stared at the other two, prompting them to join in. They glared back and remained silent. It didn't look like this little band of outlaws had their roles sorted out yet.

"So, you're not Irish?" Cuinn waved the shotgun around as he talked. "I could have sworn I saw you doing a jig just now..."

"Nah, man. I got the hair all right, but my mama was a California girl, like the surfers sing about, 'Let's go surfin'… everyone's surfin' now…' I dunno, somethin' like that." He shook his head as if the action would shake the memory loose and he'd be able to finish the lyric.

Soren squinted at the guy, genuinely wondering about his sanity. The other two vampires rolled eyes at each other, and even their captive was looking a little less panic-stricken.

"Oh, not Irish then? So, I guess there's no reason why we should keep you alive," Cuinn said.

He let go of Soren's hands and turned his shotgun toward the vampire on the right. At the same time, Soren brought his pistol around and aimed at his mate on the left. They fired in unison.

Both demons dropped, one to his knees, mouthing a scream that did not make it to the air. As the bullet hole between his eyes smoked, he fell forward. Dead. The second vampire fell to his side and then onto his back, clawing at the hole in his chest already spewing blood as the holy water from Cuinn's shotgun went to work on his flesh. He screeched so loudly that a vulture sitting on a cactus a little way away looked sharply in his direction. Blood bubbled from the vampire's mouth as his heart gave its last few frantic beats, then stilled. *Two down.*

Red stood unmoved. They'd surprised him. *Good.* Armed with just a feeding knife, he had nothing to defend himself with, and apparently had too little brainpower to run.

His victim wasn't so stupid. He pushed the vampire as hard as he could straight at Soren, then streaked over to his wife and child, who still crouched by the rock. He wrapped his arms around their backs to hold them close, then stayed right there, eyes warily flicking between Cuinn and Soren.

The vampire stumbled straight into Soren, who caught him by the shoulders and shoved him upright. The demon slashed at him with his feeding knife, opening a shallow line across his arm. Soren looked from it back to the vampire and grinned, then raised his arm to give him a clear view of the wound healing over.

"Shit, man! Really?" The vampire dropped his shoulders and shook his head. "No fair!"

"Yeah, sucks for you, dude." Soren raised his gun again and pointed it at the vampire's stomach. "Why were you harming these people?" Perhaps this was a chance encounter, a standard vampire hunting party, or maybe their motivation was different. The Advocate perhaps?

"What, man?"

Soren shot at the ground in front of the vampire, who dodged the bullet by a hair's breadth.

"Dude! The boots!" He lifted a foot and rubbed away the dust from a bright green cowboy boot with red stitching in the shape of a bull's head on the toe.

Soren raised an eyebrow. "Answer. Or those boots are gonna see blood."

"Just, cos, man." He shrugged, screwing up his face with genuine confusion.

The second shot hit the tip of his right boot and sliced a black line across the leather.

"Ow! Fuck!"

Cuinn had stood back just watching, but now he smiled. "Ah, but that was a crappy shot, Hux! Give me the gun. Sure, I won't miss."

"It's all yours." Soren said, and the two men swapped weapons.

The vampire backed away a few steps and nearly fell back over the leg of his dead companion. A vulture had hopped over and was already picking at his fingers.

"Hey! There's no need. I was just hungry all right?" The vampire finally seemed to understand the seriousness of the situation he faced.

But Cuinn was starting to enjoy himself. He shot again, and unlike Soren, it wasn't a warning shot. This one hit his foot, piercing the top of the boot just above his toes, blood splatted the shiny green leather and oozed into the dust around his foot.

The vampire shrieked and started jumping up and down, holding onto the injured foot, shouting. "Not cool, man. Not cool! I told ya, I was just hungry!"

"Yeah, but watching you dance *is* cool, man. You're doing a jig now!" Cuinn laughed and nudged his companion.

Soren double-took at the look on the Soldier's face. The grin, the laugh. *What the hell?* This was just messy. He glanced at the terrified three figures still huddled on the ground watching their saviours become monsters.

He didn't smile back at Cuinn and flicked his eyes to the victims. "Hey, man, let's finish it."

Cuinn looked at them, dropped the smile, and nodded. Both men raised their guns and fired. The impact of the duel closeup shots was instantaneous. The body fell to the ground in a heap. They both caught the spray.

"Feck! Now we'll stink of vampires as well as baby shite!" Cuinn wiped the front of his shirt, but just managed to spread the blood over a wider area.

"My baby?" The woman spoke in a weak voice.

"He's safe," Soren said.

"You're *all* safe now." Cuinn added.

As they walked away, three more vultures hopped up to the vampires' remains.

10

THE RED RIVER

FROM THE RIDGE, the Abbot of Savoy traced the path of the Red River. It stretched for hundreds of miles in each direction. The river curled over the landscape like a scarlet serpent. In places its water boiled, seething, while in others it sat placid, a static bog of melted fat and congealed blood.

It stank. Disease and dirt. He liked his blood pure.

He watched as an errant soul who'd by a miracle crawled up the bank, was tossed back in by a demon guard. The distant scream faded as his skin and flesh melted over again, his bones tumbling against the rocks until they crumbled.

He knew that pain. But at the time, he'd thought it worth it. A sacrifice for his daughter.

But his plan had failed. Now she was human.

The sigh would not come. The tension he felt in each and every muscle locked it in. He paced stiffly.

He'd pivoted the plan, but as always, not able to walk the Earth, he relied on others. How close was he now? Would he be free soon with her beside him once more?

The truth was he missed more than his daughter's obedience, and it bothered him. She had always been a means to an end, nothing more. As a baby, he'd allowed her to sup from him. It would soon be time for her to return the favour.

The Abbot forced his jaws to loosen enough to release the breath into the billowing heat around him.

He ran one hand over his hair. The wax he used to keep it in place had melted to oil and came away slick in his hand. He rubbed it over the rough fabric of the military-style jacket he wore. Then buffed the bronze epaulets adorning the shoulders to a shine, remembering the glorious battles he'd led above ground. Would he feel victories like those again?

"Stephen." The Advocate sidled up beside him.

He'd felt her eyes burning into his face long before she spoke. "Report."

"Conn O'Cuinn is doing what has been asked of him— gaining the trust of my boy. Soothing his doubts. Acting with humanity. Being a… hero." The words seemed to confuse her.

"Good. So the Assassin believes in him now?"

"He appears to be trusting him further. I believe we can make it more worth his while, however…"

"What are you suggesting, Jegudiel?"

She licked her lips and leaned into him. "Remember, my boy lost his family so tragically—"

"Thanks to you!"

The Advocate smiled, and bowed slightly, taking the comment as praise.

The Abbot bowed back—*whatever it takes*—and prompted, "About his family?"

"Yes, the Irishman is all he has. With your little Anastasia wondering the globe, and the angel curled up with his own lover, he needs to find family where he can—"

"And?" The Abbot stamped on one spot. *Hurry!*

"And, I think we can remind him of just how important this family is to him. Remind him of his losses, act on his memories… manipulate his mind." She added the last statement with a gleeful smile and wide eyes. "There are a few 'acquaintances' of mine in the vicinity that might just help."

Her enthusiasm was disarming. He brushed a finger over her cheek, and leaned in to gently lick the skin of her neck. Goosebumps erupted following the path made by the tip of his tongue. Her shoulders shivered.

"You want him broken?"

Her features turned stony. "I want to remind him of his treachery." Her voice softened, "and help our cause of course."

"He is your pet, not mine, my love. Go play. Break him if it amuses you."

"I will make a monster of him. I did it before—" she looked into the middle distance, breathing the words into the air "—and he will crawl back to me!"

She jerked her head to face the Abbot again. "When do we bring him here? You haven't said."

"Eventually. Step by step, my dear. The Tipping Point comes first, then you can have your toy back." He touched his tongue to her lips this time, looked deep into her eyes, and stroked his hand down the front of her dress, pausing between her legs. She pushed against his touch until she gasped and the air enveloped her. The Abbot was left alone.

He rubbed his hand on the side of his trouser leg, grimacing. Soon he would no longer need to pretend. Soon, she would be gone, he would have complete control and be back above ground. And Soren Huxford? Live or die, it didn't matter, he cared nothing for him.

Turning away from the view, he started his descent back to the Cells of Permanent Incarceration. "Don't let me down, Conn O'Cuinn," he muttered.

11

____

MOTHER'S BLOOD

DARK INSIDE THE STORE, the smell reached him first—blood. Fresh. Sweet. Then metal hit his tongue. As his eyes adapted from the bright sun, Soren made out the shape of the mother's body draped over the top of the shelving unit. Her blood continued to trickle weakly from the deep slash in her neck. It flowed over cans of tinned meat and vegetables before pooling on the floor in a wide, sticky puddle. Her stone-cold eyes gazed at the aisle behind her.

He crept around the shelves and tracked the direction of her eyes: her baby lay sprawled on the floor. Heart hammering, he gripped onto the shelf for balance as he absorbed the scene.

A smattering of blood patterned the baby's upper body though he had no obvious injuries, most likely sprayed from his mother. He checked twice for a pulse; his fingers shook too much on his first attempt. Nothing. He looked up from the body to see Cuinn standing inside the doorway, his gun up and ready. His head swept from body to body, then dropped the weapon to his side, looking grim.

Soren retraced his steps to where he'd started the circuit, at the spot below the woman's body where her second child lay. He stepped carefully around the large pool of blood and scooped up the young boy. He'd died at his mother's feet with a similar wound to her own.

Gipping the boy tight in his arms, he looked again at the mother, remembering the car journey just thirty minutes earlier:

"—it was just a mistake," the mother said, her voice a whisper from the front seat. She clutched the baby to her chest, skin still pink, feet still kicking, gurgling happily. "We just stopped so Michael could... you know. For a minute. Then the doors opened and they were just... there."

"Sorry, mama. I couldn't wait!"

"I know, darling. It's okay." She pushed back a hand to squeeze her son's toes.

Soren watched her reflection in the side window. It seemed important to her, this confession. She needed them to know it wasn't stupidity that had almost cost her everything. "Thank God, you both were there. Thank God..." Her voice tailed off to silence, leaving only the hum of the engine and the baby's soft noises.

In the driver's seat, the father's hands were bone-white fists on the steering wheel. The cuts on his skin were still weeping, but the tears on his cheeks had been cuffed away, replaced with streaks of dirt transferred from his hands. His gratitude was obvious, but so far, he'd only been able to stutter a single "thanks" as they walked to the car before settling into silent reflection.

Beside him in the second row of seats, the boy was the only chatty one, and Soren bore the full brunt of his curiosity.

At five years old, something he'd announced two minutes after they got into the vehicle, he already seemed to have forgotten the terror of the last hour and was more than willing to make friends. The questions came like machine-gun fire, and Soren felt each one chip away at his composure.

"Are you a soldier?"

"No."

"Policeman?"

"No."

"Why do you have a gun?"

"Because."

"Because, what?"

"Because I need to save kids like you."

"Wow! Are you a superhero?" The boy's eyes got rounder as he stared at Soren.

From the back row, Cuinn laughed. A mistake, as the boy's attention turned toward him.

"Are *you* a superhero?"

"Don't start on me, *mo chroí*."

"You talk funny."

This time Soren smiled. "He's not wrong."

"For sure I do."

"So do you." The boy turned straight back to Soren. "Why don't you talk American?"

"I'm not from here."

"Oh." The boy had paused to consider a good response. Then it came to him, "Where are you from, then?"

"Sweden."

"Is that a State?"

"No."

"I know all the States!" He then proceeded to list them, missing some and getting others confused with cities. At the end he said, "Did I get it right?"

Soren, who was pretty sure he hadn't, decided the best policy was to say, "Great job!"

At five seconds, the pause was the longest they'd had since they'd gotten into the vehicle. Soren took a breath.

"I'm thirsty." When no one responded, the boy leaned forward and pushed his mom's seat. "Mom, I'm thirsty."

"We'll stop soon. There's a gas station up ahead." She didn't look up from the baby, who was still gripped tight to her chest.

Satisfied, the boy continued, "Do you like *Transformers*?"

Soren looked at the kid's t-shirt, backpack, and runners. The *Transformers'* logo was emblazoned across them all, and assumed the correct response, "Sure!"

"Who's your favourite?"

"I dunno, kid."

"You said you liked them…"

"Yeah, I do, but don't know their names." It sounded weak, and Soren saw the boy scowl and cross his arms. It bothered him. "I know the *Turtles'* names…"

"Yeah?" Smiles again.

"Yeah. Donatello's my favourite…" Pleased to see the smile, Soren let the child's description of the different *Turtles* and their weapons lull him until they pulled up at the car rental place.

He let Cuinn give their thanks for the lift while he gave Michael a solemn salute. A giggle. "Bye, superhero!"

He met the mother's eyes from the front passenger seat. "Be safe," she mouthed. Soren nodded, watching as the van pulled away and turned onto the access road toward the gas station complex just up the hill.

The sound of its engine faded, leaving him and Cuinn standing alone in the quiet lot.

Cradling the boy's still form, Soren looked behind the counter where the young female shop assistant lay dead. She'd drawn a gun, but it hadn't done her any good. It now lay beside her on the floor, not even one round fired.

He gently placed the boy's body on top of the counter. With careful fingers, he tilted the boy's head, trying to hide the worst of the wound, and closed his eyes. *Blue. Like the baby's. Like his.*

The boy was covered in his mother's blood. It had soaked into the seat of his shorts, dripped onto his sandy blond hair, and was smeared across his legs and arms. Soren took a small towel he found beside the counter, and laid it over his face, then broke the silence. "Did you find the father?"

"Yeah, out back. Ripped to bits. The vultures were already there," Cuinn said.

"Roamers?"

"Yeah, I heard their bikes leaving after we heard the shots." Cuinn shook his head. "The women got off easy. They saw us coming."

This is easy? But Soren knew it was the truth. He looked again at the vicious wounds in their necks. A signature. He knew the clan well. They travelled from place to place looking for booze, money, and fun. Always at the expense of others.

The low wail of sirens started to get closer. Police? Private security? Hard to say in these times. It seemed the sales assistant had at least managed to press the alarm to someone.

"Let's go, Hux. We can do no more for them now, man. I'll meet you in the car." Cuinn retreated outside, making his way back to the SUV they'd just hired. Soren didn't follow. He went back to the baby's body, picked him up, and placed him beside his brother. Then he pulled their mother from the wreckage of the shelves, laying her out on the floor below her children. Together. He didn't know why. *It just mattered.*

As he went outside to the SUV, he pushed past the car rental store manager, who'd just arrived panting and stood ashen-faced in the doorway. Soren paused at the door, jerked his head over his shoulder: "The boy's name was Michael."

As Cuinn negotiated the car out of the lot, Soren stared at his hands. Blood. The boy's? The mother's?

No. Another mother. Still his hands, but smaller. Eight-years-old. Blond. Blue-eyed. Sitting on the floor beside her. **His** *mother. Daubed in her blood and staring into her frozen eyes.*

12

SKINNING A LIVE BEAR

THE SUV ROLLED down the slight incline in neutral, silent except for the crunch of sand and grit under the tires. Soren coasted to a stop at the edge of the road in deep shade. Two days of dead ends and backtracking. Now, another checkpoint. Every other route into Detroit was like this, a checkpoint with armed sentries. This one was at least fairly open. It had options.

Above them, to their left, was an old industrial warehouse perched on top of a manmade hill of concrete blocks, patches of parched scrub, and waist deep piles of the sand blown from the rich arable land now dried to desert by the demon sun. The dunes breathed and rippled with the movement of lizards and snakes just under the surface. Hunting. He shuddered.

To the south, houses stood in a typical subdivision pattern, circling a playground. The encroaching dunes had buried that place, too. The tops of rusted swing sets and a wood and rope climbing frame stuck out from the top of the sand and grit.

Below them, as the incline levelled out, the low-roofed checkpoint building straddled the centre median. For all the good they would do, weak plastic barriers stretched arms across the road on either side.

Ten guards with weapons but no body armour, milled around. Khaki pants and t-shirts. Private security, not military. Kids conscripted by government desperation and given assault rifles. Against demons, it amounted to using a Swiss Army knife to skin a live bear. A catastrophic miscalculation that left a mountain of corpses and the high-ups sitting it out in safety silos with real military and the rest of the weaponry.

"It's time to call it, Hux." Cuinn dropped the binoculars, count finished. He rubbed his injured legs. "Together we can take all ten." He wheezed the words out; even recon was tiring him.

"You sure, man? You look done in." Soren had only agreed to get Cuinn as far as Detroit. Now, it looked like he'd need to assist him further, but killing people hadn't been part of the deal.

"I'll be fine, so I will—with your help, brother." His eyes flashed light blue. A challenge.

Soren regarded the guards. "They're just kids, man," he said. Several of the men looked way under twenty. They were laughing and throwing around a football, certainly not expecting to see two armed men drive up to them. "They have mothers."

Cuinn nodded. "Sure they do. Like I did. Like you did."

"Mothers are innocent."

"Mothers always are." Cuinn sighed and watched the young men. A couple now wrestled playfully while the others looked on, laughing and cheering.

"There must be another way. Not this Tipping Point," said Soren. "Can't we leave it for the angels?"

"I wish." Cuinn twisted in his seat to face him, the cut under his jaw splitting slightly again. Almost healed, it oozed clear liquid through the crusty surface. "This is the way—the only way. You've got to stop doubting me, lad."

"If I start killing people. It could be Bali all over again. You know that would be—"

"—bad. I know." Cuinn put a hand on his arm, stopping him. "Believe me, I will never put you back there. But, you'll be grand. You're older now. Just keep a proper perspective, soldier."

He paused, then added, "Look, Hux. You're not my recruit anymore. I can't order you to follow me. I'm asking you to stand with me, to know I wouldn't lead you wrong. To trust me. I'm your feckin' family, man."

He held Soren's eyes and waited. A deeper green than Soren had ever seen them. Sincere. Though in the drawn-out pause that followed, flecks of blue flashed irritation across them, too.

"I don't—"

"Enough!" Cuinn's eyes zipped to light blue. "I'm going. Save me, or watch me die." He pushed open the door of the SUV and set off at a jog toward the men, his shotgun up and ready.

13

BROTHERS

AS SOON AS Cuinn opened the car door, Soren leaned back to retrieve his rifle from the back seat, never once taking his eyes off the demon. Was this a test to prove I'm family? *Okay then.*

He ran through scenarios. Cuinn's move was madness, but at least he'd chosen a good time. Two guards had moved down the hill on the far side of the road to throw the football over a longer distance, effectively putting them out of play. Five more were milling around city-side, maybe half a sports-field-length away. And the final three were lounging against a couple of old Jeeps parked by the checkpoint building, relaxed and chatting.

Cuinn wouldn't be able to turn into his Core form if he was attacked; he was too weak. If the three closest guards got a few good shots off first, who knew what would happen? His bones were strong, but bullets from the AKs would still do a lot of damage at that range. If they disarmed him, could he go hand-to-hand? One-on-one, yes, but if they decided to double-down. Usually, it'd be no problem. But, today?

One of the closest guards spotted Cuinn's approach. He

snapped to standing, gun in hand, but not yet in firing position. He said something to the other two, who followed suit, and all three formed a line beside the vehicles before aiming their rifles directly at the approaching demon in unison, like a choreographed move from some old cowboy movie.

"Christ, Cuinn." Soren spoke under his breath, rapidly freeing his rifle from the confines of its carrier.

At the checkpoint, the guard who'd first spotted Cuinn seemed to be in charge. He shouted, "Stay where you are!" his words drifting up the road to Soren.

Cuinn continued to approach, not even slowing his steady pace. As a concession to the command, he raised his arms out to his sides, his shotgun held at arm's length.

"I said, stay where you are!" The guard shouted the order again. Then added, "Halt," as an afterthought.

This time Cuinn came to a casual stop, talking to them all the time with his lilting Irish accent. Soren couldn't make out what he was saying. It was time for him to move. He scanned his surroundings, looking for a good spot, eased himself from the SUV, and made his way up the hill toward the dilapidated warehouse.

Boulders dotted the landscape around this part of the city outskirts, and he moved from the shadow of one to the other. The warehouse was partially demolished and scarred by fire, with a trail of black marks snaking across the breeze blocks that made up its exposed foundations.

As Soren crept closer, he sank up to his knees in the sand and had to raise them to wade through it. It trickled into the top of his loosely laced boots and glued to his sweat-soaked khaki fatigues. *Fucking sand!* Half a dozen lizards scuttled away from his approach.

Settled in the cover of a large boulder, he assessed progress below. Cuinn was being frisked by one guard while two others flanked him, guns still pointed in his direction. One by one, all his weapons were stripped away.

Eventually, the guy in charge was satisfied. He looked Cuinn square in the eyes and said something too low for Soren to hear. If they'd told him to remove his sunglasses, he'd be done for.

The two footballers had swaggered up to the little party now, too, adding their own guns and attitude to the mix. Instead of rifles, they held handguns in Cuinn's direction with a high arm and twist of the wrist that shouted, "street!"

The others, far over on the Detroit side, also approached at a run. One kid grinned like he was greeting an old friend. *Idiot.*

Soren already had his sights set on the guy a little to the right of Cuinn. Not the one doing all the talking, but another, older man. He looked jittery, his finger flexing against the trigger of his gun.

The guy in charge raised his voice. "Take off the shades!"

Shit!

The Irishman did no more than shrug in response, and, for his tardiness, the guard struck him across the side of his face with the butt of the rifle. From the boulder, it looked half-hearted; Cuinn's head barely moved.

Cuinn looked from the gun to the guard before pulling the sunglasses slowly from his face. And then… he smirked. Soren groaned. *Of course he did!*

The guard recoiled like he'd caught the stink from a hot corpse, and shouted, "Dem—" But before he could complete the word, Cuinn made a grab for the end of his rifle with his right hand, jerking it up and away, while chopping his left down on the man's forearm.

The crack as his arm broke echoed down the empty road, as did the long scream that followed.

The guard staggered back, clutching his arm to his chest,

but stayed standing. Cuinn didn't wait; he kicked out at the next guy in the line-up, his foot meeting a soft belly. The guard folded at his midriff and flew backward. He hit the dust.

While the third guard hesitated, Cuinn zipped forward and grabbed the shirt of one footballer, and the arm of the other, and swung them together, crashing heads. Blood sprayed as the skin of each forehead split, and they sank to the ground, out cold.

Four down in fifteen seconds. Soren grunted appreciatively.

The five other guards charged into the melee, their weapons raised, but it was the original third man, itchy-trigger guy, who still had Soren's attention. He finally committed: he raised his rifle to Cuinn's side and—

Soren fired.

The bullet hit his shoulder. He spun before losing his footing and hit the ground face down. The guy had gotten a shot off—a wild round that slammed into the front of one of the Jeeps. A plume of black smoke and steam belched from under the hood. Disabled.

Three of the final five charged forward at Cuinn, guns raised. Soren fired again. Still only looking to disable. The bullet punched through the heavy muscle of the oldest-looking one, kicking up a puff of dirt on the other side. The guard's leg buckled instantly, and he went down with a choked yell. He silenced himself, already clawing his way back toward cover.

The remaining two sheltered behind the Jeep and rained a barrage of shots onto the rocks, forcing Soren to wait it out. The two not firing forgot all training and sought to bring Cuinn down any way they knew how, kicking and punching, battering him with the stocks of their guns and rocks— anything they could lay their hands on.

Under their blows, Cuinn almost seemed to give up. He was handcuffed and dragged around to the other side of the checkpoint building. Soren caught a glimpse of his blood-soaked face looking in his direction—a flicker of a challenge in his eyes—before he was pulled out of sight.

The firing stopped, but two guards remained on watch behind the vehicle. It was a standoff.

14

____

SUNSET

THERE WAS ONLY one move that made sense: wait until sunset. Soren hadn't seen any night-vision kit, so hopefully, the border guards wouldn't see him coming. But even if they did, what else could he do? He couldn't leave Cuinn there to die. He couldn't leave his brother.

Annoyance grumbled low in his stomach. What the hell was he doing, going off half-cocked like that? It wasn't like him; he planned meticulously and had taught him to do the same. To keep control at all costs.

Had Cuinn deliberately been trying to force his hand? Had his brother just set him up? Soren refused to consider it.

Leaning back against the rock, he watched the lowering sun, and deliberately cut off thoughts of his anger at Cuinn. But then the space was filled with other images; the dead family at the convenience store, and from there, to *that* hallway with the tall ceiling and ornate staircase curling up to the second and third floors. Back to his childhood home in Stockholm.

He used to lie on the cold marble slabs and gaze up into the very heights of the house. He would follow the contours of the plaster decorations with his eyes and pretend he could reach up and trace the soft curves of the scrollwork.

Everything was so beautiful until:

The slap of his father's hand around her face and the thump as she hit the wall sent splintering cracks up into the plaster above. He'd thrown her around like a rag doll while Soren watched, hidden behind the bottom step of the staircase.

But they both knew he was there.

"Go to your room, baby," his mother had whispered, blood trickling from her cut lip.

"No, mama, let me help you!" He'd been brave despite his shaking legs and had planted himself between the two of them.

His father pushed him away and ordered him to his room, but still he'd resisted. If only he could stand there a little longer, he could save his mother; he knew he could. So, he'd run back and clung to her.

Then, his father had pointed the gun at him.

"Soren, move away! I'll be all right," she'd begged him, her voice cracking.

He'd looked at his father. The eyes of the man were glazed, lost. Then the next wave of anger hit him. "Get out of the way, boy!" He prodded the gun directly into his chest. "Move! That's an order!"

"Please, Soren, move away. He won't do it," she'd whispered into his ear, and even managed a little smile as she'd pushed him gently to one side.

"Move recruit—"

No, that was wrong. His father hadn't called him that. That was Cuinn.

Soren's eyes flew open. He'd closed them against the glare

of the setting sun bouncing off the roof of the vehicle below and dozed off.

He pulled his attention back to the road.

Deep shadow now spread down to the SUV while a light evening breeze blew against his sweat-soaked shirt. The dreams always left him wet through.

Taking a calming breath, Soren slunk down the hillside and back to the vehicle. Inside was Cuinn's backpack. Apart from the weapons he'd carried with him into the fight, he'd also brought a few grenades, another large hunting knife, and a short, thin, flexible blade.

Soren stared at it. Cuinn had told him before they'd left Las Vegas that he had *just in case* supplies that *could stop any wee fecker.* This blade would stop a Soldier. The last time Soren had seen one like it, he was stabbing it into Cuinn's head, up through the eye socket, around the armoured plating of his skull, and deep into his brain. Sending him to Hell.

He let out a steadying breath.

So, what if Cuinn had forced his hand? There must be a good reason, even if it meant killing kids. He had to trust him. He would not fail him again.

After removing their bags from the rental, he put it into neutral and released the brake. It began to roll forward down the slight incline to the checkpoint. He primed two grenades, dropped them onto the driver's seat, and retreated.

The two guards who'd been keeping watch saw the car creeping toward them and shouted the alarm. They opened fire. The two street kids and the guard with the shoulder injury joined them, too. When they realized no one was shooting back, but the car wasn't stopping, they ran forward to investigate. As the road levelled out, the SUV came to a slow stop. They peered into the front window. The grenades exploded.

The ground trembled below Soren's feet. A spray of rocks

and broken glass shot into the air as the explosion created twisted metal of the vehicle and dug a deep trench into the ground. Flesh too, bloody pieces slapping the ground around the SUV. Flames caught, and the stink of burning fuel and meat filled the air as a cloud of choking black smoke erupted from the vehicle.

Under its cover, Soren ran full-tilt toward the checkpoint.

As he emerged from the smoke, the four remaining guards scrambled to form a firing line. Soren didn't break stride; his arm was already in motion. The grenade landed at their feet. They saw it. A split second of frozen panic, then they scattered, diving for cover that wasn't there. Too late. The blast tore through them.

The instant the grenade left his hand, Soren had lunged for the corner of the building, tackling Cuinn and shielding him with his own body as shrapnel and debris rained down.

Sitting beside Cuinn was just one guard, the one with the bullet wound to his leg. He had no weapon and stared in shock at Soren, not moving.

Soren pointed his pistol. "Get him up."

The man fished around in his trouser pocket for the key and undid the handcuffs.

Cuinn stood with Soren's help. "You took your time, brother!" he said, and put his arm around Soren's shoulders.

Soren growled a reply and propped him up against the one remaining wall of the building. Cuinn wobbled a little, then planted his feet while Soren looked him over. New injuries on top of the old. Split earlobe and smashed lip. A deep laceration on the side of his head. Purple bruising and deep blue drills that looked like he'd been dragged across gravel. No broken bones. The damage was superficial. For a Soldier.

"What do you want done with him?" Soren asked.

Cuinn shrugged, and without a glance at the guard, he

limped to the still working Jeep and pulled himself awkwardly inside.

Soren cuffed the guard and threw the keys into the scrub. He didn't matter, they wouldn't come back this way.

He retrieved their bags and his rifle and put them into the Jeep, then climbed into the driver's seat. After turning the key, he regarded Cuinn. "Okay?"

"Yep. Talking didn't work, so it didn't." Despite the humour, Cuinn's face was grim. His right eye had almost swollen shut. He'd be feeling the soldiers' boots on his body for days.

"I just had no strength, man. Felt like I was wading through mud." He shook his head. "Thank God you were here, brother." He gave Soren a weak smile, then collapsed sideways against the window, and closed his eyes.

"Yeah. Thank God I was here..." Soren echoed as he put the vehicle in gear and moved off. As they drove over the border and into Detroit, he didn't look back. His mind was clear; his choice made.

15

ROMAN HOLIDAY

HIGH ABOVE, the painting stretched out in all its Renaissance glory. There were sighs and whispers of "beautiful," "*beau*," and "*belissimo*," by the people who stood alongside her. But Tazia, who had stood still too long, and stared so hard her neck locked, had no further admiration to give. Was five minutes enough? Ten? Could she move on now? Some people had been staring for an hour. Perhaps there was a code she was unaware of.

She rotated her neck gingerly, but feeling the grind at the top of her spine and the spasm of pain that shot across her shoulders, she stopped, and instead, bobbed it forward and back until it loosened. Being human sucked.

Around her, a couple of tiny children were chasing each other, circling a pile of prayer books balanced precariously on a rickety wooden table stupidly placed right in the middle of the open space. They were laughing, not understanding the solemnity of their surroundings. It wasn't just an occasional titter or giggle, but constant fit-to-burst laughter that shattered the concentrated silence, and seemed to come from the edge of hysteria.

Children—that was another thing she didn't understand. In the human world, they appeared to get away with murder. Give them a knife, and she'd be happy to have them stand alongside her in battle. Little energy monsters, fuelled by candy and carelessness. Perfect cannon fodder.

Dragging her attention back, Tazia stared again at Michelangelo's fresco, *Creation of Adam*. She raised both hands up to the back of her neck and dug in her fingers, massaging firmly under her hair, working her way up and down the vertebrae she could reach.

She soaked in the painting again. It was beautiful. Had God touched her like that? Had he put the spark in her at the same time that she uttered the last word of the witches' spell? Had the moment she'd said *yes* changed her from a child of the dark world, whose soul was a fallen angel's plaything, to a child of… God? How the fuck did she know? Turning human hadn't come with a *Coles Notes* on spirituality.

Her breath shortened, and she clutched at the pendant at her throat, pulling the herbal charm from side to side along the chain. It made a zipper-like sound. Back and forth. Soothing.

Aideen had insisted on the charm. "It will keep you invisible from angels and demons," she'd said, her voice full of concern. Why? *You don't know me, lady. I can look after myself.* But thinking about it, being hidden from prying eyes was too much of a gift to pass off, so she took it.

"It will wear off, but will give you time to re-balance." The witch had seemed so concerned that becoming human would be too much for her. Well, she was right. So far, nothing worked. Not the heart that beat in her chest, nor the soul that dug at her conscience, not even her own body. It felt itchy and new, like wearing an unwashed shirt fresh out of the cellophane.

Tazia pulled at the chain again. This time, holding the cool glass bottle to her cheek. She'd spent her first days trawling the city coiled tight, waiting for an attack that never came, or a flicker of recognition in the eyes of some passing Soldier or Leech. Nothing. And the humans? She didn't need a magickal charm to be invisible to them. They mostly ignored her—and each other, too. Odd. Sad.

And so boring!

Here she was at yet another tourist site, starting conversations with any damn person who stood within a couple of feet of her. Just for the *craic*, as Cuinn would say.

The children's laughter changed to ear-splitting screeches that echoed around the vast space. They grabbed at the table as they ran, making the pile of books wobble dangerously.

She raised an eyebrow and scanned the room. Everyone looked in different directions. She was not the only person being ignored. The speed those kids circled the table was dizzying. If she could just take that energy and mould it, she could churn out little soldiers so fast... Ahh, but what about their souls? The question gnawed at her.

She circled her neck to look again at the painting. "Don't look so smarmy." Her comment targeted Adam, but caused a passing tourist to lower his expensive camera with its massive lens, automatic light meters, and whirring focus, and look sideways at her.

"What?" she asked him. "Don't you think he looks smarmy? Lying there, all rock-star-like." She gestured toward the painting again.

The tourist shrugged. "I guess he does look a little... relaxed."

"Yeah, like 'God, you owe me something.' Right?"

He pursed his lips and nodded, then laughed. "I guess the entitlement generation isn't such a new thing!"

At that moment, the pile of prayer books crashed to the ground. The kids came to a shuddering halt, and the youngest, a little boy not much more than a toddler, stood in the middle of the scattered books and gave an air-rending scream. The crowd immediately stilled and looked at the kids. Some teens a few feet away burst out laughing. The little girl looked at the tourist who had been talking to Tazia, her own bottom lip shaking. "Daddy! Help!"

The tourist groaned. "You got kids?"

"No." *Just memories.*

"Lucky you!" He balanced his camera on top of his backpack, which he'd left leaning against the wall beside him, and went to their aid with hunched shoulders and a sigh.

Tazia looked up to the ceiling again and whispered, "More than a spark of a soul is needed to make a human you know. I've at least learned that in the last few weeks." She dropped her head and dangled her hands to her sides. Figuring out her place in the world was so damn hard.

Shaking her last smoke from the packet, she scrunched it up and threw it on the floor before lighting the cigarette with a match and trembling fingers. She took a long, deep draw.

As she blew out the smoke, her heartbeat slowed. She spotted another fresco on the far wall, *The Last Judgement*, and winked at the central figure. "Jesus! For the love of God, help me figure this shit out!" Her first prayer. It would have to do.

Before the docent could start shouting at her for smoking in the chapel, she turned to leave, but catching sight of the tourist's discarded camera, she paused. Her fingers twitched again.

With two steps, she was there. She bent her knees, picking up the camera in one smooth motion, and headed for the exit. As she left the chapel, she hummed "The Boys are Back in Town," while the metal studs of her boots tapped the rhythm on the hard marble floor.

16

____

SHELLING PEAS

THE STREET the newspaper seller had sent her to—*via di angelo*—wasn't what she'd expected. Tall, narrow townhouses of cream block work leaned in on either side, squeezing the sky into a bright blue ribbon. Laundry lines crisscrossed between balconies, clothes flapping in the warm breeze. It felt a world away from the tourist traps. A slice of old Italy dropped in the middle of the city. Tazia felt her shoulders loosen. This wasn't home, not Turin, but it was close enough.

A faint smile touched her lips, remembering the man who'd sent her here. He'd yelled at her in a rapid-fire stream of curses when she'd stumbled into his magazine display, too busy examining the stolen camera to watch where she was going. He'd assumed she was just another stupid tourist. Her own colourful reply had made him stop short, then burst into laughter. "*Mia piccola!*" he'd roared, pulling her into a hug so tight she almost passed out. She rubbed her ribs at the memory. He'd pointed her here, to a Signor Purletti, though what she was supposed to be looking for now, she had no idea.

The "shops" were the street-level front rooms of domestic residences with just the occasional splash of ochre paint beside their entrances to denote the nature of the establishments. She'd noticed a few symbols that made sense, like a "V" to illustrate an open book for a bookstore, and a single flower petal for an establishment littered with pots of dark red geraniums. But so far, she had seen nothing to represent a camera or electronics store of the type she sought.

Outside some houses, on blue metallic slat chairs, sat matronly ladies dressed in full Mediterranean garb, including scarves over their heads, and black skirts to their toes. Human. Faces cured to the colour of old walnut, with deep wrinkles like the bark of the same tree. Some fiddled with rosaries, others smoked or drank coffee, but most were busy with some sort of household task.

As she passed them, some muttered a few ritual words in Latin. Whether to bless, curse, or gain her attention, she wasn't sure, though there was also a fair smattering of magickal phrases she recognized sprinkled in too, enough to keep her guessing about their real purpose.

A cat, with an army of kittens following close behind, and small dogs ran from woman to woman, receiving caresses from their deep brown hands or the occasional edible tidbit. All were fat and happy, though none had collars to mark ownership.

It looked like Rome afforded strays a good life. Tazia felt she'd fit in well.

Stopping beside the lady nearest to her, she asked politely for the home of Signor Purletti, as the newspaper seller had directed her

The woman stopped her task of shelling peas and considered Tazia for a long moment before fishing the remains of a cigar from her apron pocket. She lit it and offered it to her. It was the long, thin sort that smelled of warm coffee and young wood rather than the acrid scent of an old burning shoe like her father's big fat smokes.

Tazia smiled her gratitude and sucked deeply. As she blew

out the smoke in a long reedy puff, it seemed to envelop her, wrapping her in the loving embrace of a warm winter sweater and the taste of a sweet cinnamon bun. Under the scent of the smoke, another note rose: expensive, spicy, and with the sharp metallic tang of gun oil jabbing at her playfully. *Soren Huxford!*

She spun around, expecting to see his large form bearing down on her, but the street was empty apart from the other elderly ladies who had all paused mid-task, and stared at her expectantly.

She looked back at the woman who'd given her the cigar. "*Magia?*"

As one, all the ladies nodded, their laughter echoing down the street with such affection that it put Tazia at ease. The lady took back the cigar, stubbed it out on a blackened area of the old cream block work over her shoulder, replaced it in her apron, and invited her to sit down on the seat beside her.

She passed a bowl of unshelled peas to Tazia and gestured that she should get to work.

What else was there to do? She took the bowl and cut into a pod with the short nail on her thumb. When this failed to get it open, she moved on to a twisting motion. Also, no good. Finally, she settled to snapping the pod in two, pulling up the outer shell as though unzipping a sweater, and pulling out each pea individually using her finger and thumb. It was an arduous task, and she concentrated with equal effort she would have applied to gutting a victim for her father.

After a few minutes, the lady nudged her and shook her head. She took a pod from her hand and popped it open, applying just enough pressure with her thumb about a third of the way down the length. Then she eased the rest open and pushed all the peas out with the back of one thumb into the waiting bowl. *Easy.*

Nodding, Tazia took another pod and tried again. After a couple of false starts, she popped one open. Her eyes widened with surprise as a spray of fizzy vegetable juice tickled her face, a swathe of refreshing green scent hitting her nose at the same time. Triumphant, she pushed with her thumb, as she'd seen the lady do, and a cascade of little green peas bounced into the bowl. She giggled and brushed her hair to one side with her newly green-stained fingers.

The old lady smiled, leaned forward and patted Tazia's knee, then said in broken English, "Is… small things… *le piccole cose*… to make the difference to the life. To live… *spettacolarmente!*"

She removed the bowl from Tazia's lap and gestured to the house next to her own. Daubed in ochre paint beside the front door was an infinity symbol and PURLETTI.

———

"Where did you get it, Miss?" Signor Purletti spoke perfect English, but he was most definitely Italian, from the olive of his leathery skin to the shape of his Roman nose. Tazia guessed he was around sixty years old as he peered at her from under lashes so thick and dark it looked as though his eyes were outlined in kohl.

"It's mine, just don't need it anymore." She looked at him directly, but the lie was clear. Without her demon eyes and nature, guilt washed over her regularly, and now it rose in the heat of her cheeks.

He held her gaze a little longer, then put out a hand. "Let me look at it more closely."

Tazia passed the camera to him, and for some minutes he examined it, unscrewing the long lens, unclipping the light attachment, and scrolling through the pictures from the memory card. "There is only a little battery left. The charger?"

"Oh. Um. No. I… um… lost it?" This time she looked anywhere but his eyes.

"Ah, you *lost* it." He didn't look at her as he continued scrolling, but the sarcasm was clear. "And please, Miss, tell me another thing."

"Yes?"

"If this is your camera, why are there pictures of you on it taken by someone else? Taken just an hour ago."

"What?" Tazia took the camera back from him to look.

The pictures he was referring to were of her staring at the ceiling of the Sistine Chapel. In the first couple, the angle was from the back. The next shot was a close-up of her face, and to her shame, it looked tear-stained. She didn't remember crying.

The next picture showed a different angle. Now, she was facing the camera, looking aimless and lost, staring into the middle distance, her hand to her neck. She remembered that moment. Desperate to know whether the soul that felt so strong to her now was a real chance to begin again, or yet another trick the Universe was playing on her.

"He must have been watching me…" she said under her breath.

"I'm sorry, did you say something?" Purletti's hand still outstretched, waiting.

"Um, I said, they're selfies!" *Stupid!*

"Ah, I see." He nodded and took the camera from her to peer at the images again. "And what of the gentleman in the background?"

"What gentleman?" She snatched it back and studied the picture. Behind her, standing in the shadows in the corner of the room, was the tall, broad figure of a man. He was almost translucent, as though his image had been overlaid onto the wall. But she could clearly see long fair hair swept behind his ears and a rifle balanced against his leg—the butt plate resting on the ground and the muzzle of the long barrel grasped in his fingers. He appeared to be staring at her with focus and recognition. Hux. *Again!*

Tazia took a breath and gave the camera back. "I don't know who that is. Are you interested in the camera or not?"

"You don't know him? He seems to know you, Miss. He seems to need your help, if you don't mind me saying. He looks a little… lost, don't you think?" The shopkeeper smiled, then reached into his cashbox, counted out a pile of euros and held them out to her. "That should get you home."

"Home?"

As an answer, he nodded at the photograph again. "To the man you don't know."

Tazia took the money, murmuring her thanks, and stepped back outside to the street. Why the fuck did everyone know her business? It would seem that in the human world, there was a lot more magick than she'd realized.

The sun had set now, and the only occupants left on the cobbles were a couple of magpies casually pecking at the remains of a small animal that looked like a passing vehicle had squashed it. She hoped it wasn't a kitten. Whatever it was, its light-coloured fur was now smeared with bright red blood.

Maybe it *was* time to move on.

17

——————

SILENCE

SOREN STEERED the Jeep around the wreckage of a city bus lying on its side, undercarriage charred black. It had been less than a year since he and Cuinn were last in Detroit, but the rot had deepened. Shattered windows in the high-rises winked like hollow eye sockets. A fresh litter of bones, sun-bleached and scattered across the asphalt. Human, from the looks of it. Or maybe just leftovers from another demon squabble. The carrion birds, at least, were eating well.

It was the silence that was new. Before, there had always been a low hum to the city: the growl of engines in the distance, the occasional scuffle, the caw of vultures. Now, nothing. A dome of oppressive quiet had settled over everything. It felt wrong. Unnatural.

"Even demons don't want to be here," Soren said. He'd been waiting for a comment or two from Cuinn since they'd first entered the city, but there had been none. The Irishman remained hunched in his seat, staring out the window, lost in thought.

"Cuinn!" Soren attempted to jerk him out of it.

"What?"

"It's deathly. Even the demons don't want the city."

"Oh, they want it…" Cuinn sat slightly more upright, flexing his knees against the glove box to help himself do so. "They want it bad."

"Man, push your seat back. Give yourself some space."

"Nah. I'm all right, so I am." He hunched back again. "Lemme sleep."

Soren grunted an acknowledgement.

Cuinn's light snores soon drifted to him. The sound was comforting and took the edge off the stark world outside the windows.

————

From the deep shadows of the alleyway, the church's semi-collapsed copper-green cupola looked like a twisted mouth taking a bite out of the dusk. Along the apex of the roof, what he first took for stone gargoyles resolved into a dozen vultures. Watching. The northern HQ for the Demonic Irish Resistance. Once Cuinn's place, now Kevin's. At least, what was left of it.

Between them and the entrance, twenty-some Vampires milled around a concrete barrier. *Tiocfaidh ár lá* was scrawled across it in green, then NOT FUCKING YET! underneath, complete with love hearts.

Mocking the Celtic Soldiers' loyalty with graffiti? This pathetic scrawl was like something he'd find on a textbook at boarding school. They may as well have painted a flaccid dick on the wall, scrotum hanging loose and hairy. Yeah, that sure would teach those Irish! He gave a quiet snort.

"Feckin' Leeches. How'd they get this close?" Cuinn was exhausted, but his voice carried a slight vibration. "What the fuck has Kevin been doing?" He sank back in the passenger seat, panting. He'd need at least another twenty-four hours of healing time before he could move without the stiffness of an old tree branch in a gale.

"Things feel different," Soren said. "Detroit seems dead. Everything just hanging. Waiting for the axe." He glanced up at the vultures again. They weren't moving, not shuffling a foot or shaking a wing, not even tipping their heads in his direction. But they knew he was looking.

"Sure, man. It's the Tipping Point. We're nearly there. Everyone will feel it. It'll be motivating these feckers. But until someone leads them, they won't know what to do with it—the power." He nodded at the vampires. "You still got a grenade?"

"Yep. You wanna declare war?"

"Nah. There must be a reason Kev is leaving them be. Distract them, though. So we can sneak through. That alley leads round back." He gestured to the right, to a narrow dark passage that looked like it finished in a dead end. It was a few yards over the border into the vampires' territory. "If we can get them to look the other way for a bit, we can get in."

Soren leaned over to the back seat and pulled the last grenade from Cuinn's pack. He quietly slipped from the vehicle and jogged over to the other side of the street, keeping to the shadows. The hot wind yanked at his clothing as he ran, blowing directly at the vampires. It wouldn't be long before they'd smell him.

There was an old low-roofed building to his right, once used as a mechanic's workshop by the look of the sign hanging now from just one corner, CORKTOWN CARS. It looked odd, stuck into a row of taller buildings like a broken tooth. Usually, buildings like these had flat roofs, but this one had a little angle to it. If he threw the grenade over the top, it would roll to the other side, and the explosion would happen just out of sight.

He looked back at Cuinn, who still had his head turned

toward the vampires, but now he had Soren's rifle in hand, the end of the gun leaning out of the open window, covering him.

Soren positioned himself, and made a couple of warm-up arches with his arm, then before he could think too much about what could go wrong, he pulled the pin and threw the grenade. He heard it land and paused just long enough to hear it patter down the other side of the roof, then turned tail and ran back to the car.

As he jumped back into the driver's seat, the explosion shattered the air. He glanced through the windshield. Perfect. Most of the vampires ran toward the noise, leaving the entranceway to the alley unguarded.

A cloud of dust and smoke rose into the air as Soren eased the Jeep toward the barrier and then turned right into the passageway. It was a maze. A rabbit warren of narrow streets and paths. Before the fall, he'd walked them. Then they were clean, cute artisan businesses. Now the hand-painted signs were scorched and broken, windows smashed, and doors forced.

They turned again to find the church. Cuinn breathed a heavy sigh. "There you are *mo chroí*. I missed you."

18

—————————

WELCOME HOME

THE WOODEN DOOR to the Irish Club stood at the bottom of a short flight of concrete steps flanked on either side by a solid metal railing. The whole thing sheltered under a Gothic arch made of large blocks of carved stone that looked intentionally too big for the doorway.

There were no signs or colours to mark the Club, apart from a face-high hole in the door guarded by three metal bars and a backing of shaded glass. A lookout inside would see a close-up view of whoever demanded entrance.

Cuinn rapped on the door with the stock of his shotgun. He had the other arm over Soren's broad shoulders. No sound came from inside. Soren frowned. A Friday evening, and there was no talking, no music? On a normal night, the bar would be buzzing.

He leaned forward to look through the viewing window. The fire was lit. "Someone's in there."

Cuinn rapped again, repeating the special rhythmic knocking he'd used before. Again, silence.

"No key?"

"For sure, Hux. They let me keep a feckin' key to the bar in Hell… Or should I use the one we keep under the door mat?"

Soren raised his eyebrows at the sarcasm. He matched it with his own. "We're out of grenades, or we could blast it…"

"No one's blowing anything up!" The voice from the right was underscored by the sharp, metallic sound of weapons being armed on either side of them. The hair on the back of his neck stood up. A presence behind him, close.

"Ahh, sure lads, you don't wanna be shooting me!" Cuinn spoke without turning around.

"You wanna tell me why not?" the voice asked.

"Cos then I'd have to shoot you, myself, and I don't think you'd want that beautiful child of yours going without its da —" he slowly turned, and looked to where the voice had come from in the darkness "—now, do you, Kev?"

There was a pause. Soren stiffened. He'd also recognized the voice. All these boys would know about Turin. He was on dangerous ground.

"Cu… Cuinn?" Kevin hauled himself up and over the railing so that he stood right behind the two of them.

A flashlight flicked on. Soren heard a shuffle on the steps as whoever the other gunman was, moved to one side. The light shone in Cuinn's direction.

"Sure, it's me, man. Don't you recognize me? I'm a bit battered, so I am, but this ugly mug is still mine…" He grinned, then winced in the bright light directed at him. It shone off his teeth and lit the rest of his features sufficiently to draw a gasp from the two men standing above him.

"I… I…" Was all Kevin could manage before pushing past Soren and grabbing at Cuinn to pull him into a solid embrace. As he hugged, his hands roved, slapping Cuinn's back and squeezing his arms, no doubt checking he was flesh and blood, just like Soren had done back at the hotel. "But you're dead, man. You're dead!"

"When have you known me not to bounce back?" Cuinn laughed, but he was still wincing. "Let go of me now, Kev. I'm broken, man."

Kevin stood back, hands still cemented to his shoulders. He shook his head. "Just tell me I'm not fuckin' seeing things!"

Cuinn shrugged and swayed, leaning his weight against Soren. "Unless you're seeing pink elephants, you're not seeing things. Just me, and Hux here."

Soren braced Cuinn to hold him up, then slowly turned, so the flashlight illuminated his face. "Hi, Micky—"

The blow didn't just land; it detonated. It smashed under his jaw, snapping his teeth together with a sound like a pistol shot. It didn't lift him—Cuinn's weight anchored him—but it slammed Soren backward, twisting him so his spine collided with the iron railings. The metal bit deep. He barely kept his grip on the Irishman's waist.

The hook to his temple scrambled his vision, white static flooding the dark stairwell. He ignored it, shoving Cuinn hard to the side, pinning the demon against the door where he wouldn't tumble down. Only then did Soren turn back.

He didn't attack. He couldn't. Not Kevin. Not after what he'd done to them.

Instead, Soren crouched, tucking his chin and throwing his forearms up.

The follow-up was pure blind anger. Kevin was a tank. The punches rained down, hammering into Soren's forearms, slipping through the guard to smash his ear, his jaw, the bridge of his nose.

Eyes shut, Soren took it all.

Blood slicked his lips. He tasted copper and loose bone. Trapped on the stairs, the railing vibrated against his back with every hit. *Good. Do it again.*

Then, abruptly, the battering stopped.

Soren lowered his guard an inch. His vision was still a

cascade of snow. Through it, Kevin stood over him, chest heaving, nostrils flaring. The physical fury stalled.

"You… fucking… traitor," Kevin gasped. He dragged the back of his hand across his mouth to wipe away the sweat, smearing Soren's blood across his own cheekbone in a streak of red camo paint.

As his vision cleared, Soren looked him in the eye. He offered no challenge, no defence. The heat was already rising under his skin. The wards stitched his flesh back together. His split lip sealed. The throbbing swelling in his ear deflated. The loosened tooth rooted itself back into his jaw with a wet click.

He spat a glob of blood onto the steps.

"Finished?" Soren asked. He meant it. Did he want more?

Cuinn hadn't interfered. Now he said, "Easy, Kev. You need to hear the whole story, man. And you really can't kill him. Not even if you go Core."

"I fucking can, Cuinn. I'll rip him limb from fucking limb." His eyes flashed red, teeth bared.

Soren glanced uneasily at the ground. He wiped his mouth with the heel of his hand, smearing the blood from his now-healed lip in a wide swathe across his cheek. "I wish you would."

"All right, both of yous. Enough of this blood spilling. We're brothers here—feckin' family. Let's get inside and talk it out. I need a drink." He banged again on the door. "Whoever's inside, open this fecker now!"

The door opened. Franky Lavender stood there, tears streaming down his cheeks, his arms outstretched to Cuinn. "Come in, lad. Come in. My, you're a sight for sore eyes!"

With a glance over his shoulder to Soren that said, *easy lad*, Cuinn walked into the hug, and let the old man hold him close, before pushing back and grinning. "How're you doin' Frank?"

"Good, now, lad. Welcome home! Welcome home!" He

wiped at his face with the sleeve of his jacket before stepping back from the door so they could all enter. Not one word to Soren.

"Whiskey?"

19

———————

AD NAUSEAM

DESPITE THE HEAT of the night and the log fire, Soren remained frozen. He stretched out across two easy chairs in front of the hearth, his body on one, his legs on the other, staring into the flames and wishing with all his might he was somewhere else.

After three hours of drinking, Kevin and Franky had just left the bar.

The Turin happenings were dissected *ad nauseam*, and eventually, Cuinn sent the men away so he could rest. Tomorrow was soon enough for further conversation.

As soon as Soren tried to explain, he was stonewalled. Twice, Kevin had hit out at him again, especially when he'd brought Anastasia into it. Why he needed to save her from the Advocate. How the angel had tricked him.

But Kevin remained disgusted, and in-between his flailing fists he'd spat, "You killed your comrade—your brother—to save some little vampire bitch? Man, you should hang for that."

At that point, Soren poured another large whiskey, silently slunk to the chair closest to the fire, and gave up. It was pointless.

His actions had stopped the angel from carrying out her plan, at least for a short while, and the world had continued ticking along. It hadn't lasted, but hell, he'd tried.

Deep down though, he knew he'd had more in his heart in Turin. A thin sliver of hope that Anastasia would be his again. One day. Except he'd messed that one up too. *I'll cut your fucking heart out!* echoed round and round.

Soren concluded, while staring into his glass of whiskey and hearing Kevin's distant tirade, that yes, he'd chosen a *vampire bitch* over his brother. There was no denying it.

Franky had preferred to blame himself. "I knew she was up to something, Cuinn. I told her as much—I told you, son. I should have stopped her."

Cuinn's efforts to bury the hatchet left him hunched over, his skin pale, words coming in wheezes. He'd emphasized family over and over. "Lads, come on now, let's remember who the bad guy is here. It's not Tazia, not Hux, and it's damn well not you, Frank. It's the feckin' Advocate. Let's focus on that."

It had finally sunk in a little, and before he left, Franky came to the fire and patted Soren on the shoulder. A wordless welcome. Kevin was less willing to give ground, but had told him roughly, "Thanks for getting the old man back home." It was something at least.

As the whiskey burned a path from throat to stomach, Soren felt the edges of the ice inside him melt, but the block in the centre stayed frozen.

He closed his eyes. Nine corpses crowded him. *Nine.*

Cuinn insisted they were at war. *Bullshit.* Soren hadn't been on a battlefield today. He hadn't been up against hardened soldiers. They were kids. Children hauled out of their mother's basements and told to defend a world they hadn't had a chance to grasp yet.

On a true battlefield, those kids would have been on his

side. They would have looked to him for guidance. Maybe for orders.

And he'd blown them out of existence. *For another fucking demon.*

Soren poured more whiskey. He filled the tumbler to the brim and slammed half of it back, treating the single malt like cheap tequila.

God, he hated tequila. That was Anastasia's poison. She drank whiskey when she wanted to be one of the guys, but she preferred drinks with a smear of salt and a slice of lemon. Not for the flavour, she'd insisted once, dead serious, but because the little paper umbrellas made her happy.

A burst of laughter pushed up from his chest.

Stupid.

He clamped his lips shut, trying to hold it back. He took another mouthful of whiskey to drown the noise, but the laughter blurted out the moment the glass touched his mouth. Liquid splattered up, drenching his chin, a drop flying wild to catch him right in the eye.

The sting was vicious.

He winced, rubbing his eye, laughter fading.

Voices floated to him from the back of the bar. Wasn't only himself and Cuinn left in the building?

With a small wobble, Soren got up and made his way to the open doorway between the bar and the corridor that led into the back rooms, and to Cuinn's small living quarters. His door was closed, but the gap at the bottom revealed a dimly lit interior, and his shadow pacing back and forth across the room.

Hushed Irish tones floated to him. "Everything's in hand. Don't worry yerself, darlin'."

A woman replied, the words indistinct. But he knew that voice. Soren leaned back against the wall. No! It couldn't be, not after Cuinn's speech earlier. He'd urged them all to remember the common threat.

Turning back toward the door, he listened again. Yes, there it was. The cut-glass accent, the wheedling tone. The last time he'd heard it, it had been in mid-scream, and he'd been sitting on the floor of a Boston basement, clutching the newly human Anastasia to his side.

Soren crept closer. If he wasn't careful, Cuinn's demon ears would pinpoint any sound, but he needed to hear more.

"The future of your kind is in the balance yet again, Conn O'Cuinn. There is no guarantee they will survive if you renege on our agreement. He will destroy them."

"Why are you here telling me this, yet again, angel? I know my job." Cuinn sounded irritated rather than angry, tiredness showing still.

"Because I want to see some action, pet. I'm tired of waiting. The Tipping Point is almost here, and you must be ready." She was attempting to soothe now. His skin crawled. It was a tone he recognized.

"How long?"

"Your men must be ready in a few days."

"That soon? I felt a change—especially here—but..."

"This last month has been… spectacular! So many have given up. Humans are killing their own kind at a tremendous rate—they just needed a push in the right direction. So much for God's wonderful creation!" She tittered. "Once a little energy got behind it, the cities are falling like dominoes."

There was a long pause.

"And you haven't forgotten the promise you made me, pet? Our special arrangement."

"I haven't forgotten. Though I still don't understand."

"You don't have to." Her voice came quick and sharp. "I want him ready, prepared as I asked. Will he be ready, Conn O'Cuinn? Will you be?"

"I will be. We will be." His boots crossed the floor again, and Soren heard him collapse heavily onto the bed. Shadows moved. One boot dropped to the floor, then the other. "Now leave me be, Jegudiel. I need sleep so I can fight this feckin' war for you."

There was no more conversation.

Soren crept back to the fireplace and spread again across the chairs. Cuinn had told him to trust, that there were things he couldn't reveal. Was he working with the Advocate? It made no sense.

She wanted the end of the world—she'd told Soren as much herself. Cuinn didn't want that, surely? The end of the world would mean no humans left. He'd never known Soldiers to have issues with humanity, only the Leech races. So, was he really doing it to save his kind? The Soldiers had pushed the vampires underground once before, couldn't they do it again?

Tomorrow he'd talk with him.

Soren stared into the flames of the fire, slouched further into his chair, and wished for sleep.

20

THE IRISH CONNECTION

DUBLIN WAS A MESS. Devout to its core, its few human holdouts were likely expecting beautiful angels on magickal unicorns to charge in and save them any second.

They'd be waiting a long time. Billy was the only angel in the vicinity, and too busy fighting monsters to provide an angelic uber.

It had taken them three hours to bash their way from their hideout in Clontarf, a distance of just over a mile. They'd dodged Leech-infested alleyways and fought off Tricksters who invaded their minds, finally barricading themselves into the priest's inner sanctum at the Church of St. Joseph in Coolock.

They were just moments too late. They could only watch as the poor screaming bastard of a priest got yanked through one of the three small, high windows by a Leech. There was no time to reach him before his feet vanished.

Jacob immediately slammed the warped frame down. "The catch is loose, William. It will not hold." He used the handle of his knife to wedge it shut.

"Is it fixed?" Aideen clutched her dagger tight to her chest like a security blanket. She'd fought like a bloody tiger, and the adrenaline still thrummed through her. Orange sparks fizzed behind her as she paced.

In the relative, temporary safety of the room, Billy grabbed a white surplice from a hook and scrubbed at the chaotic spatter of red and blue across his jacket. The blood made his skin crawl. He scanned their sanctuary.

The vamp would be back soon.

Jacob pulled the curtains to obscure the view. "Will you be able to transport us out of here?"

Billy shot Jacob a look. "As long as the demon-effect hasn't infiltrated the church, then yes, bruv." *If it has, we're bollocksed.*

His angelic circuitry—*not mojo, thank you very much*—had felt like running into a wall of static the moment his feet hit Irish pavement. The sheer density of demons squashing their evil arses into the city choked off the high-frequency energy he'd needed to translocate. It was the equivalent of having no bars on his phone.

Billy hoped the sanctified interior of a church would be enough to get him airborne again for the return trip, and to take a couple of passengers with him for the ride. It was also the place to find the holy oil needed to break the Fort Knox of a witches' charm protecting his girl.

Caught between panic and practicality, he faltered, watching the other two. Jacob had instinctively placed himself between Aideen and the danger from the window. The energy between them was a full-on pink and green light show.

Stunning, but not the bloody point right now. He dragged his mind back to business, turning toward the heavy oak cabinets lining the wall. "Aideen, exactly what are we looking for?"

"We need oil from the Holy Land," she said. "The sort priests would anoint themselves with, or use to sanctify a space. It's what we used to set up the angelic part of the spell. Blood from a demon, and oil from a priest. We hid Tazia from the eyes of both. To undo the spell, I have to reverse what we did, but just the angel part."

All this before breakfast. His stomach roaring, Billy started opening cupboard doors, carefully shifting piles of hymn books, candles, and packets of incense. He found an open box of communion wafers, hesitated, then shovelled a few into his mouth.

Gah! Dry as old leather.

He looked around for something to wash them down, spotted an Evian bottle still half full on a side table, and took a swig.

Still planted at the window, Jacob asked, "The charm is temporary, yes?"

"Yes. It will wear off in time. Actually, any time now I would imagine, but from what Billy said, we can't wait—"

"No, we can't," Billy said, his voice loud as he strode into the adjoining dressing room and started tearing through cupboards. "If Tazia's dad is alive, he'll want her back. And that would be the worst thing for her."

His earlier fastidiousness forgotten, he yanked items out, throwing them to the floor and kicking them aside. Finding nothing, he came back into the office, which the others were searching much more systematically. *Who even am I?*

Jacob examined a desk overflowing with paperwork. He opened its drawers and checked the items inside one by one. After fishing around in the third one, he pulled out a small dark bottle. "Here!"

Billy got to him at the same time as Aideen. "Is it what we want?" He took another hit from the water. A cold fizz bubbled low in his stomach.

She took the bottle from Jacob and scrutinized it. There was no label. She held it up to the light from the desk lamp. The substance inside shone deep amber with a slight greenish tint. Aideen nodded. "It looks right." She opened it and took a deep whiff. "Smells right, too. Let's try it."

"It looks like the stuff I use on my salad." Billy had picked up another bottle from the drawer and opened it gingerly. "Smells like it too. A bit more perfumy, though." He dabbed some on his wrists and sniffed. *Nice.*

"Well, that makes sense," Aideen said, prepping her own bottle. "It's religiously blessed olive oil with a few aromatic ingredients thrown in for good measure: myrrh, cinnamon, that sort of stuff. Let's get started!"

Outside, the demons howled.

Aideen opened her backpack, pulled out a cloth, an intricately carved wooden bowl, and a candle. She spread the cloth on the ground in front of her and put the bowl on top. She tipped in various ingredients, including the contents of three packets of chopped green herbs and a teaspoon of a powder the colour of fresh saffron.

She lit the candle and dripped both the holy oil and melted wax over the top of the ingredients. A delicious aroma kissed the air. "The wax represents the covering over Tazia's physical body…"

A heavy thump rattled the window frame. Jacob didn't flinch.

"…by melting it, the covering fades away," Aideen continued, her voice steady. "It should be fairly straightforward. I'll need a few minutes, though."

"Hurry," Jacob said, his gaze fixed on the curtains. "The demon is back and has brought *ses amis*." He hefted the shotgun, the bloodied spike on its side glinting in the dim light.

"As soon as I complete the spell, you can run your code and get her location, okay?" Aideen asked, not looking up from the bowl.

"All ready." Billy already had his phone in his hand.

As she worked, Aideen casually chatted, her Irish accent lilting. "By the way, I got a call from the Boston Resistance yesterday. Two coven members have joined to help. They're getting weak communications from the energy that spoke to us before. The one who helped us with the Advocate when we turned Tazia human."

"The demon?"

"No, not the demon. It hasn't been back in touch. The fierce one that always came through first before we could start speaking—"

"A handshake?"

"What?"

"Before two networks speak to each other, there's a handshake… like, a piece of code they exchange as one network switches to another."

"Yeah, I guess that sums it up, Billy." She laughed. "I just know that we couldn't speak directly to the demon unless this other energy turned up first to make it happen." Aideen had finished her preparations and was about to recite the spell.

"What did it say?"

"It was really weird. I'm not sure if they interpreted correctly, so I just thought I'd tell you." She closed her eyes and drew a breath to chant—

"Well?" he snapped.

She opened one eye. "It said, *Come get me, dude.*" She closed it again to start the chant.

Billy's mind reeled. Joshua. It had to be. "Aideen! Stop! For fucksakes, stop a minute, girl, this is important!"

Her eyes flew open, the green clouds of spell-casting energy around her dissipating with a frustrated sigh. "Has anyone ever told you that you are a very demanding man?"

"Yes. Frequently—in bed mostly—not the point. Did it say anything else?"

"Maybe. The coven wasn't altogether clear, but they

thought it said *super-secret hideout*, but that doesn't make sense, right? Now. Can I continue?"

Billy breathed rapidly. "Yes, go ahead. Thank you. I mean… sorry. Sorry, and thank you."

Thoughts churning, Billy paced back and forth over the dusty floor.

Jacob clicked his fingers to get his attention, and mouthed, "They're here!" He'd pushed the curtains aside for a better view.

BAM… BAM… BAM…

The demons outside rhythmically thumped at the window frame.

"Come on! Come on, Aideen!" Billy mumbled. *Isn't that a song?*

She continued to chant, unaffected by the noise, her voice low. He risked a glance at the windows: five of them now. Distorted shapes clawed and pressed against the glass, and wet, guttural sounds promised a messy death. They were seriously pissed off.

With a sound like a gunshot, a spiderweb of fractures erupted across the outer pane of the third window.

Shit. They had a minute, maybe less, before they came crashing in.

Aideen stopped speaking and grinned widely at Billy. "All done. The charm is lifted. You should be able to find her now."

Thank God.

In anticipation, a familiar pressure built in his sternum, a thrumming vibration on the peak of pain. He guzzled the remainder of the water, then sat back on his haunches, phone in hand.

Instant tingles filled his body—more powerful than when he'd run the spell before. A torrent of blue angel light erupted from his chest and flooded into the phone. He urged it on, the device glowing like a miniature sun. Dazzling. And as it did, he floated up from the ground, hovering above their heads.

Wow!

"What the hell are you drinking?" Aideen snatched the bottle from the floor, twisting it around to reveal a handwritten sticker stuck on the opposite side to the brand label: Lourdes, Holy Pilgrimage, Spring 2019. "Billy! It's miracle water!"

He heard her, but was too swept up in the strength of the sensation as he slowly rotated. Colours of all shades sparked around him, flowing into him, supporting him.

CRASH!

The first layer of glass shattered.

"Hurry up!" Jacob ordered from the window. He'd raised his shotgun, ready for the first intruder. Aideen went to stand next to him, her knife in hand.

Billy heard both exclamations and focused. A ball of golden light appeared, hovering in front of him—

A snaking crack blasted over the second pane of glass.

"Billy!" Jacob and Aideen spoke in unison.

He braced, locking his muscles against the familiar, rib-cracking wham of returning energy—

The light raced toward his chest. *Oh God, this is gonna hurt!*

But instead of knocking the wind out of him, it hit with an almost imperceptible *pop!* Like he used to do as a kid with his finger in his cheek. *Result!*

For a split second, his mind was a storm of street grids and coordinates before it all resolved into two words. He checked the screen, and there it was. A new text from his Home number: DETROIT, USA.

He landed with a bump on the floor at the exact same moment.

"Bloody hell! She's in Detroit."

The second pane of glass smashed, and a rock came hurtling into the room, narrowly missing Jacob's head. It was followed immediately by the booted foot of a large demon kicking away the remaining glass.

Jumping up, Billy shoved the phone in his pocket. Feeling the holy power coursing through him, he gave a quick, grateful wink to the image of the Virgin hanging on the wall. This was gonna be easy.

He grabbed Aideen and Jacob by the backs of their clothes. The tidal wave of energy from the sanctified building, the holy oil on his skin, and the water in his body all answered his call.

As the first demon planted his feet on the floor, a flash of blue light and a crack louder than thunder announced their passage into the ether. Even as they flew, Billy only had one thought:

Joshua!

WAITING FOR THE BEAST

"FIRE'S OUT!"

Soren opened an eye and wiped a small trail of saliva from the corner of his mouth. He'd slept the uncomfortable sleep of a semi-drunk man slung across two easy chairs.

Cuinn dropped the logs beside the fireplace with a clatter that left Soren wincing. As the Irishman eased himself straight, his breath caught, and his hand went to his ribs. Dark purple bruising bloomed at the edge of his collar, disappearing under his shirt. The guards' boots had left marks all over him.

"You could have used the guest room," Cuinn said without turning. He bent again slowly and proceeded to rake together the embers from the night before. When he was done, and they glowed bright red with promise, he set bits of twisted paper on top of them.

Soren grunted and watched as they burst into tiny licks of flame.

Cuinn added more paper to the fire, then shuffled back a bit to reach for a handful of wood shavings. His left foot caught on a whiskey bottle. It rolled away from him and clinked against an equally empty mate.

He glanced over his shoulder and raised an eyebrow. Soren looked from him to the bottles. Now the sandpaper in his throat made sense, as did the slight metallic flavour that leached through the abraded surface of his tongue. He groaned, knowing that as soon as he moved his head, the sparks of pain would begin to crackle like the flames.

Soren turned back to the fire. The little flame had eaten the paper and now curled around the wood shavings. It hissed, demanding more. Cuinn fed it with a few wood chips, then laid thin bark peelings on top, before sitting back waiting for the beast to grow. "There's aspirin in my room, in the bathroom."

"Cheers," Soren whispered the word, but still pain stabbed in his temple and squeezed the back of his eyeballs. He closed his eyes for a moment, revelling in the darkness—

An echo in his head: *the Tipping Point is almost here, and you must be ready… Our special arrangement.* The Advocate's voice and Cuinn's agreement.

He jerked upright.

Pain beat a path around to the very back of his brain where it thundered. With the blood rushing loudly in his ears, nausea overwhelmed him, and his mouth clamped down to bring his groan to an abrupt conclusion and stop the vomit he felt sure was about to erupt from him.

"Jaysus, man. You look like shite!" Cuinn was still staring at him.

He nodded slowly. "I feel…" His words faded. Words weren't worth the effort. Sweat beaded on his forehead, and there was a slight tremor in his hands as he wiped it away.

Cuinn added a few more scraps of wood to the fire, then paced out of view before Soren heard water trickling into a glass. Time flickered, and suddenly Cuinn was beside him, nudging his hand with the glass.

Soren took it and collapsed back, drinking the water in a gulp while Cuinn disappeared again. The glass clattered against his teeth, and a little spasm of pain from the one Kevin had loosened yesterday shot into his jaw. It looked like magickal wards weren't quite as effective as a dentist after all.

Cuinn returned, this time with a plastic bottle of water, and dropped a couple of aspirin into his hand before bending to the fire once more.

"Thanks." Soren swallowed the pills and downed the water. The hammering receded enough to let him wrestle with the memory of the night before. *Just do it.* "I heard you talking to the Advocate last night."

Cuinn had been arranging some long pieces of a split log on the fire, crisscrossing them over each other to raise them slightly and keep the air flowing. He paused. "Did you, now?"

"Yeah. Recognized her voice."

"Did you hear the conversation?"

"Enough to know you're working for her."

The flame had already grabbed at the new fuel and was turning it black and then gold as it started to burn. There was a loud crack as the heat aggressively forced the dampness from the wood.

Cuinn turned away from the fire to catch his eye. "Working for her?"

"Sounded that way."

The Irishmen chuckled. "How many times you known things to not be what they seem?" He stopped laughing. "We're at war, Hux. Alliances are made."

Soren bit his lip, waiting for more.

"I told you before. You're with family now. I wouldn't lead you wrong. Did I ever lead you wrong?"

"No."

"Then…"

"What?"

"Then trust me."

Trust him. The words sat like stones in Soren's gut. Cuinn

had saved him, yes, but he was also dealing with the Advocate. Alliances in war were one thing; this felt like something else. Like being a pawn in a game whose rules he didn't know.

Cuinn assessed the fire critically and placed a whole log onto the support he'd made of the split wood. Some had already been consumed to breaking point; the rest took the weight of it, and flames licked around the outside, looking for a weakness to bite into.

He leaned against the wall next to the fireplace, stretching his stiffened limbs out in front of him, and faced him. "I'll tell you again. The Tipping Point must happen, but…" He stared for a long minute at the mirror above the bar, and the drinking glasses arranged in front of it.

Soren's gaze followed Cuinn's to the mirror above the bar, and his stomach clenched. The glasses arranged in front of it gleamed. Reflections everywhere. His skin prickled at the thought of Jegudiel's face appearing in one of them, watching.

Cuinn lowered his voice. "But, it's the beginning, not the end. Just remember that."

What the fuck? The woman. In the lift in Vegas…

His heart felt fast in his throat, and he knew that Cuinn would be able to hear it. He acknowledged his tension with a big sigh.

"Okay?" said Cuinn.

"Sure."

Cuinn got up and slapped him on the back. "Good man. Now let's get some food inside you. Good greasy breakfast is what you need to settle that stomach, so it is, and there's stuff to do today. A chance for you to get the boys back onside. You got your sea legs on?" He laughed, crossed behind the bar, and turned on the old-style CD player. Soon, military drumbeats filled the air.

Before heading into the back, Cuinn turned one last time, his eyes stern. "Hux?"

"Yeah?"

"Remember, I'm your feckin' saviour, man. Don't forget it!" He disappeared out back.

Soren let the heat from the fire flow over him. Whiskey scented sweat burst from his forehead as he continued to battle with his raging pulse. The fire roared up, snapping its jaws around the sacrificial log. As it did, Soren felt his own skin sear.

22

——————

THE MONSTER IN ME

SOREN SAT on the harbour wall, not half a mile from the place where he'd found Anastasia alive and well after she blew up the vampires' warehouse months before.

The memory hadn't faded: chemical ashes in his throat, muscles screaming as he tore through concrete and vampire remains, searching. He'd been certain the piles of burning flesh were hers. Then he saw her walk away, flipping her hair, and the dread had vanished. Now it was back, a dark serpent coiled inside.

His gaze shifted back out onto the lake. A sea-going tug. Large, thick, and built to last, but looking like it had seen hard times. Scorch marks scarred the starboard side. What looked like a bomb had gone off in the wheelhouse, ripping a jagged hole into its wall and roof. It flew a tattered Canadian flag and rode the gentle waves of Lake St. Clair, spinning in slow, aimless circles.

Kevin had been monitoring its progress for a couple of days, and filled Cuinn in. Another prize for the Unit's inventory. With a boat like that, they could navigate out of Detroit by water, avoiding the armed borders, loaded down with the ammo and arms they'd been stockpiling. That was the plan. A way to give them an edge when the Tipping Point finally came.

He reflected on the bright red maple leaf, now mostly in tatters and singed with ash. Was the Great White North an option? Demons hated the cold, but was it enough of a deterrent?

The thought of escape—any escape—was a brief distraction. When the Tipping Point came, he wanted to be with Anastasia if she'd have him, holding her safe and close. But he'd given his word to stand with Cuinn. There was no going back.

A deep breath and—

The boat hit against the harbour wall with a crash of wood on stone followed by a drawn-out screech as the stern dragged heavy and long against the concrete.

The people on the boat grabbed onto each other or the sides of the vessel; some fell to the deck and lay still, dazed. Those that could, forced themselves upright and stood again, squashed in-between the lifeboats raised on each side of the boat. Others sat further off in the bow. No one made any attempt to secure the vessel.

Hollow-eyed, they carried the expressions of injured prey. They had nowhere left to run, and couldn't even if they tried. Their clothes hung off their gaunt frames, with no meat left. Demons wouldn't look to make a meal of their flesh. Their souls, though—they'd be sweet for some.

He turned to Cuinn, who now stood beside him watching too. "What about them?"

"Look at them, man. Nothing but vermin." Cuinn had been talking on the radio to Kevin, coordinating the Unit who were on their way, and broke off to reply. He shrugged. "What do you do with vermin?"

"We're exterminators now?"

"It'd be a blessing, Hux. If we leave them be, and just take the boat, the Tricksters will get them. Sure, you've seen what they do."

An image flared in Soren's mind: a woman on her knees in an alley, her head rocking back and forth, a thin, unending whimper escaping her lips as her eyes stared at nothing. Soul all gone, not a hope of redemption in this world or the next. *Not even a zombie.*

"So you're telling me we kill, to stop others playing with them?"

"Kindest thing, man."

Soren looked back at the boat. "There are children," he said. *Always kids.* A strange quiet settled over him, muffling the sound of the waves and the scrape of the boat, leaving only the gaunt faces on the deck in focus. He already knew Cuinn had seen them. That it would make no difference.

Cuinn put down the radio and nodded. "We do them a kindness and help the Tipping Point that bit more." He paused, irritation washing over him. "I'm getting sick of saying it, Hux. You with me or not?"

"I'm with you." Soren didn't hesitate. His eyes not shifting from the boat.

"Good man."

The tug hit off the wall again and finally settled against the side of a jetty that stuck out into the water, making a ninety-degree angle: a perfect trap.

"Kev's on his way." He examined something high in the sky as he continued speaking, "Why don't you get started? It doesn't look like anyone'll put up a fight."

"You want *me* to do it?" He jerked to face him. "Why me?"

Cuinn stared him down. "For the Unit, man. For me." *Another challenge.* Would he ever stop paying? Cuinn handed him an old rifle. Not his usual vampire killer, it looked like a gun better suited to life in the Wild West. The barrel glinted in the sun, polished to a shine, and there was curly script engraved into the metal.

"Nice gun." Soren said. No other words came.

Cuinn smiled. "Thanks. It was a gift."

Soren took it without another word. He walked toward the boat on leaden feet. The dark he'd felt earlier twisted in his stomach; he prayed it would soon reach his mind.

———

The Advocate watched from the tugboat's window, reflected in the one pane that wasn't cracked or broken. The exchange between the two men drifted to her across the gap that opened and closed between the vessel and the harbour wall with the movement of the waves. "Well, old girl. Which fate will you bring your cargo, death by the Soldiers or starvation at sea?" She winked at the sky, *I hope you're watching.*

As Soren approached the boat, she smiled with excitement. She could *feel* the breath rasping in his throat, in and out, in and out. *Time to decide, pet.*

He was her blue-eyed boy; she had created him. With every decision he ever made, every loss he ever suffered, she had nudged him toward this exact moment. Even if for now he was acting on the command of Conn O'Cuinn. If he did as she expected, as she'd trained him, he would be compliant again. She would have her plaything back, and God would lose yet another beautiful soul.

Soren stopped short of climbing into the vessel. Holding his gun by his side, scraping the ground with the stock, he paused.

Damn it, boy! The sheer stubborn refusal to let go of humanity. She had so much power to offer him, but still he resisted. It was infuriating.

A knot of irritation tightened the skin between her brows.

She traced the lines with her fingertips and forced the muscles to smooth. She would not let his stubbornness age her.

At least the Irishman had come round. In the past, he'd always told him to respect the kill or some such sanctimonious drivel! Talking about honour! What do demons know of honour? Now he was doing well, though. It seemed he was finally seeing things her way, their way, hers and Stephen's. *But it was taking far too long!* She needed Soren's humanity gone. Wanted him malleable. She stamped her foot, and the pane of glass that held her image creaked under the vibration.

A sweat broke on the Advocate's forehead, and her hands moved from her dress to run over her cheeks and down her neck. Absently, she sucked the moisture from her fingers, not taking her eyes off Soren as he stood beside the boat. *God, he's magnificent!* Perfect in every way. Just how she'd imagined he'd be as a man.

He took a step forward—

Her excitement rose. *Do it, Soren Huxford. Do it, my boy!*

At the side of the boat, he hesitated again. In his eyes, she saw a flicker of doubt. Was he still not convinced that murder would be justified? Did he think these rats worth saving? *You will do it. You must.*

Behind him, Cuinn stood unnervingly still, his gaze fixed on the scene. Not a word. No gesture to urge her boy on. His second, Kevin—a younger, duller copy of the first—had joined him. *Do something, Irishman.*

For a moment, Kevin looked as though he would join Soren, but Cuinn put a hand on his arm to detain him and shook his head.

Good. Now, Conn O'Cuinn, order my boy forward!

But Cuinn said nothing. The two demons turned away.

Jegudiel sighed. As usual, she would have to take charge.

She focused her will, her whisper brushing the mind of one of the stick-like humans who stood near her reflection. He was a tall, thin man, middle-aged and grey-haired. Beside him stood a woman, long blond hair hanging limply around her shoulders. A young boy stood between them, his hand in hers. Just a month ago, they could have graced the cover of any housekeeping magazine. Now they were undernourished and broken. Shadow versions of themselves.

The man snapped to attention. He faced her reflection, head bent, listening. When she finished speaking, his eyes closed into slits, and he moved his focus to the woman by his side. Without warning, he snarled and sprang at her, grabbing her by the neck, and throwing her against the wall.

The Advocate giggled. *Maybe this will be fun after all.*

The woman tried to speak, but could only push out grunts from under his hands. The more she tried, the more he squeezed. Eyes wide with shock, she desperately pulled at his wrists.

From the bank, Soren watched, his eyes narrowing, but didn't intervene. Attracted by the sound of the commotion, Cuinn had turned back too. He looked between Soren and the scene on the boat. But he remained where he was.

Jegudiel whispered again, this time giving her attention to the child.

The boy, who had cowered on the ground when his father attacked his mother, threw himself at the man, pulling on him with all his strength. His father shrugged him off, pushing him to the deck, and returned to the woman who had also sunk to the floor on all fours, and was now taking big gulps of air.

The Advocate whispered once more and, this time, the boy leaped from the deck, crossing the three-foot gap between boat and land with one jump. He raced up to Soren.

Soren's eyes fixed on the woman, his breath ragged.

The boy snatched the rifle and twisted back toward the boat. Soren looked at his hand. *What? Where?*

Just watch, my boy. Enjoy the show!

The boy jabbed the old-fashioned gun in his father's direction. It was so heavy he could hardly raise it. The man had recommenced choking his wife and had his back to the boy. "Dad! Stop!" The boy struggled to cock the gun, but finding some strength, he stuck it right into his father's back. "Daddy!"

The man turned and looked. He loosened his grip from his wife, who he'd shoved against the wall of the wheelhouse.

Tears streamed down the boy's cheeks. "Let her go, dad, please!"

The woman stretched her hands to her son. "No!" She mouthed. "Don't!"

The Advocate jiggled with excitement. This was playing out just like she'd hoped. With one eye on Soren, she whispered to the man once more.

He reacted instantly. "Give me the gun, son." He held his hands out to the boy. "Give it to me."

"Will you leave her alone?" The boy's desperate voice sounded loud in the silence.

The Advocate looked again. What will you do, Soren?

On shore, Soren blinked rapidly, appearing to wake from his daze. "No, don't give it to him," he whispered.

Only the Advocate heard him. She giggled again. *Yes! Give it to him!*

"Give it to him, Paulie." The boy's mother had recovered her voice enough to encourage him.

"No! Don't give it to him!" Soren's words were stronger, but still not loud enough to interfere.

Do it, boy, do it!

Still gulping tears, the boy passed the gun to his father. There was a moment of silence. The Advocate held her breath and knew Soren was doing likewise. She connected to him, feeling every ounce of anguish in his thoughts.

Both knew what would happen next; they'd seen it before.

The father shook his head at the boy. "You shouldn't have done that, son." He turned and, without hesitation, shot his wife directly in her chest.

The blast threw her back against the side of the wheelhouse. She slid down the wall and landed hard on the floor, her life gone.

A howl tore from the boy's throat. It echoed around the dock. A sound of pure, beautiful agony.

On the boat, the Advocate applauded and screamed with laughter, while vultures circled overhead.

———

A howl and the world went silent for Soren. He was back in the hallway, the smell of her blood in his nostrils, a scream—his scream—ripping itself from his lungs. He knew that sound. He knew the soul-deep pain that created it. And he knew what came next.

The man on the boat stared at his handiwork. A mess of blood and splinters of bone. Looking from the gun to his wife's body. A look so lost.

He turned back to the boy. The child was on his knees. He crawled forward, fixated on the gun that hung loosely from his father's hand. He reached out, his fingers grasping at the muzzle.

"No!" Soren forced out the word with what breath he had.

A voice rushed through his mind. "Yes!" *Jegudiel?* He felt the sickening familiarity but couldn't drag his attention away from the boy.

The child pulled the gun from his father's limp hand. *No!*

As though he'd been released, Soren ran full tilt onto the deck of the boat. He landed, and the boat lurched. Everyone lost their footing and swayed or fell to the deck. All but the boy, who was now on his feet with the gun in his hands, and had it pointed directly at his father.

The man stared at his son, still confused, eyes blank. He put up a hand as though a palm would prevent the shot. "What?"

No, not the boy. Ice cut into Soren's chest. He couldn't let him pull that trigger. Couldn't let him carry that stain for the rest of his life.

Just as his finger tightened, Soren clamped his hand over the boy's, wrenching the heavy rifle free. The worn stock slammed against his shoulder as he pivoted. He met the father's eyes. The shot was a single deafening crack.

The man's eyes widened; blood seeped through his t-shirt. His knees buckled, and he sank to the deck. For one brief moment, he smiled at the boy before teetering sideways. Dead.

———

The boy crawled to the spot where his mother had fallen. Sitting in her blood, he cradled her head. Red soon smeared his face and stained his clothes. Nothing had changed. Soren had saved no one.

He looked from the child and his mother to the father, who stared with empty eyes. From him, his eyes traced a path to the window; the Advocate's gaze burned into his.

A satisfied smile slithered over her face. "My boy. My pet. My little monster!"

The words slid into him, venomous. *My little monster.* And just like that, the part of him that had been fighting, the part that clung to hope, simply... broke. *She's right. I am a monster. I always have been.*

Soren's hand hovered over Anastasia's Bowie. *No. Not for...* *this.* He yanked his Izula from its plastic sheath on his hip. His gaze found Cuinn. *Tell me not to. Give me another way.* But his brother just gave a single, sharp nod and then turned away.

The passengers cowered in front of him. He met their eyes. And stepped forward.

———

When no one was left standing. He climbed from the boat and walked away from the docks, knife still in hand, dripping a steady rhythm of blood onto the concrete slabs.

After walking for what seemed like hours, he found a quiet street. Tall buildings. Blackened trees. Vultures. Shadows merged with the brick and disappeared down alleyways. He found a low wall. Sat till dark, unmoving.

Blood clung to his face. Spattered his lips. He swallowed... breathed... swallowed. His hand still grasped the knife.

He heard the crackle of a faraway fire. Caught the smell of roasting death and wood.

His eyes followed the trail of smoke into the sky. It found the breeze and swirled up, up to the beady eyes of breathing gargoyles perched stock-still in the dead trees, watching.

A slow smile stretched his lips, cracking the dried blood at the corners of his mouth. A city of monsters. *His city.* For the first time, it felt like home.

Her body slid into place beside his. She released the knife from his grasp, then put her hand in his. She rested her head on his shoulder and whispered into his ear.

When he heard her, he cried.

23

———————————

HELLO, LOVER(S)

TAZIA WIPED the man's sweat from her cheek with the back of her hand and forced the muscles of her mouth into something resembling a smile. "We good now?"

Her stomach heaved, something far worse than simple disgust. A human reaction to a pathetic human act.

A year ago, she would have snapped his neck for even looking at her wrong. Now she was meat.

The realization didn't just cut; it terrified. Is this what she was now? Just some fangless girl who got on her knees in back alleys to get a pass into Detroit?

Get a grip, Taz. You've done worse. At least it was quick.

The guard grunted, hitching up his pants. He shifted his weight, favouring his unbandaged leg. Cash hadn't worked on this bastard like the others en route. "Yeah. We're good." He lit two cigarettes and passed one to her.

She took a long drag, hoping the smoke would burn away the sour taste in her mouth and the tremble in her fingers. She'd have to work on that.

"Like I was sayin', he came through here yesterday. Tall, blond sonofabitch. Crack shot. Took out nine of my men. Blew them sky high." He spat a wad of phlegm on the ground. "Kicked the shit out of his friend, though. The other one. Monster with a weird accent. One of those tough ones. Metal bones. What a joke! We left him a bloody mess."

"You do the kicking?" She smirked before she could stop herself. Her heart juddered when his expression changed to pissed. She looked pointedly at his leg, and followed it with her sweetest smile. She still had to make it over the border, *alive*.

The information, at least, was solid. Hux. But a beat-up Soldier demon made no sense. Soldiers didn't break that easily. Still, she was on the right trail.

"Well, I did some!" With the jab to his ego, he changed the subject, and gestured vaguely northeast with his cigarette. "You want my advice, you stick to the main arteries. Avoid the old auto plants. Fucking monsters nest there."

She nodded, feigning gratitude. The charm around her neck felt blessedly cool against her skin. Monsters were the last of her worries, at least while it was still working. She just had to find Hux and figure out why it seemed all the magick in Italy pointed her back to this bitch of a city.

She took a final drag from the cigarette and flicked it onto the ground. Turned to walk away. "Thanks for the tip."

"Hey!"

She froze. "Yeah?"

"Look me up when you come back through. We can get a beer *too*, next time?"

She gave him an icy smile. Ground the butt into the dirt and jogged away, every burning, human muscle in her legs screaming. If she saw the guy again, she'd… well, what would she do exactly? Tell her dad?

The jog wasn't the belting run she was used to, but she kept it steady. She pushed past abandoned cars, ignoring keys that dangled invitingly from the ignitions. So tempting. But a running engine was a beacon in a dead city. The risk wasn't worth it.

She finally slowed, ducking behind the rusted-out husk of a city bus. The Irish Club wasn't far now. It seemed the most likely place to find Hux.

Nobody noticed her. The charm was holding, thank God. Tricksters, even Umbrae, ghosted past her and not one turned their head. The vampires were different. They were everywhere in the south, only petering out when she got close to Corktown. They knew, sniffing the air, eyes slitting to focus on her direction. She kept fast, and travelled wide around them.

When she got to the Club, it was wrong. Too quiet. No muffled shouts, no clink of glasses, no Celtic beats leaking through the boarded-up windows. Just the occasional flash of movement through the hatch in the door. She settled in to watch from the roof opposite until an old, battered truck pulled up. Tazia's breath caught. Conn O'Cuinn's rust-bucket of a Ford F-250.

Her heart stuttered. The last time she saw it, Cuinn was standing in the truck bed making cracks about the shitty weather, as they loaded the guns she'd brought him.

A stranger drove. Another Celtic Soldier. Same crew cut, same freckles. When he strode into the Club, he kept it running, and she dropped from the roof and peered into the gloomy cab. Nothing there to help her. She retreated to the doorway of the building, hidden in deep shade.

He emerged minutes later, his biceps bulging under the strain of two long khaki holdalls. Guns.

This was her chance. Hux. The Club. Guns. A job? It made sense. As he wrestled the bags into the cab, she ran low, her feet barely skimming the dusty asphalt. *Easy, Taz. Light feet.* Soldiers can smell a kicked-up stone from fifty yards.

The engine roared into life.

With a last burst of speed, she hooked her hands over the lip of the truck bed and heaved herself into the back. She landed in a clumsy heap just as the truck lurched forward into a hellish ride. Every pothole a body blow.

The route he took was like her greatest hits from the year before. She could imagine a highly made up tour guide in a tight purple skirt suit and matching fingernails: "To the right is the tenement building from where you first spied on Cuinn. He'd been blasting the hell out of a nest of vampires who'd had the temerity to challenge his territory, if you remember? Next, north to the docks. On your right, the warehouse you blew to shit! Lucky escape, Taz!"

A grin touched her lips at the sight of the blackened skeleton of the building. The memory was exhilarating—the heat, the roar, the beautiful chaos. *Fun—*

The smell of chemicals and Cuinn's sweat. His hand gripping her arm, his lips finding hers in the chaotic aftermath—

Nope.

She shoved the memory down, hard. Hux was the mission. Not this trip down memory lane.

Rome had taught her a lesson. Being human was about community and having faith in each other. Something like that, anyway. She was still hazy on the details.

When the truck pulled onto the docks, she jumped out, without even turning to examine the cluster of Soldiers gathered by the sea wall. She scrambled up a rusted fire escape on the side of a storage depot, and crouched behind the huge, dark shape of an old winch that overhung much of the dock itself. From where she was, she could see across to the water, but not directly below her.

She dug in her pack and pulled out the binoculars—a parting gift from the arsehole at the border. Holding them to her eyes, she twisted the lens until the world snapped into focus. A large tugboat bumped morosely against the harbour wall. Its passengers, like statues, thin, broken.

Then one of them moved.

A man lunged, attacking the woman beside him. His hands clamped around her neck. Tazia sucked in a breath. A boy vanished from view and reappeared a second later, dragging a rifle that was nearly as big as he was. He levelled it at the attacker with admirable stability.

She was too far to hear, but she could read the scene in their bodies. The boy, stiff with terror. The man, pure rage. Then, the boy did something that made no sense. He offered the gun to him.

"No!" She whispered. "Don't give it to him." The vulture perched on the roof alongside her squawked and shifted a wing. Then both she and the bird jumped at the shot that followed.

The woman's body blasted against the wall of the wheelhouse, and the next minute a blond giant vaulted onto the deck from the pier, moving with a fluid power Tazia knew all too well. *Hux!*

He tore the rifle from the boy's grasp, pivoted, and shot the man dead.

A fierce, proprietary pride surged through her. She almost laughed. *See? That's what humans do, take care of each other.*

But then things changed.

He didn't console the child. He didn't drop the weapon. He pulled a knife and moved through the other passengers one by one in rhythmic, perfunctory slaughter.

What... the actual... fuck?

She stood, not caring who saw, gripping the winch so hard to keep her balance that her knuckles ached. With her body trembling, her eyes locked on the scene.

This wasn't combat, not even rage. This was extermination. Not one fought back. No screaming. Only the boy slipped behind the wheelhouse and out of sight, carrying the rifle with him.

This couldn't be Hux. He killed, sure. But only when he had to. As part of the job—even in defence of others. But not this.

Was he a demon now? Had the wards on his skin finally turned him?

When it was over, he just stood there. A statue of red on the deck of the boat, his hand clutching the knife, limp at his side. The breeze shifted, carrying the tang of death to her rooftop perch. It was already souring in the heat. The vultures above smelled it too, and as they flew from the roof, they cackled in anticipation.

Tazia gagged, her stomach clenching. The binoculars trembled in her grip, and she lowered them, fighting the overwhelming urge to vomit. She'd seen death plenty of times. Christ, she'd caused it even more. But not like this; a senseless rout.

As she dropped the glasses, her eye caught it. A flicker of movement in the wheelhouse window behind Hux. She snapped them back up, her arms shaking. It wasn't a reflection. It was a face. Grey and indistinct, like a phantom through dirty glass, but the features were unmistakable. Pinched. Sharp. Female.

Jegudiel.

The Advocate wasn't just watching. Her head was thrown back, her mouth open in a wide, silent expression of pure joy. She was laughing.

The pieces slammed into place, creating a picture of such perfect, calculated cruelty that it stole Tazia's breath. *She's in control of him.*

She remembered the feeling, losing herself. Trapped in her own body while the angel operated her hands, looked through her eyes, attached herself to her mind. Utter control.

If he was her puppet now, like she had been, his soul would be screaming for freedom.

This was why she'd been brought here. Why she'd seen him in Rome. Now, Tazia had a mission.

As Hux climbed from the tug like a man in a dream, she moved. She scrambled over the shallow roofline, kicking reflexively at a vulture that landed directly in her path. The bird squawked and flapped away, not even registering her presence. The charm held.

She slid down the drainpipe on the far side of the building. He was already halfway down the block, his long-legged stride eating up the pavement. She hung back, giving him space.

Keeping up was agony. Her lungs burning, she pushed her aching body. Tricksters scattered as he approached; she saw them shooting down alleyways or behind abandoned building. *Fucksakes, he's even scaring the monsters.*

Finally, he stopped. Sat on a low wall and stared into nothing.

She approached him cautiously. Sat beside him on the wall. His fingers still clutched the knife handle, glued in place by drying blood. Gently, she pried each one open. She laid the weapon aside and slid her hand into his.

Resting her head on his shoulder, she whispered into his ear. "Hello, lover."

———

His first cry was a choked, silent tremor. Then it broke, and the sobs came in harsh, violent waves that shook his entire body. She moved her head, giving the storm room, and clutched his hand tighter.

When he quieted to ragged breaths, she said, "Tell me."

He shook his head.

"Hux. Please."

His voice was a raw whisper, words dragged from a place of absolute ruin. "The boy… on the boat. He was me."

It took her a moment. The man's sudden rage, the gun, the mother. Oh, Hux. "When you were a child?" She'd always known something, he'd talk in his nightmares, but he'd never shared.

He nodded, not looking at her. "My mother. I… let him." A tremor rocked him. "She said no… and he shot her."

Steady, Taz. Don't rush him. It made sense. The alignments with the events on the boat: the sudden change in the man's behaviour and the action of the boy. The Advocate's laughter. The bitch had set him up.

"And, all those people…"

His eyes, when they finally met hers, were a wasteland. "Became what they wanted," he rasped. "The monster. Thought it would… make the guilt stop. But it's just… more." He couldn't hold her gaze and looked away, his breath catching in his chest. "Said it was the only way. Necessary casualties."

"Why not the boy?" she asked gently. "I saw him slip away."

He frowned, the blood on his face creasing. "The boy?" The confusion was genuine. "I don't remember."

Of course he didn't. That hadn't been him up there. Just a puppet. She released his hand and dug in her pack for a dirty shirt and her drinking bottle, pouring precious water onto it. She cleaned his face, wiping away the mask of slaughter until his skin shone through.

"Who said?" She asked it softly, casually, dipping the cloth in the water again.

"What?"

"Who said it was the only way? The Advocate?"

He shook his head, a jerky, broken movement. "No. My OC."

Tazia froze, the wet shirt hovering inches from his cheek. "Your OC is dead, Hux. You killed him. Remember?"

"No." He squeezed his eyes shut. "Not dead. He's here. He gave the order."

"Hux, look at me." She grabbed his chin, forcing him to face her, panic rising in her throat. He was hallucinating. The magick had finally snapped his mind. "Who gave the order?"

"Cuinn. Conn O'Cuinn"

Tazia's heart simply stopped.

The world narrowed down to the sound of that name. Her breath stopped too. Blood rushed in her ears, drowning out the distant cackling of the vultures.

Cuinn.

It wasn't possible. She'd mourned him. She'd packed his memory away.

"He's..." Her voice failed her. She tried again, louder, sharper. "Cuinn is alive?"

Hux nodded. "Yes."

The ground seemed to tilt under her feet. *Alive! Here.*

A wild, desperate hope surged up, instantly followed by a crash of ice. If he's alive... *why didn't he come for me?*

"And he's..." She swallowed. Jagged air. "You said he gave the order? To kill those people?"

"He's with *her*, Tazia." Hux's voice was a raw whisper, tears leaking from his closed eyes. "The Advocate. He says... he says we have to help her. Accelerate the end."

"Make it make sense, Hux." She gripped his shoulders, shaking him, needing him to snap out of it. "Why would Cuinn work with the her?"

"The Tipping Point," he mumbled.

"What the fuck is the Tipping Point?"

He drifted on like he hadn't heard. "He says it's inevitable. The only way to save humans is to let the demons win fast. Break the stalemate. He told me to trust him. And I... I do."

"You don't sound sure."

"I'm following orders. Humans must die… so fewer humans die later." He looked at his hands, caked in dried red. "I don't know whose puppet I am now."

"He's not your OC anymore, Hux!"

"No… he's my… brother." Anger flashed over his face. "And I owe him for… Turin."

They locked eyes. Tazia saw the pain in the blue irises, the desperate need for forgiveness.

She pulled back, her mind reeling. There was more he wasn't saying, but he was too fragile. Pushing would only break him further. But the man who had ordered this massacre wasn't the Soldier she knew. He would never want him this way.

He put a hand on her wrist. His voice broke. "Am I a monster now?"

"God, no, Hux." The denial was fierce. "You're the most human man I know. It's why I came for you. This—" she gestured at the smoke-choked sky, stinking of flesh and wood "—this was her. She was there, on the boat. I saw her."

The Advocate had her hooks in both of them—all of them.

Fuck.

She breathed deeply. She couldn't fall apart. Not now. Hux was teetering, and if she let go, he'd fall.

"Perhaps we're all still hers." She wrapped an arm as far as she could get it around his broad form, ignoring the trembling in her own limbs. "Where the fuck is Billy?"

"He's waiting it out in London. Waiting for the angels'… orders I guess."

Something else clicked. "So if you're with Cuinn, and he wants humans to die… are you against me?"

"Never!" He turned so fast it startled her, putting his

forehead to hers, staring deep into her eyes. His lashes, studded with tears and tipped with red, tickled her skin. "Never."

She pulled back just enough to see him. "But I'm human now, Hux. I want to stay this way."

"We all want to be human…" he whispered, eyes dropping from hers.

"Cuinn told me before, he knew how to defeat an angel." She was speaking as much to herself as to him. "Maybe he has got a plan to save us. He's playing a long game. He must be."

"And until then, we kill people…" Full body tremors started up again. She was losing him to memories of the boat.

"Until then," she corrected, her voice hard, cutting through his panic, "we look out for each other."

He shifted, rocking, struggling to stay still. His thigh pushed something cold against hers. A familiar shape. She gasped, looking down. "My Bowie! How?"

For the first time, a shadow of his old smile touched his lips. "Took it from the cave. I was going to destroy it… then… I couldn't. It's yours." He unclasped the sheath and handed it to her.

The weight in her hand was a homecoming. Power. *A piece of me.* Vampire or human, it didn't care. It worked the same. He had cleaned it. The blade shone under the weak light, and the waxed handle felt smooth and solid. A wide, fierce grin spread across her face. "Thank you."

They sat in silence, Tazia with her weapon back, a dumb grin on her face—human, but armed. Whole. Him—clenching her hand, shaking, but calm.

And that was when Cuinn turned the corner and walked toward them.

———

He'd seen her, of course. A faint, laughing phantom in the wheelhouse window. Conn had turned away, his jaw clenched tight.

Let her have her fun. Let her think she's breaking him. He wished he could tell him everything, but the time wasn't yet right. Hux was too close to Tazia. It was the price of this alliance, the pound of flesh the Advocate demanded to see.

He'd agreed to let her bring Hux to the edge of the void.

But watching her push him in… that was different.

For every innocent Hux cut down, an answering fury at the laughing bitch in the wheelhouse built in Conn's gut. Not the agreement. His men shifted beside him—demons, each one— their horror palpable. One moved to intervene, and Conn had to throw out an arm to stop him, his voice a low growl. "Hold." It was an order that tasted sour. Could he bring his brother back from this?

Afterwards, as Hux walked away like a dead man, Conn gave the order. "Burn it." *Useless pile of junk.*

His men piled the bodies on the boat. By the time the fire caught, the docks were teeming with vultures, screeching as their meal went up in smoke. Some hopped near the flames, pulling at twisted limbs. One landed on the deck itself, its feathers dragging through pools of blood until they were too saturated to allow flight. The others turned on it instantly, tearing at the living carrion. As the fire engulfed the boat, Kevin finally shot the shrieking bird into silence.

Then Conn followed his brother.

He found him saturated in the blood of his kills, reeking just like that bird. "Hux!"

Hux stood up to face him, legs shaking.

"Time to go home, recruit." Conn forced a lightness he didn't feel.

"Home?"

"To the Club. Get some proper whiskey in you. You'll be grand in no time."

Conn stopped. Something was odd. He turned, eyes scanning the heat haze, trying to pin down the disruption in the air. A scent on the wind, buried under the blood... something familiar.

A sudden chill shot through his temples, his vision sharpened as his eyes flared ice blue. He barked. "Who's here with you?"

Hux glanced to his side, but said nothing, his hand gripping... something.

But he knew that scent. *Is it... ?* A wave of warmth. It built from his chest to behind his eyes, as they cascaded into a deep ocean green. Pure joy. "Tazia?" Focus shifted, but she was still blurred and difficult to pin down.

"It's me."

"Where?"

The air in front of him warmed, rippled. He felt a hand grip his, and her scent strengthened. Spicy. Buttery. Her hair oil. She slipped into focus. Eyes locking.

"You can see me?" she asked.

"Yes!"

Tazia ripped the charm from her neck and threw it to the ground. "Okay, then."

Hux dropped his gaze and shuffled a step back. Seeing it, Conn let go of Tazia's hand. *Later. All of it later.* This wasn't the time or place for reunions.

Instead, he plastered on a smile. "Well, I guess the band's back together, so it is. Let's get that drink."

24

RETURN OF THE PRODIGAL DUDE

THE LAST TIME Billy had seen this place was when he'd fought Jegudiel. It was her super-secret hideout, so-called because he'd decided that pleat in the fabric of time and space sounded too *Doctor Who*. Despite his love of bits and bytes, he was more superhero than sci-fi.

It didn't look like she'd been back. The sun hammered down on her private little pocket dimension, turning the whole place into a blinding crystalline desert. Everything was white. A dozen shades of it, from antique lace to the brilliant, over-exposed white that blew out the contrast on a cheap digital camera. *A bit much, love. Even for you.*

There was absolute silence, here. No birds squawking, no wind blowing, and no suffocating heat. It was as though the Advocate had chipped away at the rock of existence itself and created a place of intense beauty and solitude, just for her to hide in.

Shards of glass still scattered on the ground from the mirror he'd burst through before their last confrontation. That had ended in her slinking away to lick her wounds. Billy kicked roughly at the glass, remembering how close he'd come to killing her.

As well as the mirrors dotted around, great water-filled reflecting pools gleamed. She'd used them to watch and access the world beyond.

Billy faced the entrance to the cave. During that last fight, he'd propelled the Advocate with such force, she'd hit its walls and caused a rockfall. Crystalline boulders had tumbled from the roof at its centre all the way out to the entrance. The rocks remained piled high, even now, preventing access.

He closed his eyes and stood stock still. Through his body he sent out little sensors, invisible sparks that spread into the atmosphere, swelling with energy from trace matter belonging to each individual thought and event that had occurred here since this place was created. Searching.

After a few seconds, he summoned the sensors back to him, drawing them in like he was pulling on the strings of a hundred brightly coloured balloons. The air fizzed and sparkled around him with vibrant energy, and he probed every glimmer, every star before giving up. There was no trace of Joshua. Nothing.

What else could he try? What other trick could he pull out of his new angelic magickal armoury? Maybe he should reconsider calling it "mojo" after all…

He snorted, and a shudder rippled across his shoulders as he recentered himself. He started to remove his sunglasses, but replaced them briskly as his eyes reacted to the bright light, and a spasm of pain shot across his forehead. God, human beings were fragile.

For the first time, Billy considered himself something different, something other than the human body he'd been born into.

He thought about it logically. Where could Joshua be?

First, there were no newly dead bodies here for him to

jump into, to keep his soul sparking in their blood and guts for a while. Nor were there any living people around, with souls for him to temporarily displace—as necromancers do—and bodies to ride. Also, Joshua travelled so easily between worlds that if he wanted to leave this dimension, he was perfectly capable. But that message he'd left with the witches had been an SOS.

That left one option—he was a prisoner.

Billy's eyes flitted back to the cave's entrance. When he'd first flung Jegudiel from him in the early stages of the fight, she'd hit a rock wall carved into shallow shelves, and he remembered glass jars piled high on them, each with a light inside. When she'd crashed against them, hadn't the jars all broken and the lights come flying out? What if…

"Oh, bloody hell!" Billy rushed to the mouth of the cave and pushed and pulled a few of the looser rocks away. The smaller ones rolled off, but the larger ones remained stuck firm.

The mouth of the cave was massive, as tall as the entrance into Notre Dame, but the whole thing was packed solid from the fall.

"Oh, buggering bloody hell!" Without the aid of a super-charged laser beam or, more realistically, a backhoe, there was no way he'd be able to move the rocks in one go. He was an angel—strong, fast, and obviously gorgeous—not bloody Superman. He would have to remove them all by hand.

Billy groaned, but now he'd figured it out, he couldn't leave his friend in there. It wasn't only him needing Joshua.

Rolling up the sleeves on his brown leather jacket, a gift from Thomas, he began by pulling out all the rocks that weren't wedged too firmly in place. If he could get enough loose, then maybe the ones above would fall, and he could climb over, or Joshua could just fly his little multi-coloured arse through the gap.

Billy pulled and prodded at the rocks for well over an hour, all the time cajoling them to let go of their hold on the wall cursing the whole time. Eventually, he'd loosened and removed enough that a few of the larger rocks shifted. They creaked above him ominously.

"Just one more…" he muttered and pulled on a particularly sparkling rock that looked looser than the others.

As he gripped it, puffing with exertion, the whole thing shattered. His fingers suddenly only clutched little sharp shards of crystal and hard pieces of grit. Sparkling dust flew into the air and set off a sneezing fit, which left him gasping. "Fuck… ing… cool!" The lack of air beat the sarcasm down, and no sooner had he got the words out than he looked up to see the massive rock hanging over his head shift. "Not fucking cool!"

He leaped backward, covering his face and peering through his fingers in time to see the rock wobble, then fall. It crashed forward and down, hitting the other rocks on the way and shoving them out of place. They too shifted until he found himself in the middle of a full on rockfall.

Too late to move again, he dropped to his haunches and hunkered there, arms over his head, waiting for it to be over. Rocks, jagged crystalline shards, and powdered glass cascaded around him, his body protected only by his thin designer jacket.

When it was over, he stood up gingerly. The larger rocks had missed him, but several of the smaller ones had hit squarely. One had created a deep cut on his head, and blood was already seeping from the wound, soaking into his black hair, and trickling down his face. Two shards had sliced into his jacket and cut the skin beneath, one on his arm and the other on his back. More blood flowed from those wounds.

He took off the jacket and held it up so that he could clearly see the rips. "Shit!" He'd loved that jacket; it had cost Thomas a mint. His sunglasses lay on the ground in front of him, the lenses shattered. "Oh. Just. Bloody. Great."

With a big sigh, he looked up at the cave entrance. The top third was now clear, so he could easily climb inside. "Josh!" The word echoed back at him. "You'd better be in there, bruv. Or I'm gonna be so pissed off at you."

As he spoke, he clambered up the rocks now piled in front of the entranceway like a ramp, high enough to peer into the cave. It was bright inside. The sun's rays probed deep into the inner recesses of the cave, reflecting off the surfaces there too, not just from the crystal rocks, but the many mirrors Jegudiel had hung about the place.

"Josh?" Still nothing.

Billy jumped down the other side of the wall, straight onto a carpet of broken glass jars.

When the jars had smashed, Jegudiel had been beside herself, trying to gather them to her. They must have held something precious, something she couldn't replace. Every jar glowed; when they shattered, the lights spilled into the air. What if they'd held souls, human souls she'd imprisoned and hoarded? It was just what that bitch would do. Had they all smashed?

Pushing through the detritus with his feet, Billy kicked a jar, and it rolled away. There was a weak light inside, just a slight pulse that he would have missed if it hadn't rolled into the shadow of a large rock and glowed pathetically, once, twice, before fading again. "Oh, Christ! Josh?"

He chased the jar and held it up to the light. He couldn't see a thing, so he unscrewed the top carefully. There was a slight buzzing from inside the jar, not the sound of a bumblebee or angry fly, just the low, weak, buzz-like static from a radio. "Josh?"

The buzz got a little louder, then the light seemed to creep its way up the inside of the jar and sit on the lip, wobbling slightly.

After retrieving his phone from his back pocket, Billy

carefully put the jar down on the ground. He ran the code he always had loaded, one that he'd run many times to bring Joshua in and out of his computer back home, and held the phone near to the jar. The light tipped itself off the top of the jar, hauled itself over to the phone, and then slowly disappeared into the screen. It looked like a piece of ice rapidly dissolving in the sun and sinking into a crack in the pavement.

When the light had disappeared, the phone gave a weak bleep, and a text popped up on the display.

GET ME FUCK OUT DUDE!!!

Billy nodded. "Where?" He wasn't sure what Joshua needed to revive.

UNDEAD BODY

"Undead? You want a bloody zombie?"

JUST DEAD—FUCKING AUTOCORRECT

"Not a zombie then?"

NO! NEED ENERGY STUPID ARSE!

This was the last text before the light on the phone went out. The battery completely drained.

"Gotcha, bruv. Sorta. Don't you worry. I'll have you in some nice warm blood in no time. Ramp you up a treat. You hear me, Josh? Don't you fade away now. I'll get you home…" Billy kept up the monologue all the way back to London.

25

CHAIN-SMOKING BABIES

THE LITTLE GIRL lay on her back under the playground apparatus. Her eyes still carried a surprised expression as she blindly stared at the sky. From above, Billy had watched her twirling round and round the metal pole. The slip and fall ended in a head-smack onto the concrete. Sadly, it meant death for her, but for Josh, a new, warm home.

Close by, a group of older teens crowded around an ancient blue Ford Cortina held together more by rust than metal. Billy clocked the scene instantly—the furtive cash-for-goods exchange he'd grown up around. Likely knocked off cell phones. The driver was jittery as hell. Billy glanced from the man to the dead girl. Yeah, that'd be dad, then. Too distracted by the twenties thrown at him and the coke in his system, he'd missed his daughter's demise.

Of the choices available, Billy had picked this child in this place. He knew it well. The concrete tower block in East London he'd grown up in. He'd trodden the urine-stinking stairways, watched the rats trot beside the baseboards, painted the graffiti on the walls, and seen the people turn a blind eye to need and suffering. He'd been feeling nostalgic for the neglect of his past. *Fuck knows why.* Maybe he needed to remember what he'd come from, while this new angel-Billy fluffed his bloody wings.

He transferred some of his own energy to the dead phone, reversed the code to release Joshua, and put it down next to the girl's body. The necromancer's weak soul crawled its way from the screen into her body, entering through the energy centre of her heart. It shone a weak blue, fading in and out, like a dynamo that had a tiny charge left.

Billy waited with one eye on the kids around the car. If they saw a grown man sitting beside a little girl lying flat on the ground, they might just get the wrong idea. And if they saw the blood, well, the situation could get… sticky. He smirked at the joke, but then felt bad and stopped. She'd deserved more out of life.

After a few minutes of waiting, and not seeing a single pair of eyes turn in his direction, he relaxed. Joshua was taking his time, so he leaned against the bar the girl had spun around, and lit up a cigarette.

Nighttime now, the metal was chill through his jacket and soothed the cut on his back. The deeper injury on his head still dripped freely, faster angel-healing notwithstanding. Now and then, he dabbed it with the back of his hand, testing the rate of flow.

The little girl groaned and blinked.

"Josh?"

Another groan.

"Josh? You all right, bruv?"

The child's voice rose in a weedy tirade. "Of course I'm not all right you motherfucker! I've been stuck in that fucking jar for months while you ponced around down here, getting in touch with your own personal fucking angel-side. Not giving a toss about me. You've probably just been fucking some tart too, haven't you? You cu…"

His voice faded weakly just in time, saving them both from the curse word, as the girl's body took an automatic breath. "Give me a fucking fag!"

"Dude! Bruv! Sorry, okay. I tried, honest. I *have* been looking for you. Every spell I could—even got Julie searching —" he scrabbled in his jacket pocket for his pack of cigarettes, missed his lighter in the panic, so lit one from his own "—but we couldn't find you anywhere. Do you want me to prop you up or sommit?"

"No, I can do it." Joshua manipulated the girl's body to sit up and push back against the wall on the other side of the metal bar. The blue light in her centre pulsed more strongly.

As weird as it was to hear the curses dropping from the lips of the dead kid, in her own voice no less, it was even more off-putting to Billy to see the child smoking. She sucked greedily, lips making loud wet smacking sounds with each drag. "That's just so wrong, bruv." He shook his head. "Bloody freaky."

"No, what was weird was when my only option was a baby a few years back. Now that's a story." The child removed the cigarette from her mouth and stabbed it at Billy to emphasize her words.

Billy looked aghast. "Just… no… don't tell me."

He let Joshua smoke in peace for a while. It was strange; he'd never heard him use a voice other than the one he'd coded into the program that ran on the computer back home. The usual US West Coast accent was missing entirely. He sounded pure East London.

"Are you feeling a bit better now?"

"Starting to. But I'm still pissed off at you." The girl took another long drag on the cigarette, then Joshua manipulated her hand to push the hair awkwardly from her eyes. "This one's got a massive headache. How did she die?"

"Fell off the bar and splatted on the ground head first. Saw it as we got here. Her dad's over there." Billy pointed to the Cortina, where the man was now blasting pop music.

The guy was the real deal. He didn't look that old, but as he leaned from the car, Billy could see the pushed-up sleeves of his white cotton jacket, and there was way too much bouffant in his hair. Between the deals, he sang loudly to "Wake Me Up Before You Go Go." He looked like he was living in some sort of eighties nostalgia bubble.

"We'd better talk quick then, dude."

Billy was happy for the flash of old Joshua, even if he was speaking through the voice box of a young girl.

"How did you know where to find me?"

"Witches—heard your SOS."

"Ahh! Bloody witches!"

They both nodded at that, happy to agree on something, and smoked in silence for a moment.

"What's the sitch with Taz? Saw you fight the Advocate before the cave collapsed, so hoping you saved her perfectly formed skin?" The child gave a bit of a lascivious smile, tongue circling the end of the cigarette for a moment.

Billy shuddered. "She's safe. Though I think you're starting to like her just a little too much, bruv."

The little girl giggled. "S'all right. You've got no worries from me. Just glad she's safe."

"She's human now."

"Yeah?"

"Yeah."

"Good for her." The girl nodded approvingly.

"And it's Hux you've got to worry about where Taz is concerned. He sort of declared himself to her. Love— apparently."

"Really? Bet that grated your cheese."

"That's a fucking horrible expression."

"I learned it from your code, dude."

"Yeah?"

"Yeah."

"Remind me to delete it. It pissed me right off at first—Hux with Taz—but… I dunno. She needs a human now I guess. And I've got Thomas." He glanced at Joshua to see how that one sat with him. "It's sorta serious."

"Really? You? Serious." The child threw her head back and laughed, her eyes open and staring. She looked possessed like in the films.

"Don't do that. Too bloody spooky." Billy squinted at him and looked away, then looked back. With blood still running from the wound in her head, she was that bad thing people can't resist staring at. "And what's wrong with me and Tom? We work well together."

Joshua snorted. "That's good, dude. I just, I don't know… you turn angel and suddenly you're finding, what? Commitment?" He cracked up again, laughing so much the little girl lost her balance and slipped slightly to one side. Joshua wrestled her upright again.

"All right. Enough. Let's talk about more important things." Billy stubbed his cigarette out on the ground and launched it into the trash can a few feet away. "I've got to catch you up. First, the Tipping Point's almost here. I'm waiting on—"

"Ahh, The Plan's in play then?"

"What?"

"The Plan," the child whispered conspiratorially.

"What fucking plan?" Billy was lost. They didn't have a plan yet. He was still waiting for Julie to fill him in on that.

"Cuinn's Plan. Give us another fag."

Billy threw another over. Impressively, the girl caught it in her mouth and grinned, gripping it between her teeth. She lit it with the remains of the other. *Great, now the kid's chain-smoking.*

"Conn O'Cuinn? The Irish demon that Hux killed? The *dead* Irish demon?"

"Yeah. Only he's not dead. He was in Hell when I was there."

"When the fuck were you in Hell?" For a moment, Billy felt he was losing his mind. He twisted to face the girl—

The music from the car surged, it had switched to nineties techno. Had the guy changed his hairstyle too? Is this whole thing a fever dream? *Am I lying in a coma somewhere, concerned relatives begging me to wake—*

"Before Jegudiel left me in the cave." The girl took another long drag. "Look, she's known about me for a long time. Apparently, I'm quite famous." The pride in his tone was undermined by a smile that drooped on one side then continuously twitched.

"When she got hold of me I was outside Vegas. She took me downstairs and gave me to that fucking Abbot—Taz's dad. My God, he's a bastard—"

"Yes! Thank you!" Billy felt momentarily vindicated for all the times he'd insulted the Abbot and had to put up with hearing Tazia defend him. Then it hit him. "You saw Taz's dad?" Julie had said he was involved. This was more proof.

"Yeah. We got to know each other far too well— unfortunately. He tried to persuade me to the dark side. He wants demons to take over topside. Yada yada. Usual story. He tried being nice to me—to get my help. Gave me free rein to wander the cells for a bit, and I found Cuinn, locked up. Great guy! Hot in that dirty army type way." The girl stopped talking and sat for a while, lost in thought.

"Okay. So. Dead Soldier. Nice guy…" Billy prompted, and rolled his hand over and over to indicate he should continue.

"Yeah. Sorry. Lost my train. Is that techno getting closer?"

"Fuck, yes! Talk quickly, then we can get out of here." Billy turned slightly and raised his palm toward the car as it approached the playground. It stopped abruptly in stasis. The driver's face was a perfect picture of shock; he must have spotted his daughter smoking and talking to a stranger.

"Good trick." Joshua continued. "He'd been there for a while—Cuinn—had heard lots of stuff. Agreements between the Advocate and the Abbot. Thought they were well in cahoots. But seems the Abbot's as sick and tired of the angel as the rest of us and wants rid. So he was trying to set up a deal with Cuinn to lead the Soldiers topside and help get to the Tipping Point. Then go their separate ways. Minimizes the destruction—saves the world."

"What about Jegudiel, though? Doesn't she want the world to end?"

"Yep. The Abbot is playing her. He needs her help to rise out of Hell at the Tipping Point—there's a ritual or something. It's the only way. It's all a big pile of stink, to be honest. Certain events need to happen in a certain order. But Cuinn's got hold of it. He's got a plan of his own—playing them both. That's what he said, anyway. Demon though, so you never really know."

"So why was he telling you all this?"

"Because he needed me to help Tazia. For the plan. For him, maybe. He seemed quite taken with her. I facilitated his chat with a coven in Boston to tell them the spell they needed to make Tazia human. For a low density demon he's got a good handle on possession. I created the opening, he slipped in—as it were."

"Oh my God. You were the handshake protocol!"

"Yep." The girl grinned. "Good analogy, dude. We better get outta here. He looks like he's starting to move again." The car was inching forward.

"Yeah, I still haven't got all this angel mojo sorted out." Billy stood up. "Look, I've got to get to Tazia in Detroit, tell her about her dad! Soren's there too." He held out his phone and shook it, as though the action would give it some more battery power. "You want a lift in this?"

"Nah! I'm all jizzed up now—"

"Really, bruv? Jizzed? Did ya have to?"

"I seem to remember, you gave me that word too…"

"Jazzed or juiced, sure, but not fuckin' jizzed. Look at the company you're keeping!" He gestured toward the kid's body. He needed to go through that code.

"Oh right, my bad, the dead girl I'm wearing might hear me! Like I was saying, I'm all juiced up so can get there on my own. Let me scout ahead. Test the energy. Find Cuinn. I know he was going to need our help to pull it off, but I don't know how."

Now fully recharged, Joshua flew from the girl in a bright flash, bounced off the first streetlight he came to, and was gone.

Billy turned and saw the car pulling up to a stop, still in slow-mo. He looked back at the girl, leaned over and gently stroked her eyes closed with the side of his hand, then picked up the cigarette butts, and threw them after the others into the trash can. Her dad didn't have to find her that way. "God bless, little girl," he said, and melted away.

26

GOODBYE GIRL

THE SCENE in the Irish Club was subdued. When Soren walked through the door, still covered head to toe in blood, there was a distinct shuffling of feet, and no one would catch his eye. All but Kevin, who poured him a large whiskey and put it straight into his hand.

"Drink it all down, man." He served him even before he poured a glass for Cuinn.

Mary Black played softly in the background. Her voice scratched under Soren's skin, bugging him almost as much as the rousing drumbeats of earlier.

He took the tumbler of whiskey to the same chair by the fire he'd slept in awkwardly last night. He just couldn't settle in the guest quarters. It felt wrong to be comfortable.

That morning, finding him slouched in the chair, Cuinn had asked if he wanted to turn suffering into an art. Soren had just shrugged, but in retrospect, he reckoned today could end up on the walls of the Louvre.

He downed more than half the glass. There was no burn, no feeling at all. The Club was blistering, but inside he was yet to thaw. He wasn't sure if he even wanted to.

Anastasia sidled up beside him. Before she settled on the arm of his chair, he'd monitored her progress through the bar by the locations of the whispers.

The last time they'd been here together, she'd almost died. Because of him. Breaking her bones. Spraying her blood. Setting a fucking monster on her! He scrubbed a hand down his face, feeling the heat crawl up his neck. Shame. It burned worse than the whiskey.

She pulled up a low footstool and settled beside him, her eyes darting between the curious faces of the still mumbling Celtic Soldiers. Soren noted her changing expressions depending on whose eyes she caught. They shifted between stern challenges and then nervous glances. She finally settled into a soft-eyed gaze.

She'd seen Cuinn.

He took a shallow breath—it wouldn't make it past his diaphragm anyway—and shoved the whiskey glass into her hand. She drank from it, her lips in the same place his own had been a second before. A pang of pride and a grin flickered.

Not ownership. This was just... familiarity. The quiet language they shared. Two years in Turin and he knew the tension in her shoulders meant she was tired, the slight parting of her lips that she was thirsty. He read her body like a map. One she allowed him to read. She hid nothing from him.

He still couldn't stop the sigh as she gave the glass back to him without looking. Dismissive. Too busy watching the Soldier who'd come up behind them. He looked up to see him reflected in the deep, deep brown of her eyes.

Knocking back the remaining liquid from the glass, he licked it from his lips, finally enjoying the transformation as the burn turned to sweetness on his tongue. "Can I use your shower, Cuinn?"

"Sure you can, man."

Soren pushed himself upright, noticing cramps in the

muscles of his right shoulder. He rubbed at the spot. What was that? Even as the thought formed, he was back in the boat stabbing and slicing, his muscles held taut to maximize his strength. To make it go quicker.

A shudder went through him and brought him back to the bar with a start. All eyes were on him. Dozens of them. Watching. Judging. The feeling of being cornered, of being assessed like some wounded animal, made his skin crawl.

He glared at each man. "What the fuck! Do you all wanna come watch?" He straightened to his full height. Hands clenched into fists at his sides while anger pooled in his stomach like acid. It brimmed into his throat. A shout was coming—a scream!

"Easy, Hux. It's not their fault." Cuinn put a hand on his arm.

"No, Cuinn, you're right. It's yours." He spat the words at him, and from the corner of his eye, he saw Kevin's hand move toward the gun holstered on his chest.

Cuinn saw it too and put a hand up to him. "No guns." Then he turned back to Soren. "We'll talk once you've cleaned up. Go scrub it off." It was clear he wasn't just talking about the blood.

Still scowling, Soren took a step away. Anastasia jumped up beside him.

"You coming?" His voice had no edge, but if she turned him down, he felt he might just plead.

"Sure." To her credit, she didn't look to Cuinn before answering.

But God, he felt the pull. It was clear she wanted to be with his brother, not him.

For now, though, Soren wouldn't give her that. Not yet. Hadn't they just promised to look out for each other?

———

When Soren left the shower, with his lower body wrapped in a towel, skin scrubbed raw, and smelling of medical soap, Anastasia wrinkled her nose in objection. She'd stretched out on Cuinn's bed, smoking a stress-relieving cigarette.

He raised an eyebrow at the stink of her smoke and waved a hand through the blue cloud polluting the bathroom steam.

She just shrugged.

The shower had improved his mood slightly. "Those things will kill you. You're not immortal anymore." He pulled a comb from his backpack and sat on the edge of the bed, drawing it through his wet hair.

"Vampires aren't immortal. No demon is." She took a longer drag, inhaling deeply, and smiled in a way he could only classify as sinful.

He pursed his lips to stop the smile. "Who's the oldest vamp you've met?"

"There was one. Years ago. I was just a kid myself. He was supposed to be the age of the angels. He was all wrinkly and dried up." She grimaced. "Icky."

"Icky?"

"Yeah! He had blood sorta leaching from the cracks in his face, but I couldn't tell if it was coming out of him, or that's the way he fed now. You know, got it dripped on him and absorbed it through his skin." She blew out a long, controlled stream of smoke at the ceiling.

Soren paused with the comb and made a face. "Yeah, that's icky!"

She giggled.

He liked that he could still make her laugh. His sense of humour was of the driest kind—non-existent, Billy would argue—but she'd always been able to coax it from him.

He finished raking through his hair and pulled clean underwear and combat pants from his bag. "What happened to him?"

"Dead."

"Murdered?"

"Nope. I think he just got bored and gave up. Crumbled to dust." She reached out and stubbed the cigarette directly onto Cuinn's bedside table, leaving the butt sitting in the ash. "See, we all die sooner or later."

She sat up, grabbed the comb he'd left on the bed, and dragged it through her own hair. Hitting a knot, she gave up, threw the comb back down, and just pulled a bunch to one side.

He'd dressed in his clean clothes and looked around for the t-shirt he'd rinsed through earlier, then put that on too. "You just ruined an original example of early Colonial furniture." He nodded at the scorched black wood under the butt.

"Really? Do you think Cuinn'll be pissed?"

"He won't notice." He would, but Soren didn't care.

"You have a stain on your shirt." She pointed at a light yellow mark smeared near the hem.

Soren looked down, then sat on the bed heavily.

The baby.

"Yeah."

"What is it?"

"You wouldn't believe me." He pushed away the image of blood sprayed on innocent skin, and put a hand on her leg. "You want to be with Cuinn, don't you?"

Anastasia shifted. "Can we talk about icky vampires again?"

"No."

"Okay. We have... unfinished business, I guess." She held his gaze, but blinked several times in succession.

"I don't know if we can trust him, Anastasia. After today, I don't know."

Sowilo Skye's voice echoed in his head. *Things aren't always what they seem.* "I was warned. Told I needed to trust… but I don't know."

"Who warned you?"

He shrugged. "Doesn't matter. May not be important. It's just—"

"Spidey-sense tingling?"

"Yeah."

"You sound like Billy."

"Billy makes a lot of sense."

"Wow! Things have changed." She smiled. "You two used to hate each other."

"We got… closer. Cared about the same person." He winked, though his stomach churned. "You should talk to him. Cuinn, I mean."

He held her look of surprise.

Compassion is the key to humanity, the Escort had said. *Let her see it.*

Well, he'd lost his humanity today. Out there on the lake, he'd become more monster than the demons standing watching. If he wanted it back, this was his price.

Even if it meant he was fighting on the wrong side, he'd die knowing he'd done right by her.

That was compassion. Wasn't it?

"I'm going out. Get some air, even it is the thick stench of Detroit. Better than your smoke anyway." He finally allowed himself to smile. Humour again, sort of.

He headed to the door, then stopped and turned back. She frowned, looking like she wanted to say something. The frown faded, and she gave him a small smile instead.

He wanted to tell her he loved her. But didn't.

That wouldn't be fair. He didn't even know if it would mean anything to her now.

So he left the words unsaid, and the silence hanging.

27

A JEEP AFFAIR

TAZIA LAY on Cuinn's bed staring at the ceiling until her body wouldn't let her stay still anymore. It didn't take long. She flexed her feet and rotated her wrists, then the shadows of her old tattoos itched down her back. Even rubbing against the quilt did nothing to ease it.

The itch dragged the memories up with it. Cuinn's bloody body cradled in her arms. Hux's blank eyes. That bitch laughing. The agony as the ink lifted from her flesh. *Fuck it!*

Eventually, she sat up and half-twisted her body to give her hand a little more reach and shoved it down the back of her t-shirt, blunt nails frantically scratching. Still unable to relieve it, she growled in frustration, and pulled her knees up to her chest to hug them tight.

Hux was right: she had to talk to Cuinn. But with so much obvious antagonism toward her from members of his Unit, she couldn't just walk out into the bar and strike up a conversation: *Hey, babe, miss me?* But she didn't want to stay in Cuinn's room. Without Hux with her, it sent a message, like she thought she belonged there. Jesus Christ! Being soulless was a hell of a lot easier.

She thought back to Rome: the hand of God stretching to Adam across the ceiling of the Sistine Chapel and the camera she'd stolen. It had been Hux's image in that picture, behind her in shadowy outline, and Hux she'd seen under the influence of the magick of the cigar she'd puffed on. Not Cuinn.

Perhaps that was all she needed to know. What had she been telling Billy all these years? That a human couldn't be with a demon! Perhaps it was time to tell herself the same thing.

But a talk was in order. Just seeing him had knocked the wind out of her. Hux had seen it. He'd always called her an open book.

And what the fuck was all this about him working with the Advocate? She needed answers.

A knock on the door made her snap her head to attention, eyes wide. The door opened a crack, and Cuinn looked in. He pushed it open wider, but didn't enter. She didn't smile, just stared.

He smirked. "You look like you're up to no good."

"No! Just… thinking."

He nodded. "You wanna take a supply run with me? Tell me what you're thinking in the Jeep."

"Supplies?"

"Yeah, some of the guys are hungry."

"Can I drive?" She needed to keep busy, didn't just want to sit in the car staring at the road—or at him.

Cuinn looked surprised. "Sure, *mo chroí*. If you can manage the beast, you can."

Tazia widened her eyes. The last time she'd met Cuinn's beast, it was trying to kill her.

He smiled and said gently, "I meant the Jeep. She's an old beast, so she is. We could take the truck, but Hux just took off in it."

"He'll be back. Just needed some space."

"Yeah. I'm not surprised, after… well… you know. So you want to?"

She was already standing. "Let's go."

———

They set off late afternoon. Still plenty of light. Tazia aggressively attacked the tarmac, hitting bumps at such a speed that eventually Cuinn told her to lay off the gas. Apparently, the big cloud of dust and howling engine sent a signal to all the demons in the vicinity that Soldiers were on the hunt. When she griped back at him, he gave her a wide grin and lightly squeezed her knee. Her skin juddered like a cat's.

With her sunglasses shifting because of the bumpy ride, she pushed them up to the bridge of her nose and glanced at him. "What are we looking for?"

"A Shifter—sort of. Female. Name of Rebecca. She has a lead on some whiskey and steak. As in cow."

She blurted out a laugh. "I know you don't eat people, Cuinn!"

"Yeah, well. Since I've been gone, it seems the supply route has got a little lean. So there's been a few changes to the rules apparently. A couple of the guys were saying you looked really tasty."

Her knuckles gripped the steering wheel more tightly. "You're joking right?"

He said nothing.

"Right?" She demanded.

He grinned. "Gotcha."

Tazia breathed out. *Arsehole!*

Cuinn continued. "We used Rebecca occasionally in the past, but Kev's been relying on her more of late. She's sound. But with that said, is there silver in your knife?"

Tazia's hand automatically shifted to the Bowie strapped to the outside of her right thigh. "Of course."

"And what about now you're… human. Still strong?"

"Guess we'll find out?" She winked at him. "What does she shift to?"

"What?" It seemed the wink had distracted him.

"Shifter, you said. So, what does she shift to? Animal, object… and why 'sort of'?"

"Another human form. Hobo-type mainly unless she wants something. Deceitful bastards, the lot of them—the Fey. Some kind of mix, I never pinned it down."

There was something he wasn't saying, but she didn't push more. "You really only like other Soldiers, don't you Cuinn?" She laughed.

"True enough." He held her gaze, and his eyes warmed from blue to deep sea-green and back. "There are some humans who aren't too bad." He looked back at the road. "We're nearly there. Pull in around this corner."

They'd driven to another area by the docks, further west this time. Their position looked straight across the water. Tazia pulled to a stop, but didn't turn off the engine. She was already weighing up the terrain. Buildings jutted out everywhere, storage containers set at odd intervals, some stacked to tower over them. It looked fake, like a narrow man-made ravine. *A kill box.* It would funnel them against the walls of a warehouse with no obvious exit.

"Flash the headlights three times."

"You serious? This *Bugsy-fucking-Malone!*"

He tutted. "Just do it, please, darlin'."

That was the first time he'd called her *darlin'* since she'd arrived. The familiarity warmed her heart a little. That damn Irish lilt.

She flashed the lights. Immediately, three flashes returned

from the vehicle parked by the warehouse. Tazia snorted. "Do we have a code phrase too? Don't tell me it's 'The rooster sings at dawn' or, 'the cheese monkeys are dressed for Christmas', right? Wait. No. I know. It's a mission name like 'Operation Steak Attack' or 'Operation Let's Just Get The Fucking Whiskey'."

He ignored her. "Drive slowly toward them. There'll be a lot of guns pointed at us between here and there."

On cue, to their right, the music of a shotgun being cocked came from behind one container. The beat continued down both walls. He put his hand on her arm. "And, Tazia. Stay in the Jeep. And no risks."

She'd heard that one before. Right before she'd blown up a warehouse.

She smirked and eased the Jeep forward. As Cuinn had predicted, there was at least one shooter behind each. This Shifter took her protection seriously.

"This 'Rebecca'..." said Tazia.

"Yeah?" His eyes were swivelling back and forth.

"You know her, don't you?"

He sighed, but maintained his watch. "Can't get anything past you, darlin', can I?"

They pulled up in front of the vehicle that had flashed at them. It was a top of the line, sleek black pickup with a pimped-out paint job and lift kit. The massive wheels had deep treads that looked like they'd never seen an ounce of mud. Tazia wondered if it had steel balls hanging from its tow bar too. One in every town.

A woman got out, looking like she'd just stepped off the set of that old movie, *Grease*. Dressed head to toe in sleek black leather—tight pants and halter top—her shiny long blonde locks bounced with relish. She was even more of an advert for L'Oréal than Hux.

Now Tazia knew the code word: Operation Deep Throat —with emphasis on the deep.

She walked over to them, high-heeled black boots clipping in the dust, giving her another three inches she didn't really need. There was more bouncing than just her hair. Tazia looked to see if Cuinn's tongue was hanging out as far as hers. To her surprise, it wasn't. In fact, he looked pretty bored.

"Conn O'Cuinn. What a *total* pleasure." Rebecca flung the greeting in a Southern drawl at the same time as her eyes raked over him. Her gaze hung around his eyes for a moment, then dropped pointedly to his groin. "It's been far too long."

Tazia looked from him to the woman. So they knew each other very well indeed. She felt no jealousy. In fact, for a moment, her imagination jumped to a threesome. *Wouldn't that be fun?*

Cuinn got out of the Jeep, shotgun in hand. It was a different one than usual, most likely packing silver shot.

He took a step toward her. "How have you been, now, Rebecca?"

"Missing you, sweetie." She tilted her head to the side. "I heard you were dead, sugar. Done in by some *gorgeous Swedish hunk*."

Odd emphasis, but this time she bristled a little. Not a threesome then. And definitely not a foursome.

"A temporary setback." Cuinn gave an easy smile.

"And Vegas? How is my old stomping ground? Surviving the Risings?"

"You tracking me, Beccy?"

Rebecca shifted her weight and sniffed. "Don't flatter yourself, sugar. You pop up, and a girl like me gets to hear."

"Ah yeah. The Good Folk like to talk, and I noticed the place was overrun."

"Family stays in touch."

"Well, I'm here now and—" he put out his arms, his palms out "—all alive and in one piece as you can see."

"Well, I can't see everything, can I?" She managed to giggle, lick her lips, bat her eyelashes, and flick her hair all at the same time.

"Wow!" Tazia was impressed. If she tried that, it would look like she was having a seizure. This woman could teach her a thing or two.

They both turned to look at her. Cuinn rolled his eyes at Tazia.

"Who's this?" Rebecca addressed Cuinn. Her smile stayed fixed but dropped from her eyes.

Tazia jumped from the vehicle and came forward. "Hi, I'm Tazia. Just lovely to meet you, sugar." She offered her hand and lost the mock Southern accent. "That whole flirty thing you've got going on—it's just awesome, lady!"

"I don't do handshakes."

"Oh, of course. You probably just go straight for the dick." Tazia gave a wide smile and winked. "Good move. Used that one myself." She let her eyes flit to Cuinn and back to ensure Rebecca got the message.

The woman wiped the smile from her mouth.

Cuinn groaned. "This is Anastasia—my driver—she'll be getting back in the Jeep now." He glared at her.

"Sure. Just wanted to say hi." Tazia got back into the driver's seat while Cuinn pushed Rebecca aside with a gentle hand, and started talking to her in a low voice.

God, she missed her demon hearing. She watched through slitted eyes as his hand brushed away the hair from her face and then wandered up and down the naked flesh of Rebecca's back.

After a short while, the overhead door to the warehouse rose. Guys in dark blue overalls brought out flat boxes of frozen meat marked with a triple A, and square boxes full of whiskey bottles. It was a good Irish single malt.

The men loaded up the Jeep while Tazia kept an eye on them. It seemed the situation was going their way, but still Cuinn chatted to the woman, leaning ever closer to her ear. Even from thirty feet away, Tazia could hear her laughing—squeaking like an excited gerbil.

Suddenly impatient, she leaned heavily on the horn, making both Cuinn and Rebecca jump. *Tick-tock, loverboy. Tick-fucking-tock.* The henchmen closest to the vehicle immediately aimed their guns at her.

Putting up her hand to signal to the men to lower their weapons, Rebecca slowly swung her way up to Tazia's side of the Jeep.

Cuinn put his hands on his hips and glared, mouthing, "What the fuck?"

Rebecca leaned into the open window, shoving her not inconsequential bosom forward so it rested on top of the lowered glass. "Do we have a problem, sugar?"

Tazia looked from the cleavage to her face and grinned. "Nope. It all looks good to me."

Rebecca did a double take at the grin. "I just thought… cos we have stakes in the same game—" She flicked her head back at Cuinn.

"Nope. No stakes." Tazia shook her head. "That game's already been played."

"Then why with the honking car, sweetie?"

"I was bored." Tazia shrugged.

Rebecca dropped her head and laughed. "Bored?"

She moved away from the car for a moment, and shouted to one of her men. "Get the lady a few boxes of tequila." Then she moved back in, and whispered in Tazia's ear, "I like you, little human. Enjoy your gift, and if you want to come back later—on your own—you know the way." She pressed her full red-lipstick lips against Tazia's naked pink ones.

Tazia's lips buzzed, a strange coldness beneath Rebecca's warmth. The world swam for a split second. Not the grimy Detroit street, but the scent of old silver and the impossible sensation of kissing her own reflection. An intense, dizzying surge of total acceptance shot through her. Then it was gone, leaving only the ghost of the feeling. Comforting. Yet deeply disturbing.

Rebecca smiled and backed away. She walked toward the warehouse at a fast clip. Level with Cuinn, she paused, said something to him, and then continued into the building.

Well that was fucking weird.

Cuinn stared after her retreating form, then back to Tazia, both with their mouths open. Shaking herself, Tazia shrugged and busied herself starting the engine and checking the mirrors, humming.

He climbed back into the Jeep as the last of the tequila was loaded and wiped his thumb over the red smear of lipstick that had been transferred to Tazia's lips. He regarded her, shaking his head.

Under his scrutiny, Tazia felt the colour rise into her cheeks. "What?"

"Nothing, darlin'. Just marvelling at you."

Tazia backed the Jeep out of the alley at extra fast speed, keeping a perfectly straight line, all the time licking her lips. *Mmmm, cherries.*

———

"So, darlin', at the risk of sounding like a fil-um we should talk." Cuinn had laid his arm over the back of the driver's seat.

She flashed a glance at him. "Now?"

"Now."

Tazia slammed her foot on the brake, and the Jeep came to a skidding stop, rattling the boxes of liquor in the back so much that Cuinn moved his arm quickly to brace the boxes.

They'd stopped in the middle of the road, overlooked by the broken windows of abandoned tenements, and a fair number of vultures who stared listlessly down from their roofs at the scene below.

Dropping her eyes from the birds to him, she turned in her seat to face him. This was one conversation she would not start.

Cuinn took a moment. He smiled at the ground before turning to her. "You're an odd girl, so you are."

"Odd?"

"Unusual."

"Is that good or bad?" She frowned at him.

"Good. But you take some getting used to. You're a bit of a wild card, Tazia. And, as a rule, I like to know what's in my hand. Rebecca seems to like you though. Said something strange before we left."

"What?"

"That you would never be mine."

Tazia let the sentence hang for a while. She suddenly wasn't sure she wanted to have that particular conversation. "And do you think that's true?"

He shrugged.

Good. He didn't have her figured out yet. It felt safer somehow.

Still uncomfortable, she tossed her hair back, just like she'd seen Rebecca do. "Okay. Is this what you wanted to talk about?" They seemed to have started at a tangent.

"No." He shook his head, and his tone changed. All business. "Let's start over. Did Hux tell you about the Tipping Point?"

"Some. He said you were working with the Advocate to

make it happen." She looked up. Were the vultures watching more closely now? They were very alone out here. She checked the rearview mirror.

"Up to a point. There's a plan in play."

"And?"

"And I want you on my side."

She didn't answer him directly. "You let Hux become a monster on that boat. Let him lose himself. Is that your plan? To make us all like you?"

"Like me?"

"Monsters." *Fuck, where did that come from?* She bit her lip.

Cuinn took a breath. "Seems it wasn't that long ago, you would have been called a monster too, darlin'."

Tazia nodded. "I guess. But even as a demon, I never did what Hux did."

"Maybe not. But you watched him do it and didn't interfere, just like me."

"You knew I was there?"

"I was told later. The angel—"

Her temper flared. "See, Cuinn, this is what I've got a problem with. Not only did you let the man you told me in the past you needed to save from himself, turn into… that! But you're also working with the bitch that wanted to use me to destroy the fucking world. What do I do with that?"

Tazia flung the question, but fixedly faced the road. Not those eyes. *I just can't...*

He touched her chin gently and turned her head to look at him. "Trust me."

And there they were. Green, beautiful. *Deceitful?*

"But why did you need that?" She asked.

"*She* needed it. I won't let him stay there, Tazia. I'll bring him back—*we'll* bring him back."

Tazia breathed deeply, still staring at him, processing his

comment. Was this true? Could she trust him? "Anything else I should know?"

"No, darlin'." He leaned closer and said the words again, "Trust me." Then he kissed her, wiping the last of the cherry-flavoured lipstick from her lips.

For a moment she heard cackling and wings beating, then lost the sounds as the moment extended on.

28

A NECESSARY SACRIFICE

AS THE JEEP pulled up in front of the Irish Club, and Cuinn and Anastasia went inside, Soren scrutinized every movement they made, jealousy hollowing his stomach.

He'd watched them leave the Club earlier, and circled the block in Cuinn's truck. *Follow or not?* When they drove away in the Jeep, he put his foot down and left in the opposite direction.

In the time he'd been gone, he'd rebalanced. The boat was still with him, flooding his thoughts, but to stay sharp, he had to accept and move on. For now, he would box it up. Stop blaming Cuinn, the Advocate, whoever. The blood stained his hands alone.

Now, seeing them together chatting, smiling. Shit. He blew out a slow breath and forced his stomach to relax. *Remember compassion, Huxford.*

No strings was hard. But it gave her what she deserved—a life on her terms—and him a chance to cling to that final speck of humanity.

That was as far as he could get. Focus on Anastasia. First always.

Could Cuinn say the same? For him, it was country first, family second. So, would she be third? Last? Where would Soren be when this was over? Likely, nowhere.

No, they couldn't rely on Cuinn and his plan. They'd have a better chance at surviving the Tipping Point together.

Decision made.

He'd parked the truck around the corner from the Club with a good view of the front door, engine running, not yet willing to go inside. He'd get more shifty looks from Kevin and the others, perhaps even pity. That was unacceptable. Distracting. His hands still shook if he didn't focus.

A couple of Cuinn's men came out of the bar and started unloading boxes. It looked like they'd got a haul. Meat. Whiskey. The Club would buzz tonight.

Soren moved the truck. He took the side turning that ended at the back of the church; the cemetery ran along one side, and on the other, burned-out garages Cuinn used for his vehicles.

Fire had scorched their walls and their ceilings were collapsing, but the padlocked metal doors were only warped a little by the heat. He parked the truck in the one furthest away, leaving the closer one for the Jeep. Then started back to the Club on foot.

As he got closer, he saw a movement in the shadows. It was just for a moment, a flash of a man standing in the doorway of the old pawn shop across from the back entrance to the church. Like someone had pulled back a black curtain, revealing the figure, and then let it drop back into place.

He halted. Took two steps back so that he, too, was in the shadows of the road against the walls of the buildings to his left. If this was a vampire, he was far too close to the Club for comfort, and it was something he'd be happy to dispatch—without guilt. Knife in hand even before his smile completely formed, he slunk forward, feeling his way along the wall.

Another movement: someone walking up the centre of the road toward him. He recognized the gait. Cuinn. Alone. No weapon. His head swivelled from side to side. Looking.

Soren waited. He was downwind; Cuinn wouldn't pick up his scent this far away.

As Cuinn got level with the doorway where Soren had seen the shadow, he stopped and looked sideways. His lips moved. Just a mumble from here. Soren sucked in a breath. It was too tempting; he had to get closer.

On light feet, he crossed the road, finding mounds of dried grass and weeds poking above the sand to dampen his steps. He kept to the shadow of an old oak tree cast by the angle of the moon in a rare moment of cloudless sky.

On this side of the Club, the cemetery stretched wide for more than a hundred feet before it butted up against the back wall of the church. Headstones, large sculptures of angels, and a few semi-destroyed tombs provided plenty of cover. Vines of dead ivy blanketed the paths deadening the sound of his approach. Soren inched his way closer to the two who were now deep in conversation. *Close enough.*

Their voices drifted to him.

"You here by magick?" Cuinn asked.

"A temporary situation. I will not be able to hold the spell for long."

"Then talk quickly, I'll be missed." Cuinn shuffled his feet and glanced around, including a sweeping look into the darkness of the cemetery.

Soren ducked behind a large concrete angel that was standing on one foot and trumpeting to Heaven. He took a breath, then peered around the base of the statue.

Cuinn's voice rose. A tone of agitation cut through the air. "Why didn't you tell me about this until now?"

"Because, my dear Cuinn, I did not want it to prevent you from finding her. You have a soft spot for the girl despite whatever else is at stake, do you not?" The voice had an antiquated tone. Slightly accented. Confident, with each word precise and clean.

Soren shuffled closer, hoping he could catch sight of the speaker.

"Sure, it makes things more difficult… on a number of levels." Cuinn had his back to Soren, but the sudden stiffness in his shoulders made his irritation obvious. Whatever this speaker wanted, it had come as an unwelcome surprise.

"I had another plan, but it failed." He sighed and added, "the help is not what it once was."

"By 'help' I assume you mean your cronies and slaves?"

"Supporters and devotees, Cuinn. Don't confuse me with the Advocate." He continued, "Regardless of what you think of me, the girl must be handed over for our alliance to continue. And if you decide otherwise—" The man snapped his fingers in Cuinn's face. The hand flashed in the moonlight. *Rings.* Lots of them. One large red stone stood out.

Soren recognized it. *No, it isn't possible!* He had to get closer.

On hands and knees, head held low, Soren crept forward to a crumbling tombstone even closer to the roadside, hoping to get a clearer view.

"What do you need her for?"

"That is my affair, Conn O'Cuinn. It is enough for you to know, she is necessary to me—and to our success."

"The angel doesn't know about this, does she, you auld fecker?"

"Was that a threat, Irishman?"

"I'm asking. If this is something you need and I can't give it, then maybe I'm on the wrong side…"

"You would do well to remember your place, Soldier." The words hissed. When he spoke again, his tone was cajoling. "Give me the girl, Cuinn. You have my word she will be well looked after. As soon as the Tipping Point comes, I will be free of Jegudiel, and you will be free of me. Then we can each of us be to our own lands, and you will be home. Free from the rule of all but yourself."

Crossing his arms in front of his chest, Cuinn sounded steady, not to be messed with. "I'm asking again, what do you need her for?"

The wind changed slightly and blew away the man's reply. *Fuck!*

It looked like the conversation was over. Cuinn's shoulders drooped as he nodded and took a few steps backward.

"Come on, come on," Soren muttered under his breath, willing the man to step forward. He needed to have his suspicions confirmed.

The wind dropped.

"Cuinn!" This time the man's words travelled clearly to Soren. "I want my daughter. Do not let me down." The man stepped forward, and for a moment the light hit his face. *The Abbot of Savoy.*

Soren held his breath, not daring to let it out.

"You'll have her," Cuinn said. He walked away without glancing back.

The Abbot called after him, "Forty-eight hours, Conn O'Cuinn, until the Tipping Point. I need her before then."

He looked up, eyes closed and arms out like he was greeting the moon. His chest expanded, as he sucked in the rank Detroit air. He let the breath out in silence and faded into nothing.

———

Soren walked back through the cemetery towards the Club. Far ahead, Cuinn opened the door. An old Irish folk song blared into the night before being cut off as the door slammed shut.

Soren stopped short. *Think, soldier!*

He couldn't just breeze in there, grab Anastasia, and run. Cuinn would be on him in an instant. And where could they go? His boys were everywhere, and with the Tipping Point about to hit, everyone was jumpy.

He'd seen it that afternoon. Groups of demons gathered on street corners and patrolled their borders. Everyone planning —waiting. Just like them. The damn heat rising every second.

Soren took a few steps forward. Inside, he would have to act normal and look for an opportunity to pull Anastasia aside.

That's it, they'd plan an escape together, just like in the old days!

He walked more purposefully for four, five, six paces. But if the Abbot is involved in the Tipping Point, Cuinn was out of his depth. He's Satan's Second, for Godsakes. Evil!

Abruptly, Soren's feet dragged on the ground.

Control it, Huxford. Cuinn will read you in an instant.

Doing a deal with the Devil to get out of Hell was one thing, but Cuinn just agreed to give Anastasia back to that monster. Her torturer. Was he about to hand her over just so he could get back to his fucking green fields and flag?

Outside the Club door, Soren paused. He took a deep breath. It was easier to hate now. Hate the man he'd trusted. Followed.

His brother. Yeah, a brother who was using them both!

Soren bent double with the effort not to roar his anger aloud. As he wrestled to regain his equilibrium, his thoughts tumbled away from him one after another. He'd been played. All his own plans were useless. *A fantasy.*

He dragged in another breath, all the hairs on his skin sticking up, and his blood ran ice-cold. *Hatred. Yes. Use it!*

He could not let Cuinn influence him anymore. Soren was on the wrong fucking side and needed to get himself, and Anastasia, out. He would not let her be handed over like a chess piece. They'd fought so hard to keep her alive—him,

Billy, and the others. They'd sacrificed so much. And she'd sacrificed everything.

No, he would get her out. Cuinn and his plan could go straight back to Hell.

Soren opened the door.

29

RUN AWAY

CUINN WAS behind the bar when Soren entered the Club. It was busy with more recruits coming inside in a steady stream. He hovered by a barstool, but didn't sit. Loud, smokey, stinking of sweat. Soren's head thumped.

Cuinn pushed beers across the counter to a waiting Soldier, each glass accompanied by a tumbler of whiskey. It could have been any other night in the bar.

He skidded a beer across the counter towards Soren and nodded a greeting. Soren met his eyes for a moment and nodded back. He hovered longer, sipping from the glass. *Keep it casual.*

Piecing together snippets from conversations around him, Soren figured out Kevin had rounded up a couple of prisoners —humans who'd strayed into the city. Now and then, ear-splitting screams carried from the back rooms. The interrogation had started.

While serving, Cuinn chewed on his lip, eyes darting toward the booth in the furthest corner of the room. Anastasia sat there on her own, knocking back a bottle of tequila that already looked half empty. She was pale, her eyes flicking to the door to the back when the screams rose. Nerves. Fear. Or maybe guilt. He couldn't tell which. It was new for her.

Cuinn cranked up the music before shouting, "How're you doin', man?" and poured Soren a whiskey from the good bottle kept under the counter, a ten-year-old single malt. It followed the path of the beer straight into Soren's hand.

"Better."

"Yeah?" Cuinn's shoulders released. He leaned over the bar and spoke normally. "Good. Why don't you go keep your girl happy? She did good today—supply run—but she's looking peaky now."

"She's her own girl, Cuinn. Not mine." He spat the words out, couldn't hold it in.

A flicker of confusion crossed Cuinn's face. "Come again?"

"Nothing. Where did she get the tequila?"

"Used her charm, so she did." He grinned. "My contact seemed quite taken with her—"

Soren raised his eyebrows.

"Old flame of mine. Nice lass, but I didn't seem to be doing it for her today." He shrugged. "Tazia played it up nicely though."

Sounded about right. Anastasia wouldn't balk at an opportunity if it gained her something. She had an opportunist streak a mile wide, and it didn't look like that had changed with the onset of humanity. "Any reason she's knocking it back?"

Cuinn shrugged again. "I think the action out back is disturbing her. That human soul of hers is pretty sensitive now, isn't it?"

Soren nodded. "So is Kevin just playing, or is there a reason for it?" He couldn't keep the tone from his voice.

Cuinn's eyes flashed ice blue for a moment, but he kept his voice level. "Reason for it. Borders are down. Finally. Humans are short of food. Hungry people are dangerous."

It was true. They'd heard bomb blasts the night before.

Even Soldiers might not survive that—homemade or military grade. Right now, there would be more food inside the cordon than outside.

"I guess suggesting we share supplies wouldn't go down well." *Cut it out, Huxford. Why are you goading him?*

"Fuck, Hux! Are we still doing this?" Cuinn came close to raising his voice.

"No—" Soren knocked back the whiskey and pushed his glass forward for another "—we're not."

He got it, but Cuinn banged the bottle back down with unnecessary force. "Good man. We should talk later. Tipping Point's almost here. We need to get ready."

Soren took the glass, raised an acknowledgement and turned away. He slipped into the booth alongside Anastasia. She hunched over the table and didn't look up, but slid the bottle of tequila toward him.

"I've got whiskey, Anastasia." He pushed his glass under her nose for a moment, then took it back.

"Cocktail?"

He smirked. "No," and sipped from his glass. "Good idea to keep our wits about us tonight, lover." His voice was loaded, and he deliberately used the endearment to get her attention, but the tequila had already taken effect.

"Nope." She shook her head. "I'm only about Mexico tonight." She raised her glass and gave him a big smacking kiss on the lips, then looked again into its depths.

It threw him off guard for a moment, and he glanced toward Cuinn to see if he was watching. He was. Carefully.

"Last time I was here, drinking like this, there was a talking dragon."

"Yeah?" He moved the tequila bottle to his side of the table.

She glared at him and moved it back. "I'm not drunk, and I'm not lying!" She raised her voice, and for a moment she seemed surprised at the sound of it. She tried again, and this time hissed almost as loudly, "I think it was the angel. I think she was in my glass, watching me." She shuffled closer to Soren, her eyes wide. "Do you think she's here now?"

He shrugged. "I've stopped worrying about her. Bigger fish to fry." Again, he tried to get her attention as subtly as he could.

"Fish? Who's frying fucking fish?" she practically shouted, earning a few glances her way. He met their eyes, unblinking, while she giggled. "Hey, that's funny. All the frying fucking fish. Could be our band name."

She laughed again, knocked back her glass, and refilled it before he could stop her. Then she put the bottle beside her on the bench instead of returning it to the table and stuck her tongue out at him, daring him to reach for it.

It was time for a new strategy; subtlety wasn't working. "Drink it. I won't take it away again," he said. "Just remember you're human now." A drunk woman could be carried outside to a waiting vehicle. Maybe it would be better that way. Take action and explain why later.

"You promise?" She held up the bottle, uncertain whether to return it to the table.

"I promise."

"Cross your heart and hope to die?"

"No."

She frowned. "You're supposed to say yes, then kiss me to seal the deal."

"You're making that last bit up." He pecked a kiss on her lips anyway.

She put down the bottle gingerly, but still on her side of the table, in reach of her hand. She looked again into her glass, staring closely at the little dragon stamp on the base. "I miss Billy." She leaned her head in her hand, and a tear dribbled from eye to nose, then fell on the table.

"You crying?" He couldn't keep the surprise from his voice. Generally, she wasn't a sad drunk. She was more likely to dance on the table.

She rubbed roughly at her face, and gulped more tequila, avoiding eye contact with him. "They're killing those people out back. Torturing them, then killing them." She sounded totally sober.

"I know."

"I used to do that. Kill people just because they knew something I didn't. And sometimes just for fun."

"That was a long time ago."

"Yes," she agreed. "But I did it, Hux. My father liked it when I did."

They were silent for a while until Soren reached for the tequila, topped up her glass, and poured some into his own, which was now empty of whiskey.

"Do you really love me?" she whispered.

"Yes." He'd never been so sure.

"Good." She took a big gulp from her glass, put her head on his shoulder, and started snoring.

———

Once Anastasia was sleeping, Franky Lavender came over and sat opposite Soren. The old empathy demon looked tired; grey shadows under his eyes and creases on his face not there even a few months before. "How are you doing, son?"

"Wishing everyone would stop asking me that." Soren offered the bottle of tequila to him.

"Nah! You really wanna drink that stuff?" He screwed up his face as though it was poison.

"No, but I can't get up." Soren looked at the sleeping Anastasia. His right arm squashed underneath her.

Franky shuffled back down the bench and crossed to the

bar. He fished around under the counter and brought out a bottle, then headed back to the booth. Cuinn had disappeared out back, and in the gaps in the music the sounds of wailing filled the room again.

"He's really going for it." Soren gestured toward the door.

"Situation calls for it, kid."

Soren shrugged. "No judgement." *Careful. He'll read you.*

"So you standing with him, Hux?" Franky swirled whiskey around his glass, clinking the ice cubes noisily.

"You checking me out, Frank?"

"No, just asking the question. It must be conflicting for you —human asked to kill humans. I'd have a problem with being asked to kill my kind."

Despite the denial, Soren was on his guard. "It was. Is. But for now, I'm supporting my brothers." He chose his words carefully.

Franky looked him over and was scrutinized in return.

"You're looking older suddenly, Franky."

"Feel it, kid. The months without Cuinn, it was hard. His loss was a big one. Not just for me, for the entire Unit. Kevin did well, stepping up, but it's not a job he wanted or asked for. But he owed it to him." He slurped from his glass. "The bosses came over. Considered putting someone new in his place. Kevin had to fight for it—literally. Prove he was up to the job. He came home battered as hell, but made it. That baby of his could have lost his pops."

"I didn't know any of that."

"No, Kev doesn't talk about it. He suffered though, and all the time missing his brother."

Soren hung his head. "I was tricked. The same angel that Cuinn's working with now—she had me."

"I know, son. Not saying it to make you feel bad. I'm telling you so you understand what's at risk for us here. Cuinn knows it. He'll fight to the death for what's right. Kevin too."

"So, you want to know if I will?"

"Yeah. I guess I do."

"I'll fight to the death for what's right." He glanced at Anastasia, couldn't resist it.

Franky saw. "You putting the girl above Cuinn—again?"

Shit. Make it convincing.

"No. Not above Cuinn. But keeping her safe is part of keeping the rest of us alive, Frank—including Cuinn. Not a matter of choosing. It's all or nothing."

Franky was quiet and swished his whiskey once more. "You love her. Cuinn loves her. That'll end badly."

"You reading the future now, Frank?"

"Nope. Two men, one woman. Seen it too many times."

"You think Cuinn loves her?" *Really?* His gut clenched. He'd thought about Anastasia's feelings for Cuinn, but not the other way round.

"Closest he's come since Kathleen was murdered."

They were silent again.

Anastasia stirred a little, then sank back against Soren's shoulder. "I think this one needs some water." He smiled at the old man.

Franky nodded. "I'll get it for you, from out back. Bottles of better stuff out there."

"Thanks, man." He waited until Franky disappeared through the door to the back and then pulled her onto her feet. "Anastasia, we've got to go!" When she didn't respond, he pulled her out from between the table and the bench, picked her up, and threw her over his shoulder in a fireman's lift.

She groaned and banged a weak fist on his back. Ignoring her, he walked determinedly out of the Club door, up the steps, and jogged as fast as he could around the back of the church towards the truck. He still had the keys in his pocket.

Reaching it in a fraction of the time it'd taken him to walk back earlier, even with her weight to carry, he lowered her into the passenger seat.

"What the hell, Hux?" She'd woken up after all the bouncing and was holding a hand to her mouth. "God, I'm going to throw up."

"Do it in the truck."

"What? You serious?"

"Yes, we've got to get out of here." He started the engine and pulled forward.

As he headed out of the garage, he turned on the lights and skidded to a stop. A Jeep pulled up in front of him, blocking his path. Two shotguns pointed at them through the open side windows of the truck: Cuinn held the one on him, Kevin had his on Anastasia. Still blood covered from their efforts in the back room, their faces were stony.

Franky got out of the passenger side of the Jeep, shaking his head and muttering, "Sorry, son. So sorry."

Soren sat back and closed his eyes. *Stupid.*

"What the fuck is going on?" Anastasia looked from one to the other, then she vomited spectacularly all over the dashboard.

30

____

BIG PICTURE TIME

AFTER TWO HOURS chained in the heat with a dead man, Soren was done. No, he was fucking bored. He was getting no conversation from his cellmate, who sat slumped against the opposite wall, naked from the waist up, skin covered in black and blue bruises, sitting in a pool of blood and piss. A deep slash severed his throat, and the digits from his right hand lay scattered on the concrete floor.

Christ, what secret did this poor bastard die for?

The air weighed on him. Ammonia, blood, and rot cooked in the heat, creating a stench so thick it felt like breathing soup. It coated his tongue and made his eyes water. For the hundredth time, Soren stretched his arms up and pulled, testing the long chains attached to his wrists and threaded through a metal loop above his head. Solid.

What were they doing to Anastasia?

He'd heard raised voices twice in the last hour, but no one had returned. Delay was good for him, but not for her.

The words weren't clear, but Kevin sounded mad as hell. He would argue to finish him. But Cuinn and Franky sounded conciliatory. Cuinn would win.

A last chance then.

Franky was the problem. He'd seen into his mind, seen his devotion to Anastasia. Try as he might, there was no way he could just turn his emotions off where she was concerned. He couldn't deceive the old man; he'd have to lean in. *Own it.*

He'd seen what he'd seen—Cuinn talking with the Abbot. It changed everything. How could he justify that? "Unthinkable!" He blurted the word aloud before he could stop himself.

He stared again at the dead guy. Billy would find a joke—a better joke than he had. For a while he tried to come up with something. Nothing. Perhaps Billy was right, and he didn't have a sense of humour—

Billy!

What if he could reach out to him? Maybe he could fly in with his angel powers and save the day? At least get to Anastasia.

Feeling stupid, Soren closed his eyes and clasped his fingers together above his head like he was praying. *Billy, come find me. Pathetic.*

Trying again, he mumbled aloud this time, "Billy, Anastasia needs you. Desperately. Help her." He paused. "Bruv, help her!" Maybe it was just a matter of speaking the right words… "Amen."

The ammonia in the air slammed the back of his throat as soon as he'd opened his mouth, and now it soaked into the membranes, forcing a gagging cough. He longed for cool water.

A few moments later, footsteps approached, then a key scraped the metal lock, and the door creaked open. Cuinn entered with a bottle of water, walked to him, and dropped it in his lap. "You wanted this?"

"Franky?"

"Yeah." Cuinn sat down on the floor on the other side of the door, leaving it open.

Soren opened the bottle, drank it all down in a couple of gulps, then smirked as much to himself as at Cuinn. "If I wish for whiskey, do I get that too?"

"Yeah, but just the blend."

"Fair enough."

Cuinn was playing with a knife, the sort used for skinning a deer. He ran his fingers along the blade and rolled bits of dried blood forward with his thumbnail before flicking the little balls away. He looked like he wanted to say something.

"That what you used on him?" Soren gestured with the empty water bottle at the dead man on the opposite wall.

Cuinn nodded. "Your point?"

"Haven't got one. Just making conversation. Not with him though—" *Was it funny?* "—Obviously." He added.

Cuinn's eyes narrowed. "Let me tell you something about yer lad there, Hux. He deserved everything he got."

Not funny, then.

The Soldier stabbed the knife into the wooden frame of the door. It stuck there, vibrating slightly. "He and his friend next door were trading humans for food with the vamps over on the west side. In turn, the Leeches sewed up our supply lines forcing prices up for us. We needed the names of the vamps."

If he had been hoping for understanding, he didn't get it. "Did you get them?" Soren didn't wait for a reply. "What was he doing with the food? Selling it on? Feeding his family? Or didn't you ask before you cut his fingers off?"

Cuinn shook his head. "Seems you're judging now, Hux."

"Yeah, maybe I am. You think a human is any match for two Soldier demons? A bit one-sided, man. Did he tell you?"

Cuinn held his look. His eyes glittered red within the blue.

Soren saw, but didn't care. "That's a no, then. For a man not to tell in those circumstances, suggests he knew there'd be retribution on loved ones. Family, maybe. Or he just didn't know." He shrugged.

Since Cuinn had entered the room, it felt like the heat had turned up a notch. Soren ignored the silence that hung in the humid air and used the bottom of his shirt to wipe the sweat from his face. "You're burning hotter than a fucking oven."

"Getting hotter. Tipping Point's almost here."

"How long?"

"Forty-eight hours max. Probably less."

Soren took a breath. "So, what do you have planned for me?"

"Kevin wants you dead."

"Don't blame him. And you?"

"One more chance. Franky read conflict in you. Said it wasn't too late, that it's all about the girl."

His words landed like a slap. Dismissing the woman he was supposed to love according to Franky. "By 'the girl' I take it you mean Anastasia?" His voice was icy.

Cuinn got up and stood in the middle of the room. He retrieved his knife from the door frame, and this time threw it at the door itself, over and over. Each time the point struck within a fraction of the last. Each time he stamped harder as he marched forward to retrieve it.

The temperature in the room rose still higher.

After ten throws. He sat again just a few feet away from Soren. His eyes were a steady blue. "You're allowing your affection for her to distract you. You got just hearts and feckin' roses in your eyes, Hux. This is big picture time. What's the point of saving your girl if there's no world left to save her for?"

"You still expect me to trust you?"

"Yes!" His voice rose, cut with a desperate edge which was unusual to hear.

"You won't let anything happen to her?"

Cuinn didn't hesitate. "No."

The sheer, breathtaking hypocrisy of it all struck Soren as funny. Genuinely funny. A bubble of pure, caustic laughter rose in his throat, and he buried his face in his hands as his body trembled with the suppressed force of it. He couldn't keep it in. The noise blurted out, ragged and broken, echoing in the quiet room exactly like a sob.

Through his fingers, he saw Cuinn shift. The demon leaned forward, a large, heavy hand wrapping around the toe of Soren's dirty boot. It was the only part of him within reach. Cuinn squeezed the leather—a firm, steadying grip. *He thinks I'm breaking.*

At the contact, Soren dropped his hands and looked up, his eyes gleaming with bitter amusement. He dragged his foot out of Cuinn's grasp as though the touch was sickening.

"Cuinn. You're a fucking liar." Soren felt pumped that he'd finally found his voice. "I saw you—heard you—talking with that bastard father of hers. You said you'd give her to him. After everything you know he did to her, you're giving her back? He'll kill her—or worse. You told me in Vegas you were against the vamps, and now here you are working with one. The one who killed your wife and kid, man. How the hell can I believe anything you say?"

"There is a plan in play." Cuinn held onto a level tone, but his jaw set hard.

"Yeah, sure. Sacrifice Anastasia. Kill humans. Demons rule. That's the fucking plan, right? You played on my guilt. Turned me into one of you. But I'm not a monster—" his voice broke for real this time, and he took a breath to get a hold of it again "—I'm not. She showed me that. I'm done with you and your plan. So let me go or kill me. Just try to find some fucking compassion in your—whatever passes for a heart in there." He poked a finger toward his chest.

"Compassion, man? That's new for you."

"Yeah. Someone in Vegas gave me some advice. Didn't get it at the time. I understand it now."

"No space for that here. Big picture counts." Without a word, Cuinn heaved himself up from the floor and left the room.

Soren struggled to get a hold of himself again. This was it. This could be his last minute left alive. Jegudiel knew how to bring down the wards. She would have told him or do it herself. Yeah, Cuinn would know how to kill him.

Two sets of feet thumped down the corridor toward the cell. His body clenched, waiting. He was ready.

Kevin entered swinging a metal baton. Another Soldier accompanied him with a taser. They didn't hesitate, and Soren didn't fight.

The taser hit first. Stuck into Soren's side, he fell sideways to the floor, jerking and kicking out at the wall. The pain from the site spiralled through his body, but the charge dissipated quickly.

Before his muscles relaxed, Kevin raised the baton—

A sun detonated behind his eyes, swallowing all thought in white fire before he sank into darkness.

31

REMEMBER MILAN?

THE SCENT HIT HIM FIRST: a wave of sweet nuts, hot spice, and citrus. Anastasia. Even human, she used the same skin oil —the one that protected her skin from the sun when she was a vampire. He loved that smell. Slipped some through his own hair sometimes to remind him of her… *Darkness.*

He came to with a start again. Blood this time. Sticky on his face. Hot, heavy air rushing past. The pillow beneath his head was firm, warm, and shifted with his movement. Her lap.

Thank God, the Abbot hasn't got her. *Fading. No!*

"Anass… sta…?" His tongue was swollen, useless.

He tried to shift. Agony clawed at the back of his skull. Bone grabbing bone, knitting.

Kevin—metal. Groaning. Was that him? *Sounded miles away.* His skull breaking! *Jesus.* Each thud of his pulse was a fresh hammer blow of pain. Stars in his vision. *Need to stay awake.*

Ruts in the road juddered through the vehicle's frame. Ropes bit into his wrists. He pulled. *Weak.* They would break. They didn't expect him to wake up.

"Shh, Hux." Anastasia breathed in his ear. "Stay quiet." Her hand clamped down on his arm, a clear signal.

He obeyed, lying still. *Focus.* Spilled whiskey, gun oil, stale smoke. Cuinn's Jeep. Open top.

He tapped her knee. "Where?" he whispered, the single word a monumental effort.

Her hair brushed his cheek as she bent low. "Out of the city. Airport, I think. Shh!"

Time?

He risked a glance upward, ignoring the early morning sun shooting into his eyes. About four hours since the Club.

Who was driving? He swivelled his eyes forward. The driver had a fresh crew cut against dark skin. *A recruit. Good.*

"Take the right turn, man. It's quicker." Cuinn's voice from the passenger seat. Just the two of them. A rookie and Cuinn, still injured. They had the element of surprise.

Soren thumped her knee with his knuckles.

"What?" she hissed.

"Remember Milan?" He breathed.

She gasped. "Oh God, Hux. No."

"Yes."

"Oh fuck!"

"On three."

"Fuck! Fuck! Fuck!"

"Three!"

They launched forward.

———

As Soren looped his roped wrists toward Cuinn's head, his knees pushed hard against the back of the passenger seat for leverage. The Irish demon must have felt the pressure; he twisted, eyes widening in surprise as Soren loomed over him. It was too late. The ropes dropped over Cuinn's neck, and Soren pulled back with all his might. *Don't break now!*

The coarse bindings bit into the thin new skin of Cuinn's

old wounds. The Soldier yelped as they burst open, spilling blue blood.

Soren anchored his feet and pulled, the skin on his own wrists splitting. Red blood mixed with blue, saturating the rope. It stretched. He yanked harder.

Beside him, Anastasia fought with the driver using her own restraints, her human strength focused entirely on pulling the vehicle off the road. Distract the driver, disable the vehicle, run like hell. That was the play.

Cuinn fought back, his hands crushing Soren's wrists. Soren sucked the pain between his teeth and used it, pushing harder. A deep, guttural growl rumbled from Cuinn's chest. It went on and on. Soren and Anastasia exchanged a panicked glance. *Core.*

Seeing his look, she desperately pulled on the driver's neck. She groaned, squeezing her eyes shut, but held on. Choking, the driver abandoned the wheel, his foot slamming the accelerator, and grabbed at her hands.

The Jeep careened wildly. Cuinn reached for the wheel, but Soren yanked him back. A crack like a gunshot—a tire blew. The vehicle dragged hard to the right.

"Now!" Soren yelled.

They let go, pulling their arms back over their victims' heads, and vaulting out of the vehicle.

As they rolled away, the Jeep's front right wheel hit the deep curb, tipped, and landed hard on its side. It twisted, sliding across the sidewalk and crashing tail-first into the plate-glass window of a clothing store, ending its journey in a cascade of glass and naked mannequins.

Soren landed and rolled, halting his momentum in a sitting position. He scanned for Anastasia, spotting her sprawled on the road.

Adrenaline numbed the pounding in his head. The car

creaked. Any moment, he expected to hear the howl of the Core.

"Anastasia!" He pushed to his feet and ran. "Tazia! Get up!"

He got to her and hauled her upright. "Wake up!"

Her eyes cracked open, then widened as they focused over his shoulder. "Cuinn," she mumbled.

Soren looked back. The Soldier was crawling from the wreckage, his left arm hanging loose. He shook his head like a dog, and his eyes, burning pure red, locked onto them.

Without looking away from Cuinn, Soren asked, "Can you run?"

She answered by pulling on his arm. "Let's fucking go!"

They took off, sprinting across the road and into a maze of back alleys.

Behind them, an animal roar split the morning air.

32

REVELATIONS

WRESTLING with every instinct he had, Conn saw them run and howled. Anger, frustration, betrayal. All let loose in an animalistic scream. He could already feel the change: red mist fogged his vision, talons pierced his fingertips. He hunched over, coiled, ready to chase them on four legs.

No, I will not.

Collapsing to his knees, he fought back for control, dragging in a huge breath. Then rolled onto his back. He stared at the morning sky. A few streaks of blue remained above him. The sun, already heating the thick grey cloud cover. The heavy air pressed on his face. That few precious minutes of morning air gone already. *Fucking Detroit!*

He closed his eyes. All he wanted was the fresh green of home. It'd been so long. He was so close. Almost feel the spring rain on his face, and the soft grass under his feet. Cork held the last memories of family, friends. A brigade that fought so hard to remain free. An honest fight. Not like this.

Michael, the driver, groaned from the Jeep, and the sound brought Conn back to the moment of impact. The kid had clung to the doorframe until the Jeep had stopped, then his grip had failed, dropping him bone-jarringly hard onto Conn's left shoulder.

Conn pulled himself upright, using a sidewalk fire hydrant for leverage. "You all right, recruit?"

"Yeah. What the fuck? She's just a girl." He shook his head.

"She's an ex-demon, son, vampire, and he's the highest paid assassin in the feckin' world. I should have known better." He looked away and stared at the sky again, muttering, "I just had to keep them safe for another couple of days."

"What, Sir?"

"Nothin' recruit. Nothin'. Help me with this shoulder. You feckin' did it, you can put it back." His arm hung at his side, dislocated at his shoulder.

Michael approached. "You sure, Sir?"

"How the hell else will we fix it? Find some bollocks, son. And don't call me Sir, its Cuinn."

"Yes, Sir… erm Cuinn."

Giving further instructions, Conn grimly studied the fallen mannequins to distract himself. One had been squashed under the back wheels of the car. She stared at him with wide, indignant eyes and pointed a ridiculously long and red-painted fingernail at the sky. *Jesus, is it an omen?*

Michael manipulated Conn's arm a little, then shoved with force. As the shoulder slipped back into the socket, he didn't even groan.

Conn tested the arm gingerly before removing his belt and making a makeshift sling to support it across his front until healing kicked in. It wouldn't take long. The Hell-made wounds on his neck though were different, they still oozed blood from the rope, and he cursed Hux again. That was twice he'd knocked off the scabs.

He'd known no one to have such a death wish and survival instinct mixed so close. Despite himself, Conn smiled.

"The boy's got guts, Conn O'Cuinn, you trained him well."

Conn's smile dropped, and he walked toward the voice, speaking low. "Thought you'd feckin' turn up. Come to gloat?"

"No, pet. Came to help. Time's ticking away, and you can't be wasting it, so you can't." Jegudiel mimicked a terrible Irish accent.

He ignored her. "They won't get far…"

"Do you know that for sure? Remember, they've got the angels on their side. I have it on very good authority that the beautiful Billy is looking for them as we speak. Once he's here Conn, it'll be over. He can take them wherever he wants."

"Not from Detroit—the energy is too low."

She tutted. "Did you ever hear about, oh, I don't know, cars?" She licked her index finger and ran it over her eyebrows. "Would you like my help or not, pet?"

"Cuinn, you okay?" Michael looked from Conn to the only pane of glass in the shop doorway that hadn't smashed when they crashed into it.

Conn stared at the Advocate's reflection and then back to Michael. "Get on the radio and get Kevin McInnes here. We'd better go after them." While the Soldier was busy, he turned back to the window. "Get them somewhere I can find them. Get him… compliant."

"Sir. Yes, Sir." She mock saluted, and faded away giggling.

"Compliant don't mean dead, Jegudiel!" he shouted after her. His words likely useless, she wanted Hux alive too.

For fucksakes, man, just behave, will yer?

"We need a vehicle." Soren flew from one abandoned car to another, wrenching on handle after handle.

They'd run far and fast before they'd both stopped, bent double with fire-filled lungs. No Core was chasing them. But it certainly wasn't over.

"Hux."

He ignored her, pulling at the door of a custom Dodge Ram pickup. Chrome everything. Stupid bull horns on the front. Old, but manual transmission, diesel, no flats. *Perfect.* He could get it working if it just had a bit of viable gas.

He smashed open the passenger's side window with a crowbar he'd found in the back of the truck bed, reached through and yanked open the door lock. He climbed in and shifted to the driver's side, and searched for the keys. "Get in."

She jumped in beside him, worked the ropes on her wrists against the broken glass until they snapped, and rooted through the glove box. Coming up trumps, she held out the keys but pulled them away as he went to snatch them from her. "Tell me."

"What?" His tone was icy calm. *Not now.*

"Tell me what you found out to make Cuinn do this."

"We don't have time, Anastasia. We need to keep moving." He eyed the keys, assessing how quickly he could grab them from her.

She held them further away.

"Alright! I found something out about Cuinn."

"Well, doh!" She put the keys in the pocket of her jacket, then made a display of sitting on it.

"Oh, very mature."

"Tell me."

"It'll hurt…"

"Everything hurts. I have a soul now. Tell me!"

Soren took a breath. *Steady.* "He's working with more than the Advocate."

"Who?"

Blinking rapidly, he remained silent. This was the last thing he wanted to do to her. Betrayal on two levels, Cuinn and—

"Fucksakes, Hux!" She pulled out the keys again, and opened the truck door ready to throw them out onto the road.

"No!"

"Tell me," she hissed, but dropped her hand slightly.

"The Abbot."

"Wha… what?"

"The Abbot. Your father. He's back—telling Cuinn what to do. All three of them are in it together."

"How—"

"I saw them talking. Heard them. Confronted Cuinn. He didn't deny it."

"But—"

"He wants you back, Anastasia. Your father. I didn't hear why. He told Cuinn to hand you over."

He looked her straight on. Saw pure pain.

"And…?"

He nodded and held out his hand. "Give me the keys."

She handed them to him and faced the windscreen.

He turned the engine over; it tried to catch, then nothing. "They won't have us again. Not the Advocate, not the Abbot. We stay free."

"When we went on the supply run, he told me that there was no future for us—me and him." Her voice was small but resigned.

He glanced over; she was staring at her knees.

"He said that Hell had changed him, and that a demon had no place with a human. Told me you were a better man for me than he was."

Soren's head jerked. "He did?"

"Yeah."

Elation surged, filling his chest, butterflies in his stomach. The feeling died instantly. "Is that why you got so drunk? To forget him? You were upset."

She looked him full on. "That? God no. I just needed a drink." She paused, and added, "Fucking tequila, Hux! Come on! What did you expect?" Her smile faded with the flippancy.

So much pain. "We talk. Properly. Later. Okay?" he said.

She nodded.

"Let's get out of here." He turned the key in the ignition again, and this time it turned over, and fired!

"Yes!" He banged on the steering wheel in celebration and turned on the wipers to clear the thick layer of sand on the windshield.

Then he froze.

As the glass cleared, the face of Jegudiel grinned at him. "Not so fast, boy."

Soren grabbed Anastasia's arm, ready to pull her from the truck and start running again, but she was stuck, eyes open wide and mouth already forming the words, one finger pointing forward. The stasis had trapped her warning.

"I don't have time for you." Soren put his foot on the accelerator. The engine screamed at him as though he was pushing it into something solid. Clouds of dust and the smell of burning rubber rose from the tires, but it didn't even inch forward. "Fuck it, Jegudiel. Let us go!"

"Language, Soren Huxford. Swearing is so uncouth. Let's leave that to your little friend there." She glanced at Anastasia and pouted. "I do miss her so. We used to have fun back in her psychiatric days. Those drugs really did make her nicely compliant."

Her reflection on the windshield leaned closer, her voice a whisper that echoed inside his skull. "But compliance can be given... or it can be *taken*. Now, watch, pet." She tapped a single, long finger against the glass.

The truck vanished. The world outside dissolved. He was home—

He was small, sitting on his mother's lap in his father's study. Laughter—warm and real. The waxy smell of a new crayon. And his proud voice, high and childish, as he showed the picture. "You papa, you!"

A golden moment. One of the few he had left. It was just in his head. He knew it. Blinked. Fumbled for the keys again. But the vision stayed. *No not this.*

"A beautiful little domestic scene, pet," Jegudiel's voice sang. Then she hissed. "Shame it all went so wrong."

The laughter soured into shouts. His parents' faces twisted with anger. "You're no true wife. The child's not mine!"

"A seed was sown that night, Soren Huxford," the Advocate hissed in his mind. "A ruse, of course, you were his son. And your mother? She was the most loyal wife any man could wish for. But men's egos are fragile things. It didn't take long from there…"

He was ten years old, hiding, small and terrified, in the hallway. Shouting. Screaming. Purple blotches on her arms and neck.

"I don't want to see the rest," he gasped, slamming his eyes shut, but it didn't matter. The vision wrapped around him—

Gunmetal glinting. His mother's pleading voice. His father's rage. Then, the impossible moment. His father calmed, taking the weapon, then locking eyes onto his. But they weren't seeing him. They were staring at something else reflected there.

He said the words Soren only remembered in his dreams. "I'll do what you say," his father's voice echoed, hollow. "Yes, of course… She must die… I'll do it for you, son."

The blast. The recoil. The silence.

In the hallway mirror, a flicker of purple and red, a cruel smile watching him cry. "There, there, my boy. I'll always be here for my little monster."

Soren's eyes snapped open, fixed on the smirking face in the windshield. "He saw *you*," he whispered, the words cracking. Hot tears stung his face as the last piece clicked into place. "He saw you in my eyes. And he thought he was doing what *I* wanted."

"Oh yes, my dear. I was right there, goading him on. And

he did just what I—you—told him to. Your poor mother, she didn't stand a chance with both of us against her—"

"I wasn't against her. I loved her. Just trying to protect her." He gripped onto his seat with both hands, his whole body shaking.

Her voice dropped to a whisper. "You told him to kill her, Soren. He looked into your eyes, and he saw your soul." She shrugged. "Well, at least he thought that was what he saw. How does it feel, my boy? Being responsible for your own mother's death—oh, isn't there a word for that? Matricide, isn't it? We could even get Oedipal, Soren. Did you want to fuck her too?" Jegudiel screamed with laughter.

A vulture landed on the road in front of the vehicle just in Soren's field of vision. A ball of dried up grass drifted over the sand in the corner of his eye. The stasis was weakening.

"You betrayed me, boy. Put the girl above me! Time for you to beg forgiveness, or I will never stop. I will be with you and the little bitch, forever!"

Soren exploded from the truck, images still burning behind his eyes. All his life, a puppet for this thing. Now he remembered.

He snatched up the crowbar and circled to the windshield.

The first blow crashed down, spiderwebbing the glass. He was back at school, seeing her image flash across the bathroom mirror, his classmate bloody and broken on the ground.

In the army, raining hell down on his barrack buddies for messing with his stuff. Just a joke, they'd said. Her laugh echoing in his head.

Bali. A simple job. A fucking simple job. And suddenly picking off civilians like they were ducks at a fairground shooting range. Her walking through the blood in her purple boots.

On the tugboat, slicing into the passengers, to play nice for fucking demons. Not even angry. Not lost. But a monster.

With each memory, he brought the crowbar down on the windscreen, wiping out her image, her voice, her memory. He would finally free himself even if it killed him—

The first taser blast shot through his side, forcing him to drop the crowbar. With the second, he fell to his knees. The third held him, jerking uncontrollably, as Cuinn leaned into him, weapon on max, his face a blank mask.

Other Soldiers swarmed, forcing his arms into cuffs while he still convulsed. A canvas bag shoved over his head. Just before he lost his view, he saw Anastasia pulled from the truck by Kevin, his hand clamped over her mouth. Her eyes searching for his. Blood pouring from cuts on her arms and legs as he dragged her, kicking and fighting, to a waiting vehicle.

The glass! Oh God, what did I do?

Under the darkness of the bag, Soren heard the truck speed away. Then metal hit his skull. For the second time that day, he sank into nothing.

33

─────────

QUICKSAND

SOREN WOKE UP CHOKING. The heavy, chemical stink of burning diesel invaded his nostrils, and thick, acrid black smoke spewed into the confined air. By the time he'd kicked open the back door of the vehicle and crawled away to a safe distance, tears stung his soot-stained skin.

Getting up, he circled the car warily, like it was a wild animal that would leap at him if he got too close.

Now just a skeleton of jagged, twisted metal and shattered windows, it had once been someone's pride and joy. Plastic stickers depicting a man, woman, little girl, and two dogs still clung to the inside of the back window, curled and shrunken by an older fire.

The vehicle's badge shone proudly on the front of the hood, like someone had recently buffed it. A Volvo. Was this a joke—or a threat? He'd been beaten, bruised, and dumped in the epitome of a Swedish family vehicle. The safest car manufacturer in the world—or so they said.

He coughed and spat. Blackened phlegm splatted on the ground. *Fuck. How long was I out?*

A stream of dense smoke billowed from the front footwell.

Someone had tossed a shop rag, heavily soaked in diesel, onto the rusted floorboards. A slow burn. A deliberate message meant to smoke him out or choke him in his sleep.

Bristling, Soren picked up a rock and threw it directly at the right-side headlamp. The remaining plastic casing around the lamp smashed and fell to the ground, making a pirate of the smug, grinning car.

"You bastard, Conn O'Cuinn," he muttered. Then, overcome with sudden anger, he repeated the curse, this time shouting and flinging a stone with full force. The rock fluked a hit on the narrow metal that once had supported the side of the windshield. It rebounded and hit him directly on his right cheekbone, gouging a deep cut. Blood trickled down his face before the skin healed.

Hands on hips, he closed his eyes to gather himself, vibrations of anger rocking his body. After several deep breaths, he opened his eyes and lifted his head to the bright blue sky. Far above, vultures silently circled in the updrafts.

After another cough and spit, he felt more in control.

He gazed around.

A giant irrigation pivot stood frozen in the distance, stretching rusted arms across the fields of dead cornstalks and cracked earth. Apart from that, just a long stretch of highway, wide and empty in both directions.

With no discernible skyline, he had nothing. Detroit could be in any direction. The sun gave him east from west, but that was all. He needed a road marker, a town, a damn phone! Billy must be looking for him by now, surely. With the Advocate and Abbot making appearances on Earth, the angels should be mobilizing. But if not, Soren would have to get to him. Somehow.

He wiped the blood from his cheek with the bottom of his tee. It was so ripped and stained, the patches of blood kept it glued together. The last time he'd changed clothes had been at the Irish Club. He'd lost track of his weapons too. He may as well be standing there naked. Would have preferred it. *Jesus, a hot shower and soap—*

"Focus!" He barked the order out loud. Nothing reacted. No bird took flight or lizard froze on the road. Did he exist?

Disturbed by the weirdness of the thought, Soren inhaled for a count of four, holding the air until his pounding pulse settled. There was still a chance Billy could find him. He may already know what Cuinn had been up to and taken steps. Maybe there were a million golden angels riding the wind to help him, or running a rescue mission to save Anastasia before her father got her.

He scanned the horizon. Nothing. No angels, just the sun reddening his pale skin. He'd be crispy pink in no time if he didn't get out of the heat. At the thought, his temperature surged again. *Do something.*

He took a step forward. Then stopped, and about-turned. "Make up your bloody mind, Huxford!" For a moment he stood still, then barked once more. "Commit to the action, soldier!"

But he didn't move. He put his hands behind his head and paced back and forth over the same six feet, then dropped to his haunches, hands falling forward to cover his eyes. His mind was blank but for one thing, one question. Had he killed his mother?

He knew all the Advocate's tricks by now. Knew she could distort reality and memory if it suited her purposes. But at the back of his mind, there was a seed of doubt. Had he said those words to his father? Had he told him to kill her? "No! Of course I didn't."

He got up and marched faster, shaking his head as his boots hit the road. "No! No! No!" *But what if I did?*

Soren stopped for the third time. He gagged, but with only a little whiskey in his stomach, he didn't vomit. When had he last eaten? Yesterday? Before that? Knees buckled. He staggered and leaned over, resting his hands on his thighs. More deep breaths. One, two, three—

Too late. Here it was. *Quicksand.*

The world slowed, and he was sinking. Blood roaring. Mouth dry. Down and down. Not moving. His mind pelted with images.

Boarding school corridors. A blur of bodies ran to class while he stood frozen, invisible. A ghost who should have died with his parents. How many times had he wished for it? Then, she whispered. *I'm your friend. I'm here for you, pet.*

How could he have forgotten that?

His mind recoiled. No, their beginning was the London flat. That was the story he'd clung to. Her proposition: *Kill for me, and I will make you strong.* The sting of the wards burned into his skin, sealing the pact.

But she hadn't been a stranger at all. He'd already tasted her poison.

Had she ripped the memories out of him, or had he done it himself, so desperate to forget the truth—

His blood howled, not just in his ears, but shrieking all around him like it had taken form and screamed into each ear. Could he feel its hot breath against his skin?

More images. Death. His own body swinging.

It was something he'd wanted for so long. Until he'd found Cuinn. Found his brother. But that wasn't true either. They'd all tricked him! All these fucking demons and angels—

The blood screeched, and now, he felt the definite tug of the wind against his body, pulling him around, almost raising him off his feet.

No, this is real—

Soren snapped his eyes open. Hundreds of vultures circled him at breakneck speed, calling with savage squawks, stretched wings swiping against him, sharp feathers slicing into his skin.

How could that be? The razor-like cuts opened for a second to release a little blood and then healed again, ready to be torn open with the next feather strike.

And then he was rising, touching the ground with only the very tips of his boots.

In a panic, Soren punched out at the birds, yelling. A gap opened up in the feathered tornado. A large armoured Humvee hurtled toward him. The horn blasted over the cacophony of the birds' cries. The horn again: long, hard, and loud.

The birds rose toward the sun, their noise receding, just as the vehicle screeched to a halt a few feet from him.

Soren collapsed onto his knees and stared at his hands. Shredded to ribbons by beaks and talons. Blood dropped onto the dust of the highway. He wiped his healed palms on the remains of his combats and looked up at the occupants.

Billy was in the driving seat, dark mirrored shades placed perfectly under his pristine hair, the sun finding golden highlights on his skin. "Need a lift, soldier?" He raised the shades for a moment and winked a deep brown eye.

"Anastasia!" He needed to know.

"She is fine, Soren," Jacob answered him, and grinned. "I feel her energy strongly."

Wordless, he got up, and eased himself into the bench seating beside Aideen. She smiled at him too, her hair glowing so red and shiny that to his blurred vision it looked like a beautiful pink halo. She patted his arm.

"Everyone is so… clean," he mumbled.

As they turned and drove west along the highway, raising dust in their wake, vultures stared from telephone poles and fence posts along each side of the road.

Soren leaned back, closed his eyes, and slept.

34

LEMON VERBENA CREAMSICLE

WHEN SOREN WOKE, the sun was low over the horizon. They were still driving through interminable fields of dead crops and blackened trees; the heat lifting as they built up the miles away from the cities. Every time they got near another fallen town, though, the fucking sand and heat claimed it again.

He woke just as they bypassed a town where the water tower screamed with dripping red letters: **REPENT THE GATES ARE OPEN.** The on-ramp beneath it was blocked by a wall of crushed vehicles welded together, a rusty iron curtain erected by the terrified locals. It wasn't the first makeshift barrier he'd seen.

The roar of the powerful engine made conversation impossible. Instead, he caught reassuring glances from Aideen and Jacob in the rearview mirror, and an occasional thumbs-up from Billy.

At one point, Billy and Jacob changed places. Billy's attention fixed on his laptop, his fingers flying across the keyboard as he coded a spell. From Billy's muttered curses— "Fucksakes, stay connected!"—Soren gathered the satellites were fading in and out. More than once they had to change direction to find higher ground, or retreat further from a fallen city.

He got the briefest of explanations on the road: Anastasia was alive, Jacob was tracking her energy. Billy and Joshua were trying to pinpoint her—a combination of technomancy and Josh's natural ability to follow a signal: "Don't worry, bruv. Just a matter of time." They were heading for Fort Worth—"Operational airport with bloody great satellite connections"—plus it had good angel mojo for jumping countries when the time came.

A second search was looking for Cuinn, but demon energies were becoming blurred and indistinct based on the sheer volume above ground.

Billy squeezed his knee. "More soon, bruv. Promise." He then rammed headphones on his ears and started dictating a stream of numbers, letters, and Latin words into the microphone. The laptop crunched out the code at amazing speed.

Soren allowed the familiarity. It was comforting to be with genuine friends again. And they seemed organized, efficient. *Mission ready*.

For another hour after they hit Fort Worth, they circled the city slowly trying to maintain contact with the satellite while Billy completed his working. For some reason, the demons had kept out of the city, and it almost looked normal. They passed a discount mall with a stream of shoppers ambling in and out with overspilling carts. *Surreal.*

Now and then, there would be a hopeful bleep from the GPS on the dashboard, but it was always a false alarm. The low energy frequency was frustrating even to Joshua. He'd zip off, riding the energies, only to hit a wall that sent him hurtling back to Earth. Then they'd try the next route, all the time looking for Anastasia's trace signature.

Once the satellite seemed stable enough, Billy suggested they stop at a motel for food and rest. Less than thirty minutes later, Soren stood in a scalding hot shower, scrubbing his body from head to toe in cheap motel body wash. According to the bottle, it was supposed to be Lemon Verbena Creamsicle, but it smelled more like citrus toilet freshener. At least it wasn't pine.

Billy came into the bathroom while Soren was finishing off, dropping a pile of mall shopping bags on the floor. "Fresh clothes for you, mate. Camo pants, couple of t-shirts, and socks." He laid the new clothes over the towel rail, then closed the lid on the toilet and settled himself there. "You'll have to go commando, Commando. They had no cacks. Seems in the apocalypse everyone goes through a lot of underwear."

Soren looked at him over the top of the shower curtain. It had pink roses on it to match the fluffy pink rug on the floor. "I've never been a Commando."

"No?"

"No. Do you even know what a Commando is, Billy?"

"Nah. Just funny innit?"

Soren looked away, not finding it in the least bit funny.

"What do you find funny, bruv? Just so I know."

Soren thought about it for a while. "I like *Friends*."

"Seriously?"

"Yes!" He glared at Billy. "What's wrong with that? I like the miserable one…"

"Ross?"

"Yeah."

"Wow. A little piece of the Ice Man persona comes tumbling down."

"Don't call me that." He stepped out of the shower with a pink towel wrapped around his middle, hair dripping, to examine the clothes Billy had got for him.

Despite looking military in style, they were a far cry from

the rough fabrics of the army surplus; all exclusive brands. It wasn't just Anastasia they had in common.

He pulled the tee over his head and sat on the side of the bath to pull on the pants. The fit was good enough around the waist, and the trouser legs reached his ankles, often not the case.

While he dressed, Billy texted. Without looking up, he said, "Josh says 'HI' and sent you a smiley face."

"Did he find her yet?"

"Nope."

"Tell him to hurry up."

Billy tutted and typed a reply. It took a while. He then put the phone down and watched Soren run his fingers through his wet hair.

"'Hurry up' took a long time."

"That was rude, Hux, so I wrote something different."

He sighed. "What?"

"I said: HUX SAYS THANKS. PLEASE FIND HER SOON. LOOKING FORWARD TO SEEING YOU." He paused and shifted a little under Soren's stern look. "Then I added an emoji—the little gorilla one with the red heart." He gave him a beaming smile. "I got you lots of socks. I remember how much your feet stink."

Soren opened up a packet of the socks, pulling apart the stapled cardboard at the top, and inspecting the fabric, then looked toward Billy. "They don't."

Billy rolled his eyes and nodded. "Bruv, they do!"

"Once! We'd been stuck in a car for days without a shower." He sniffed the fresh socks like a monkey would check out some unknown foodstuff, then pulled one over his right foot.

"Mine didn't smell," Billy mumbled.

Soren sent a low growl in the angel's direction.

"Just sayin'…"

Dressing completed, he stood, towering over Billy, who, despite his own height, looked tiny perched on the toilet seat. "We need to talk about Anastasia," he said. He walked back into the bedroom and grabbed a bottle of water from the mini-fridge.

"No, bruv, we need to talk about Conn O'Cuinn." Billy followed and sat on the end of the king-sized bed that dominated the small motel room. Jacob and Aideen were in their own room next door.

"He's working with the Advocate and the Abbot—" Soren licked his lips, his mouth suddenly going dry despite the water he'd guzzled from the bottle. He tossed it into the garbage bin and got another full one from the fridge.

"You already know that?" Billy asked.

"Yes. He told me we had to wait for the Tipping Point. Said it was part of some sort of plan. But I saw him with the Advocate—then the Abbot. That's when Anastasia and I made a run for it. He got her anyway…"

"Did he tell you about The Plan with a capital P?"

"What? No. The bastard just told me to trust him. I did, to a point. Then stuff happened." He remembered the flash of his blade, blood, screaming—what Cuinn had pushed him toward. "Then I doubted him and—"

"You ran with her?"

"After I saw him talking to her father. He's going to give her back to him. That's why we have to find her." He saw Billy raise his eyebrows. This was obviously news to him. "You didn't know that part?"

"No. I think we have to start over, bruv."

Billy was being surprisingly calm after hearing the news that Anastasia would be handed back to the Abbot. "Okay, you tell me this time."

Billy stretched and took a big breath. "Okay, listen. When you killed Cuinn—"

"Jesus, did you have to start there?" Soren hunched his shoulders and hit the empty bottle off his knees.

"It's relevant. When you killed Cuinn, he went to Hell. The Abbot pulled him out of whatever stinking hole he went to and chained him up, threw away the key. At the same time, the Advocate captured Josh."

Interested, Soren looked up from contemplating the bottle. "He didn't just disappear?"

"No, she took him to Hell and gave him to the Abbot. He wanted his assistance to help bring off the whole Tipping Point thing more quickly—reckoned they could use his abilities to infiltrate a few influential souls. He played along with them, it's a long story. Upshot was, he had his freedom for a while, and found Cuinn rotting in a cell." Billy slid closer along the end of the bed toward Soren's seat. "This is the interesting bit…"

"Go on."

"He and Cuinn worked together on a plan—The Plan—"

"With a capital P."

"Exactly."

"He doesn't know everything," Billy continued, "but Cuinn told him there was a 'long game' in play. Had been for a while. He needed his help to talk with the witches."

Soren's mind raced back to the coven, the strange rituals Jacob had seen.

"Josh facilitated a connection to Aideen's coven. Then Cuinn worked through him to possess the witch."

"The possessed witch in Boston?"

"Yeah. The two of them—Cuinn and Josh—passed messages to the witches. They told them about the idea to make Tazia human, told them how to kill an angel with an angelic weapon. All that stuff came directly from Cuinn."

Cuinn working with witches! *No way.*

But that intel had saved them. The angel weapon. How to

use it. How to complete the spell to make Anastasia human. All that came from the man who'd betrayed them.

Soren frowned. "It makes no sense. Why help Anastasia one minute, then give her back to the man who tortured her—the man who wants to end the world?"

"I don't know. The other thing though, bruv, is that Cuinn is not working *with* the Abbot or the Advocate. Josh is bloody sure of that. There's something else going on, something bigger." Billy got up and paced a little in front of the motel room window. "Josh says we should trust him."

Soren shook his head slowly. "I've heard that a lot. But Cuinn's done too much. Why give Anastasia back to her father?" The question hung between them.

"Jacob said that I would be there at the beginning and the end. Do you remember?"

"I remember you telling me. You were online, in a Jeep, sand in your hair, tight tee shirt…"

Soren raised his eyebrows.

Billy shrugged, "Hey, it was a thing. What about it?"

"At the beginning it was me and Anastasia and the Abbot. That's when this all went wrong. I have to get back to her. If the end is coming, I can't let her face him alone. You have to help me, man."

There was a long pause. Billy took a deep breath, then he nodded. "I know. I'm trying."

"Nothing from the angels?" Soren desperately searched for faith in something.

"Nothing."

"It's less than thirty-six hours to the Tipping Point, Billy. The Abbot told Cuinn he had forty-eight hours to get her to Turin, so she'd be there on time."

"They'll need to fly then. Unless the Advocate helps them. But she won't—she can't. Too much of a risk that the angels will pick up on that amount of energy…" Billy paced, talking to himself under his breath.

Soren watched him, praying for a breakthrough.

Billy snatched up his phone and sent a text. He exchanged a few quick messages, then sat back down on the bed and smiled at Soren. "We'll get them. Josh is going to check the private airports nearest to Detroit and the military bases. He's already done the internationals. If they're boarding a plane, we'll get them."

"Then what?"

"Angel mojo. I'm getting good," Billy winked at him. "It's time that Irish dude and I had a little face time. I hear he's hot."

35

RABIES

THE TRANSPORTER WAS large enough to carry twenty soldiers and a Jeep. It was one of fifty cocooned in a blistering heat haze rising from the airport tarmac two hundred miles south of Detroit. The scene buzzed with Soldiers. War was coming, and they were preparing for the oncoming battle, piling equipment and supplies into the depths of the plane's cargo bay like shovelling sacrificial blood victims into the open mouth of some enormous beast.

The army base had been appropriated for the Soldiers' use some forty-eight hours earlier, after a short skirmish with the handful of US military left on site. They hadn't stood a chance.

Kevin hadn't been involved. Like Cuinn, he'd been too busy tracking down an errant Swedish ex-soldier, who in his opinion had been given one too many chances, and dragging away his pain-in-the-arse bitch of a companion. Kevin rubbed his right arm. A bite mark stood proud against his flesh, each individual tooth clearly defined, the skin broken in places. Thank God his tetanus shot was up to date. Though, she'd probably given him something worse: syphilis maybe or fucking rabies.

Not only had she taken lumps out of his neck and shoulder, spitting the flesh into his face. She'd pulled out handfuls of his hair, and scraped bitten nails into his unprotected skin, finding at least some sharpness in their chewed edges. She'd kicked and thumped him too. For a human, she was surprisingly apt at finding his weak spots. He rubbed his tender groin. *Ouch.*

After wrestling with her for a few minutes, and feeling her desperation to be free, he'd thumped her soundly around the face until she'd finally fallen silent. The flash of ice in Cuinn's eyes told him he'd gone too far, but he was too busy hauling Hux into their vehicle to intercede.

Cuinn had shouted for him to cut it out and take care of her, that she was valuable. Kevin still didn't know whether that meant she was important for the mission, or for his heart. He hoped for the former.

By chance, they'd found the Volvo sitting right in front of them on the highway, already burned out. It looked like a couple of people had tried to make a final escape run. They couldn't tell how the car had caught fire, but the corpses remained belted in place in the front seats, flesh rotten underneath the crust of their burned skin.

Leading the convoy, Cuinn had stopped his transporter—it had seemed prudent to keep him and Tazia separate this time —and got out to examine the two front passengers of the car, shotgun at the ready.

Together, they'd pulled the corpses from the car, and thrown them into the ditch by the side of the road. Within seconds, vultures were taking exploratory bites of the burned flesh.

Cuinn and the two Soldiers then shoved the still unconscious body of Hux into the back seat of the Volvo. Kevin wondered if the choice of vehicle was a joke or a "fuck-you." Cuinn wasn't saying.

After he was in place, Cuinn crossed to Kevin. "Let's get

out of here, man. Straight to the airport. Flights leave at twenty-two hundred."

"How many?"

"We've got a hundred of ours, and fifty from the south. Meeting up with more in the field. Same everywhere. It'll be a rout." He grinned, then glanced at Tazia, who still slept on the back seat. His smile dropped. With her wrists and ankles now tied, she moaned softly under the gag. "Remember, be gentle with her. She's not like us now."

"Look at these!" Kevin had shown him the bite marks and gouges in his shoulder and neck. "She's a fucking animal!"

Cuinn smiled at him. "Yep, some things don't change." Then serious again, he said, "Keep her safe. Please."

Looking back, Kevin thought that was the only time Cuinn had ever said "please" to him.

Now, here they were. Tazia had come to a few minutes ago. Still gagged, she sat strapped to her seat on the plane, glaring at anyone who came near. Two Soldiers had made lewd comments, which she'd ignored, but when one put a hand on her thigh, she brought her still-tied legs up from the ground with such swiftness that he would have noticed the pain shooting through his bollocks a fraction before he even noticed her feet had moved.

Kevin was happy he hadn't been the only one to fall victim, but before he could intervene, the injured Soldier dropped to the ground like a stone and puked over her boots.

With a growl any demon would have been proud of, she kicked up again, this time catching him under his jaw, and sent him flying. Vomit from her boots, and that still retching from his mouth, splattered each man within six feet.

The other Soldiers swore. A couple released their seat belts and ran at her. Kevin couldn't stop feeling a little admiration as she glared further defiance at them, and raised her legs again. She had fucking balls.

He placed himself between her and the oncoming charge. "Sit!" He addressed the Soldiers who stopped in their tracks but eyed him, unsure.

"And you," he ordered Tazia, "calm down, or I'll send you back to sleepy byes." He raised a hand to her, but didn't strike this time. Instead, he swung around and reprimanded the Soldier who'd started it all with a punch to the gut.

The man stepped back from the force of the punch, and the rest of his supper flew, making a beeline for his fellows.

It didn't get there.

In the middle of the altercation, their radios started crackling, then a high-pitched squeal arced around the aircraft, starting at the cockpit controls and jumping from walkie to walkie. The Soldiers' hands went to their ears, and Tazia grimaced in pain.

The atmosphere gelled into thick treacle.

Kevin looked to the front of the plane just in time to see a tall young East Asian lad materialize beside Cuinn, who sat just behind the pilot. Headphones on, he'd been communicating with the base as they revved the engines to prepare for take-off. It didn't look like he'd noticed anything odd, and appeared to be mouthing words in slow-motion.

The man with dark eyes and a shock of pristine black hair shot Kevin a look, then winked; he said something under his breath.

Kevin tried to jump at him, but couldn't shift his feet. Perturbed, he attempted to reach for his sidearm. His hand wouldn't respond to the instruction and just vibrated slightly like it was caught in a wind tunnel.

From his vantage point, he saw the man walk over to Tazia. She looked at him with wide, hopeful eyes, and he gently stroked her hair and kissed the large swelling on her cheek from Kevin's earlier punch. She visibly relaxed under his touch. The man looked back at Kevin and shook his head, admonishing him, then he removed her gag, and whispered a few more words into her ear. She nodded.

The stranger turned back and walked across to Cuinn, who was still talking into his radio, and gripped his arm. The image of the two men glitched a few times, then disappeared like a switched off hologram.

The atmosphere on the plane returned to normal; the loud screech was gone, and everyone could move. The remaining gobbets of vomit completed their trajectory onto the uniforms of the seated Soldiers.

Still confused, Kevin looked from Tazia to the now empty seat behind the pilot.

"Billy got Cuinn," she said, and grinned.

36

—————

SPILL IT

"FIRST THING you should know is that I'm an angel, and if you try any of that Core shit, I'll blast you into next year."

Billy appeared in a shimmer of displaced air, shoving Cuinn ahead of him. The Irishman stumbled but didn't lose his footing. Billy pushed him toward the bed. "Sit."

Soren watched from the bathroom door of the motel room. "Is she okay?" he asked Billy, without taking his eyes from Cuinn.

"Yeah. She was gagged—" Billy glared at Cuinn "—but fine."

"You didn't see what she'd just done to one of my men, so you didn't. He'll not be pissing for a week." Cuinn eyed them both with a little smile. Soren didn't return it.

The Irishman's usual colour was off, a pale tinge beneath his tan skin. "You look green."

A blast from the cranked air conditioning hit Soren full in the face. He swiped a hand through his hair. *Useless.* It flew straight back into his eyes.

"Angel highway doesn't agree with demon energy, so it doesn't. I'm grand. Don't you worry about me, recruit."

"Not worried in the slightest, guv." An English insult. *Cold.* He missed his brother.

Their eyes locked.

Silence.

While the wind battered the world outside, in the motel room, the TV provided a low drone from the only local news channel still broadcasting. Its screen filled with grainy footage of demon attacks and abnormal weather reports. Joshua had explained earlier—the rising demons rode the wind to scatter across the globe. Seemed that of the Elementals, Air had picked a side.

Cuinn broke eye contact with Soren first and surveyed the room. He settled on his abductor, who'd sat on an easy chair by the front door. "Now, I'm betting you're Billy. Not what I was expecting, but still… angels, you never know now, do you?"

"What the bloody hell does that mean?"

"Nothin' lad. I've just seen some weird-looking angels in my time."

"You think I'm weird?" Billy looked down at himself, frowning.

Soren resisted the urge to grind his teeth. "He's messing with you." *And wasting time.*

Cuinn grinned at Billy, then turned back to Soren. "So, did you like the Volvo?"

Soren raised his middle finger.

Still smirking, Cuinn's gaze caught the laptop on the table, turned to face the room. A genuine smile lit his face. The fatigue in his eyes momentarily gone. "Josh?"

Joshua's face glitched, then settled into a grin. "He… y, Cui… nn."

"Processor's screwed," Billy muttered. "Dropped it when I got here."

"Well, it's better than the poor bastard he was in the last

time I saw him. Been dead a few hours. Axe to the head. Brain dripping out of his eye socket."

A sharp breath came from the corner. Aideen. Soren rolled his eyes while Cuinn turned. "Sorry darlin', didn't see you there." He winked and smiled. "Nice to see you again." His gaze moved on, "And Jacob. Good to meet yer properly, so it is."

Jacob gave a slow nod, recognizing the dark energy he'd encountered in the Boston coven.

Enough. Soren grabbed a dining chair, turned it backwards, and straddled it. He rested his arms on the back, owning the space in front of the Irish demon.

His voice stayed soft. "Josh told us you're on the right side. So spill it. The whole plan, Cuinn. And no more 'trust me' bollocks. The whole damn thing."

———

Cuinn rubbed his chin stubble, his gaze finding the mirror above the dressing table. He gave it a hard stare.

"Angel glamour," Soren confirmed instantly. "She can't see or hear. And Aideen added to it to confuse things—"

"Wrapped tighter than a donkey's dick in a Featherlite." Billy nodded sagely.

Aideen tutted. Jacob snorted.

Cuinn dropped his hand. "I like you, Billy. You're all right for an angel."

Soren's heart hammered—a furious drumbeat he knew the demon could hear. "Get on with it," he said, his voice dangerously low.

"Okay, man." Cuinn rubbed his hands together. "I'm on the right side, and you would have been, too, if you hadn't been such a pain in my arse the last while." He shook his head. "Jaysus, I'm not saying it hasn't been hard, Hux. But I'd never have left you there. I'd have brought you back from anything, man."

The words hit. Soren flinched. *Don't go there.*

Billy looked from him to Cuinn, confused. "This is like some subtext, right?"

"Something like that," Soren bit out. "Move on, Cuinn."

Cuinn sighed, then leaned forward, forearms resting on his knees and hands clasped in front of him. His eyes shot to deep blue as he looked from Soren to Billy, with the odd glance at Joshua.

"In Hell, the Abbot approached me with a plan to oust the Advocate. He's been in her pocket since she turned him demon years back, since before that too, he suspects. He's had enough."

Soren's jaw clenched at the mention of Anastasia's father.

"Now, don't you get me wrong," Cuinn continued, "he's an evil auld bugger—loves being the nasty piece of shite he is—but doesn't want to do it on her terms anymore."

He stopped, sat straighter, circled his neck then hunched back over. "She's all about the revenge. Revenge on God, the world—the feckin' President, it doesn't matter—she just wants it all gone. Ezequiel especially. She hates his angelic arsehole and the only thing she's been focused on is The End. For her, that's what the Tipping Point represents—the beginning of the end of humanity. Then she can finally give a big 'fuck you' to the lot of us—but especially him. It's been her one intention since she jumped ship, Billy, it's her Faith."

Billy grunted. "An angel has to be driven by something. Seems like she found something enough to energize her—"

"Yeah, but that's the only thing that does. Remember that, lads. It's important." His eyes flitted from blue to green rapidly before they focused again in deep blue. "So, the Advocate thinks the Abbot is on her side, that he wants the Tipping Point too. Only then the war happened—"

"The Demon War?" Aideen chimed in from the back of the room.

"Bingo, darlin'." Cuinn glanced over his shoulder. "And the Soldiers pushed the Leeches underground. We won, and suddenly, the Abbot wasn't in pole position anymore—"

"You were." Soren cut in, the pieces snapping into place. "So she had to get you in on the plan for the Tipping Point."

"Something like that. I've never wanted that sort of power, Hux. Just want my country back, man. You know that. For sure, though, they wanted me in on it. So, the whole thing—the Abbot dying, you killing me—it was all to get me into Hell and into their pocket." He shrugged. "Other stuff too, but we'd be here all day."

Soren's hands tightened on the back of his chair. *What's he not saying?*

"Tell me, Mr. Cuinn, are these beings responsible for the Demon Risings that started the Tipping Point?" Jacob asked.

The acrid smell of sweat rose from all of them, a scent everyone had grown used to over the last few months, but now it sharpened. Jacob rose and fetched water from the mini fridge and handed the bottles out.

"Nah! They just took advantage."

"It was us then? The people. We caused our own destruction. We saw it, and we did nothing."

The Precog's words hung in the sweltering air, and everyone but Soren shifted uneasily. *Not helpful.*

Cuinn looked from one miserable face to the next. "Hey, it's not over yet! There's a plan—"

"That involves the Tipping Point happening." Soren interrupted. He took a sharp breath, forcing control. "Okay. What's the plan?"

"All right. There are a few things we need to help the Abbot achieve—before we end him. Sure, the first is to make the Tipping Point happen—"

Everyone apart from Soren raised voices in protest. He shouted them all down. "Let him finish."

"The reason is because of a few things. When the clock chimes, or the wind blows, or the fires of Hell rise up, or whatever it is that announces the time has arrived, the Advocate will finally believe she's won. She'll be at her strongest, psychologically—" he grinned "—then we can rip the feckin' rug right out from under her."

"How?" Billy asked.

"You."

"Me? I couldn't kill her last time." Billy stared at his feet.

"I heard. I was down there, remember. You lost because the Abbot stepped in. Did some major magick, called in favours from the Main Man. He won't be there this time."

Soren's eyes flicked to Billy's defeated posture. Remembered his final request after that fight: *Take care of my girl.* His eyes dropped too. He'd failed him.

"Besides, there's more than one way to kill an angel, not just a dagger to the heart." He winked at Billy, ignoring his confused frown. "But that's not the only reason the Tipping Point has to happen. In that moment, when it happens, the Abbot will be reborn. Literally. The Advocate doesn't know— he's kept this bit secret from her—but he won't just rise from Hell as a demon, he'll become human again."

Cuinn smiled around at everyone. "That's our chance! If we can kill him then, he can't come back. Ever. He's dead for good. His soul will regenerate, too. If we can kill him then, the soul will feck off back to Heaven where he can finally be dealt with."

He leaned back. "Well, I didn't expect feckin' applause, but Jaysus. This is a good thing, lads."

Billy stood. "Yes. This is good. Makes sense." He paced back and forth. "If his human soul gets shunted back to Heaven, then we own his arse!"

The strategy was sound. But, what about her? "Okay, I get it. But you still haven't explained about Anastasia. If you're going to kill him, why are you giving her back?" Soren asked.

Cuinn said nothing for a moment. He interlocked his fingers and looked at his feet. "Sure, it's like this, Hux. That one came out of left field. He calls her 'the failsafe.' Part of the process to make him human. It's in her blood. He'd already collected some when she was a kid, but it was lost, he says—some accident. Then she was supposed to return to him willingly. That was the whole Saviour plan. When she became human, though, that was all screwed up. Now he has to do this ritual—that's all I know. But it won't kill her—"

"And you believe him?" Soren was on his feet and took back his spot by the door under the air-conditioning vent, desperate for air. Sweat trickling from under his hair.

"We've got to risk it—"

"No! She's always the one we're risking."

"Hux." Cuinn crossed to him. He put a hand on his shoulder. "We've got no choice now. The Tipping Point is going to happen. We can't stop it, man. But the ritual is our opportunity: he turns, he dies—she's free!"

"If it—or he—doesn't kill her in the process!" He pushed Cuinn off with a violent shrug of his shoulder. "Do you care about her at all?"

"Yes."

"When you gonna start showing it?"

Out of nowhere, Cuinn shoved Soren back against the wall. "I'm fucking sick of you telling me I don't care. And I'm more than fucking sick of you putting your feelings for her over the mission. When did you turn into such a fucking pussy?" He slammed Soren back again, this time with enough force to bounce his head against the wall.

Still in pain from his earlier beatings, Soren saw red. The mission *was* Anastasia. Nothing else mattered. He smashed his fist into the Irishman's jaw and followed up with a punch to his gut that threw him forward. In the small space of the door frame, the two men cracked heads and grunted out the pain.

Jacob and Billy flew to separate them, but the scuffle was already over.

Still holding his head, Soren pushed past Billy and strode out the motel room door.

37

PICKING SIDES

OUTSIDE, Soren grappled with his temper. A gust of southerly wind hit him as he stepped through the door, nearly taking his feet from under him. It knocked the remaining breath from his chest. In the distance, thunder rumbled and lightning lit up the horizon.

He sank onto his heels, gasping, one hand braced on the grimy ground. Cuinn's blue blood still burned his knuckles, gluing the dust to his skin.

The door to the room creaked open. A rustle of paper, then the strike of a lighter. Cigarette smoke drifted past before the wind tore it away. "Why aren't you backing me, Billy?"

Billy sighed. "You once told me that I underestimated Tazia. That she was a soldier. That she was stronger than I gave her credit for. And you were right."

Soren heard him drag deeply on the cigarette again and hold the smoke. When he blew it out, they were both ready for it. On the next drag, Soren breathed in too.

"She fought like hell, and then, when the chips were down, she made the right bloody decision. She chose humanity, Hux." He dropped beside him, his voice close. "If she was here right now, she'd tell us to give her a chance. Just cos she's not a vampire anymore doesn't mean she's lost her courage. From what you've told me about the last week, it sounds like she's even stronger, bruv. Being human is her strength now."

"But on her own? Against that bastard?"

"Who says she'll be on her own? Cuinn's plan isn't that she's on her own—"

Soren looked at him sharply.

Billy put a hand on his shoulder. "I spoke to Julie. She's been told to trust him, and I trust her. Come in and hear him out." He stood and offered his hand.

Soren stared at the offered hand, then at Billy's face. *Trust. Again.* He wasn't sure he had any left to give. But it was Billy. He took it, and the angel hauled him to his feet.

Before he stepped back inside, the wind howled under the long motel porch. Another flash of lightning lit the horizon, and for a second he saw them. A dark, seething mass swirled across the sky, riding those same gusts. *Damn birds.* They shrieked and screamed, turning in slow zigzags on the undulating air currents.

He went back inside to hear what else Cuinn had to say.

———

The light from the motel room spilled over into the passageway outside. Jegudiel watched from the windscreen of the Humvee. Her anger gained ground with each breath she'd seen Soren take. She couldn't hear what they were saying; their lips moving in silent conversation made her rip at her hair in frustration. Her boy was making plans with that angel! *Infuriating.*

Conn O'Cuinn was inside that room, too, but she couldn't gain entrance. Every time she tried, the witch's magick had flung her back.

It had taken so much effort to find him. She felt raw from her attempts to break through the spell. It took slices from her, cut into her flesh even though she was just a shadow in this world.

At first, she'd persisted, thrown herself against it over and over, but as the spell sliced deeper and her blood flowed dark red against her pale skin, she'd stopped. Her shouts of frustration had excited the winds and attracted the attention of the birds for miles. Now they circled the motel, flashing black wings and sharp beaks in the moonlight.

"It's time you picked a side!" She shrieked at them, inciting yet more winds to blow.

What was Conn O'Cuinn doing? Was this part of the plan? Was he deceiving them? Why were all these men so obsessed with that girl! She had created her after all. If anyone had first rights over Anastasia, it was she.

"Less than twenty-four hours, and we will see where your allegiance is Irishman! Stephen and I will stand together and watch this planet burn—whether you are on our side or not. And the boy and girl will trot along behind!"

The Advocate shook her hair, smoothed her eyebrows— and screamed. Cracks snaked over the windscreen, and she disappeared. There were things to do.

38

DUNGEONS AND DRAGONS

TAZIA COULD DEAL with being manhandled. It wasn't the Soldier's wandering hands, or even the avenging punch she got in the stomach from the recruit she'd be leaving with swollen balls. The real problem was that Billy had told her she was about to be handed over to her father.

The last time she'd seen him alive was in the cave in Turin. He'd whispered words of encouragement in her ear as she'd pulled the fangs from his jaw, and before Hux shot him. The last time she'd seen him dead, he'd been standing in Billy's flat, his body disintegrating and reforming in front of her eyes.

Now what did he want? Not to play a version of daddy and daughter that ended in her living happily ever after.

As a Soldier dragged her towards Conn O'Cuinn, she wriggled to free herself from his sex-starved hands for the third time, scraping down hard with her metal-studded boot against his shin. He gave a yowl and lashed out. She dodged, but he still made contact, the blow glancing off her mouth and splitting her lip, drawing a sharp yelp of pain from her.

In response, his superior rabbit-punched him directly on the nose, leaving him gasping for breath. The two Soldiers exchanged deep red demon eyes for two seconds. The recruit looked away.

Tazia smirked at him. "Wasn't expecting that woz ya!"

"Shut up, Tazia." Cuinn walked off the ramp and down onto the runway, pulling her by the arm alongside him.

They'd landed in Turin an hour before and dropped into what looked like a major military manoeuvre. Demons everywhere, dressed in a mishmash of military-style clothes, with neither colour nor badge aligning them. Most of the planes were taking off, crowds of Leeches and Soldiers piling into transporters, and heading off to God knows where. Some big fucking plan was in play that she wasn't in on.

She spat her disgust at the ground. This was her city. Things were peaceful here; everyone got along just fine. Why mess with that?

The planes took off into a clear blue sky, crossing over the mountain peaks, heading north. Her skin sung in the fresh breeze. *Bliss!*

Sucking hard on the coolest air she'd experienced in a long while. *One last shot.* "He'll kill me, Cuinn."

Ignoring her, Cuinn pulled her along, heading toward a large black Audi waiting at the side of the runway just a few yards away.

She could just about pick out its purring engine in between the shouts of the Soldiers and roaring of the planes overhead. She dragged her feet until she got some purchase with her heels and dug in. "He'll *kill* me!"

Brought up short, Cuinn stopped, and turned her to face him. He grasped both of her arms just below the shoulders and squeezed gently. "He will not. Do what he says. Tell him what he needs to hear to keep yourself alive. But, understand this darlin', there's no choice. Submit to him."

He drew her to him so that his two-day-old sandpaper stubble rubbed her cheek, minuscule flakes of skin flying between them, mixing their scents, and whispered, "Help will be there. Trust me."

She caught the look of his eyes before he looked away. They were clear green with a concentrated ring of ice blue at the edges of the irises. She'd never seen the effect before. It wasn't just focus; it was a promise frozen in concentration. She had no choice.

As they reached the car, the back door swung open, and its shiny black paintwork reflected the sun for a moment, causing both herself and Cuinn to turn away from the glare. Before her vision had even cleared, the waft of lavender gave away the identity of the occupant.

She groaned. "You are fucking kidding me!"

Cuinn pushed her gently the final few stumbling steps to the car, her hands tied in front of her. She got in, keeping as far as she could from the occupant who shared the back seat, before demanding, "What the fuck do you want?"

———

"When did you replace the white crystal with this *Dungeons and Dragons* shit?" Billy stood twenty feet away from the High Advocate who sat sideways over an ornate wooden throne, her butt centred in the middle and her legs casually splayed over the left-side arm

She turned her head a little toward him and smirked. She still wore the God-awful purple dress. It looked worse for wear, with dark stains patterning the skirt and bodice, and rips crudely patched with childlike stitches. Her high-heeled purple boots reeked of blood and bobbed in time to the sound of the tip of a black crystal dagger she hit off the hard ground.

From under her bottom, tassels from a red tapestry cushion trailed onto the floor, looking very much like the unfurled tail of a mythical beast. Billy couldn't be sure, but thought he even spied the tip of a long tongue peeking out from behind the back of the gold-studded chair.

Behind her, the black landscape, bruised in shadows of deep purple, red, and blue, seethed under the lightning flashes that forked across the distant sky.

As the scorching wind rolled in with the thunder, Billy could feel the wax on his hair melting in an itchy thin trickle down each temple and onto his cheekbones.

He too, tapped out a rhythm with the tip of his onyx blade against his leg. "Got a better knife this time, love." He held up the dagger in front of him and ran a finger along the middle of the blade. On either side of the central ridge gleamed eight black diamonds, only one of which was needed to reach her heart and kill her. "Fully studded!" He winked.

Her knife sparkled with seven studs. "I have more than enough here, angel. Don't you fret."

"You killed an angel, Jegudiel? That knife had eight diamonds last time we met…"

"No one you knew, pet." She glanced up at the sky, then twisted around until her boots sat solidly on the ground in front of the chair. She pointed her dagger up as though indicating some words hanging in the night air. "Tipping Point's almost here, Billy."

She grinned, teeth gleaming in the same light that caught the blade, her pale bony face almost skull-like, her long red hair, now grabbed by the wind, swept crazily around her head like a moving whirlwind of blood. "Aren't you excited for me? After all this time, pet, it's almost here. The end—God's world about to destroy itself."

All at once, she stood, and her right foot tapped on the spot. "Are you ready, Billy?"

"I'm ready." He kept his face blank, but her glee lit a fuse in his gut. He wanted to lunge, to bury the blade in her and be done with it. *No. Not yet.* That wasn't the best revenge, was it, love? After all this waiting, he wanted true vengeance—the worst kind of death for her. His job, for now, was simple. Delay. Get past the Tipping Point, and then show her what Fate—or God, whatever—had cooked up just for her.

Cuinn had told him the secret, a proper little gem even Julie hadn't known. The real way to kill an angel. A trick so old the Advocate herself might've forgotten it even existed. And it was perfect for her. Complete annihilation. Exactly what the bitch wanted for the world, coming right back at her. Anything else, and she'd just pop back to Heaven for a slap on the wrist. Too good for her. And far too bloody risky.

No, this way he would twist her own desires around, bringing destruction down on her. His skin buzzed with the sheer need of it. The energy was building. Yes, he could feel the Tipping Point about to strike, but he could also feel her death coming into reach. And he was so fucking ready.

Billy stepped forward, dagger in his hand, his grin matching hers. "Come on, Advocate. Let's go!"

———

"Ahh *mia bella*, Miss Dune, how are you today?" Signor Bello slid his eyes sideways towards her. At the same time, he struck the driver's seat in front of him to signal they should leave.

As the car pulled away and headed at speed out of the airport, toward the mountains, Tazia faced him. He hadn't changed.

He was still squashed into his white suit, purple shirt darkened with sweat from his chest and the constant trickle that poured down into his neck from his head. The soul from his most recent meal pressed against his left cheek, distending it with features of their nose and screaming mouth.

"I'm just peachy," she said, and stared instead at the back of the goon's head in the front passenger seat. He was running the tip of his hand gun up and down his right side cheek, and sporadically across his forehead, the cool of the steel chilling him, she guessed. Maybe he would accidentally shoot himself.

She giggled at the thought before turning back to her captor. "So, you working for my father now? That's a little freaky don't you think? The last time we had dealings, I'd arranged his murder—just for you."

"Ah well, bella. Things change. I am not a stupid man. We will all adapt when it is of our benefit. Your father has been very courteous of late. He will need support. I have money and —" he shrugged "—he has a bella daughter who could bring me much… pleasure."

He attempted a smile, but only shifted the fat of his cheeks slightly, and flashed a tiny glance of gold covered teeth. He did reach over and squeeze her thigh, however. These guys seemed obsessed with her damn legs—what was that? They weren't even that great.

"Do that again and I'll puke!"

He chuckled, then set his mouth hard again. "It would be as well for you to treat me with a little respect. Whether or not you are amenable to such an arrangement means little to me."

With surprising swiftness, he reached out and spanned her face with one hand, grabbing her cheeks, and squeezing hard. As he forced her lips into a pucker, he dragged her toward him. "I rule Turin now that you killed the worst of my enemies —your father and Giovanetti. You left the path clear for me, *mia* Sahara. I am grateful, and would be pleased to show you—"

He pushed his lips to hers, and she felt his thin, hard tongue force its way into her mouth, probing even between the teeth she was doing her best to clench together. Withdrawing, a trail of saliva dripping from his mouth to hers. He flung her back in the seat.

Gagging, Tazia wiped at her face and spat on the floor. His

spit carried the taste of pond water, wine, and lavender. Did he drink the stuff as well as disguise his body odour with it?

Hands still tied, she kicked out at the seat in front of her, a burst of raw frustration. The goon swung around, pistol first, and glared. She kicked at him again, but only dented the cushion now that his full weight was on the back of the chair. These guys were just so enormous, unless she could get a weapon, she was helpless.

Gritting her teeth, she sank back into her seat and stared out of the window while Signor Bello chuckled beside her. Is this what Cuinn meant about going along with the plan? *No fucking way!* She would not sleep with this monster voluntarily. The world could burn.

The scenery outside whipped past as night fell. When she twisted and looked out of the back of the car, she could see the lights of Turin come on behind her, the spires and tower blocks stretching up into the air. Home. That's where she should be heading, but from the route, Tazia already knew where she was going. Of course. He would rise in the same place that he had descended. It made perfect fucking sense.

The car pulled off the road at the bottom of a path, which led further into the foothills. "Time for you to walk, *mia bella*. Be sure to remind your father of my proposal. I am prepared to formalize it of course. You will be my principal wife."

"Glad to know I'll be at the front of the queue," she muttered under her breath.

Bello's men pulled her from the car. One of them attached another rope to the one that bound her wrists, then started the trek up the hill, pulling her after him. The second kept behind her, jabbing her with the nose of his weapon anytime she resisted or walked too slowly.

The climb was a long, brutal grind up the hillside. By the time they reached the top, her lungs burned, and the two demons were puffing.

The cave's entrance was partially blocked by the boulders she'd pounded out of her way last spring. Then, she'd climbed out after the rockfall that marked her father's descent into Hell. To her shame, she also remembered that she'd wished for Hux's death. *Things change.*

There was no sound coming from the tunnel, and looking inside, it was pitch black. "I'll need my hands free."

The two demons exchanged looks, then the one who had been pulling her along removed a penknife from his pocket and cut the ropes. The other pointed the gun at her and ordered her into the tunnel.

She had no weapons, and no choice. The air cracked with thunder directly overhead, and the cloud of birds that had followed them since the airport flew down and settled on the rocks and trees around them. They were silent apart from a few squawks as they vied for space.

"You come for the show too?" she shouted at them and clapped her hands violently. They didn't move. "Oh, fuck you then!" She turned and gazed down into the darkness of the hole again. It dropped vertically and then levelled off before ending in a huge cavern. The first part would be the hardest.

She sat on the edge of the entrance and slid inside, feeling for hand and footholds as she started the descent. Just before she disappeared, she flipped the bird at the two demons, and slipped into the darkness.

39

____

THE FAILSAFE

TAZIA'S FOOTING GAVE WAY, and she slid the last few feet on her butt, the back of her head cracking against stone. Lights exploded behind her eyes. Lying there for a second, gasping, she squinted against the thumping in her skull.

She'd landed halfway down the ramp that spiralled to the cavern floor. It looked the same with the flat ritual stones in the centre. The opening in the ground that had swallowed her father was now healed over, a seamless scar of rock. Tunnels, black mouths leading to her old prison, stared back at her from the far wall. All was silent but for the familiar drip... drip... drip of water, which collected in a deep dark pool.

Tazia made her way to it and took up a handful to rinse out her mouth and the last vestiges of Bello's foul taste. She washed her arm too. Sliced by the sharp edge of a rock as she fell, the blood now leached into the remains of her sleeve. As fast as she rinsed, it bled more.

"Let me help you, my dear." He'd arrived on silent feet, and stood a few paces away, one hand held out to her, the other hanging easily at his side. He looked grey. From head to foot, the colour layered his clothes, streaked his hair, and bloomed on his skin. And, for the first time, she could count every one of his eight hundred years in his eyes. Hell had been cruel.

For a moment, Tazia felt sympathy for him. She gave him her hand, and he pulled her to his side where he pushed up the remnants of her sleeve and licked her wound. She shivered as the anesthetic effect of his saliva seeped into the cut to ease the pain and suppress the flow of blood. *So familiar.*

"Dog spit does that too, father," she said dryly, knowing she'd used up her free pass with that one comment.

He ignored her insolence and led her to the centre of the cave where he lit two candles, using melted wax to place them sturdily on the flat of one of the large stones. Between the candles lay a ritual knife. With the blade sharpened to thinness, it was gold, ornate. Flashy.

Her father spoke again. "Let me see you." He pulled her into the light and ran ancient fingers over her face and down her neck, surprising her with how soft they felt. She remembered them as coarse, scratching at her skin when he'd touched her in the past. He ran them through her hair. "I like your hair longer like this, Anastasia. It elevates your appearance. Better than the street urchin you usually resemble."

Oh, so familiar: the compliment given, then immediately withdrawn.

She snatched up the knife, pulled her hair to one side, and hacked it off. When the bunch hung loosely in her hand, she threw it at him.

Strands separated and cascaded onto his face and clothes like thin strings of confetti; others hit the flames of the candles and burned, sending puffs of acrid smoke into the air.

Briefly the Abbot smiled too, then he pulled the hair from his face, threw it to the ground, and dusted down the front of his jacket to loosen the rest. When he was done, and without a pause, he backhanded her across the cheek and mouth.

The blow made a sound like a whiplash and extended the split the Soldier had given her earlier. He licked her blood from the back of his hand, his eyes locked on hers.

She staggered but held her ground, holding his gaze as her mouth filled with blood and swelling flesh. "That's better, daddy," she slurred. "I know you now."

Lightning tore the sky open, bleaching the cavern in a stark, momentary white. It carved out the hollows of his face, gaunt and menacing. The false warmth gone.

As darkness snapped back, his hand shot out.

He grabbed her by the neck, lifting her clear off her feet before smashing her down onto the cold rock of the altar. The candles flickered wildly. He leaned in, his whisper a foul heat in her ear. "I was hoping we could do this nicely, Anastasia. That for once in your life, you could be cooperative. But I see my mistake."

Thunder cracked directly overhead, the vibration travelling from the stone right through her spine.

A flicker of tension crossed his face. He wrenched the knife from her fist and brought his mouth low to her ear again. His words were a low rumble against her skull.

"Long ago, an angel believed herself to be in love with me." He shifted his thumb, pressing it over the frantic pulse in her neck. Her heartbeat hammered against his chest. "She said she could save me, daughter. Save me from the evil that travelled in my blood. I wanted forgiveness for my ungodly ways, and she told me she could get it for me."

He drove the tip of the knife into her neck, just under his thumb.

Pain, white-hot and blinding, flashed into her temple and down into her shoulder. Blood spurted against his face. He rubbed his cheek against hers, smearing her own life back onto her skin. Her hands clawed at his back. *Let me go!*

"But she couldn't save me." He latched onto the wound,

sucking deeply. A wet, rhythmic drumming echoed in her head, punctuated by the thick glug of his swallows. Her own flesh muffled his words. "In Heaven, she argued for my soul... and they refused her. But still, she wouldn't let me go."

Another deep pull. Bubbles burst behind her eyes, the world fizzing at the edges. It felt like being held under water, the air in her lungs turning to poison. His voice broke through the roaring in her ears, fading in and out with her vision. Her arms collapsed at her sides.

"I wanted to pray Anastasia... to beg forgiveness... to gain the sacrament... cried and begged her to let me go..."

He sucked her earlobe. *Jesus, no!* Revulsion cut through the haze. Weakly, she kicked down with the heel of her boot against his leg. He did not relent.

His grip on her neck made each breath a shallow, ragged gasp. He whispered on, his story and her suffocation becoming one. "But she forbade it. Promised immortality... a place by Satan's side. And in my weakness, my grief... I obeyed. I became a vampire."

He took another mouthful, a gurgling sound deep in his throat. She could taste it now, her own blood slick and sweet at the back of her throat.

"To make it happen," he murmured against the wound, "all I had to do was create a child."

Her eyes rolled back. The blackness was a blanket, heavy and welcoming. *Dying then.*

He eased the pressure on her neck just enough for her to reflexively drag in a desperate, burning gasp of air. He laid his head next to hers, stroking back the hair that stuck to her forehead, and made patterns in her cold sweat with his finger.

"So, I did what she wanted. But by then, I could see her for what she was. A harpy. A liar. More evil than even I."

He licked again on her neck, the tip of his tongue probing deep into the wound he'd made until she moaned and he pushed his hard body against her side, pinning her between the rock and his own form.

"So I built a failsafe into her plan. I made the child she wanted—I made you, Anastasia. But I conjured my freedom in your blood. She never knew. I ensured your existence would give me the ability to start over. To be human again."

He spat on the cut to still the bleeding, then began to lick her neck and face clean. The strokes were wide and slow, like a cat cleaning a kitten.

Letting go of her neck, the Abbot walked away. Without his support, Tazia slumped from the altar, collapsing to the ground. She gasped, dragging air into her burning lungs, the cavern swimming in and out of focus. Through the dark blur, she watched him.

He stepped to the pool and washed his face and hands with a chilling calmness. His voice echoed across the chamber, distant to her ringing ears. "When the Tipping Point comes, daughter, your blood will transform me to human. I will live again as a man. I will no longer be owned by her. I will be free... free to lead a good life... and when I die a natural death, I will beg and pray my way to Heaven."

He returned to her side and cradled her to him. "I may not have been the kindest father, Anastasia, but I have made you strong. I have prepared a life for us. We will live under the protection of Conn O'Cuinn. I have given him the vampire race... You and I will live together in our human lives."

The sheer, insane arrogance of it gave her a spark. Dragging air into her lungs, she pushed against him. She'd had enough of his rough clothes, the scent of death and blood that clung to him. His incessant voice, droning and whining.

She clawed at his jacket, using him as an anchor to pull herself up, up onto her knees until her eyes were level with his. Every muscle screamed.

"F... F... uck you!"

She spat in his face.

For a heartbeat, there was only the shocked widening of his eyes—

Blinding light struck from above. A fierce bolt of lightning blasted all hearing from her ears, piercing the cavern's roof and hitting the altar in a thick, silver ribbon. The stone where she had just lain split in two with a deafening crack.

The shockwave threw them both across the cavern like dolls.

40

———————————

THE TIPPING POINT

SOLDIERS AND LEECHES HAD BEEN COLLECTING for days. Masses of the demons arrived in the small glorious corner of Ireland that used to be Conn O'Cuinn's home, and still they came, marching as one unstoppable band of brothers and beasts.

In the sky, millions of birds followed them. They swooped and circled in a never-ending ribbon of undulating blackness, and created a cacophony of shrieks and cries that were only ever dampened when the thunder crashed above.

The demons had herded thousands of people to a narrow spit of land that dropped both sides into the deep water of the ocean. There was no escape: they would die at the hands of their captors or take their own lives by jumping into the sea. He knew similar scenes were taking place all over the world; he'd planned it that way.

Conn's plane had landed in an adjoining field just a moment ago. Now, he surveyed the scene from the higher ground at the top of the spit. It was already dark, but the entire promontory was lit by thousands of flaming torches that bobbed and danced with the movement of the people who carried them. Smoke swirled into the air, combining with the scents of blood and fear.

The rain continued to pour, temporarily beating the heat of the Rising and soaking all who walked and flew. It filled the dried-out ruts of the roads so that, in places, the water flowed fast like rivers. He'd seen it pull the feet out from under the prisoners, children swept away from the desperate hands of their parents.

Like demons the world over, he waited for the moment when that final human death would tip the balance in favour of the monsters. And standing there, watching the Soldiers stabbing and shooting their way through the crowds of people, he knew for the first time in his long life; he was a monster, too.

For a moment, he raised his face to the sky, rain pouring down on his head and chilling his cheeks. He watched the birds dip and wheel, screeching either in pain or celebration, and then rise again to ride the air currents. He wanted that freedom. *Soon, man, soon.*

On the cliff edge to his right, a woman screamed. Her cry pierced through the shrieks of the birds, the shouts of the demons, and the mournful wails of those already dying.

A sudden, ringing silence fell over the spit of land, so complete it felt as if the world itself had stopped breathing and the sky paused its rumbles and cracks of thunder.

A young boy had lost his footing. He balanced right on the edge of the cliff, cartwheeling his arms forward from instinct. The man closest to him held out his hand, and the child grabbed it. For a moment they made contact, but the boy's hand was covered in the slippery mud and water that had first swept him away, and he slipped from his grasp.

His mother cried out, "No!" She was too far from him; nothing could be done.

The boy fell, spinning onto the rocks below. His life extinguished.

The balance gone.

The people stilled; the demons stopped the massacre. High above their heads, the rolling clouds clashed, and a huge silver lightning bolt shot out of the mass of ebony. It blasted the clouds apart, revealing a low slung moon, and hit the ground out of sight, thousands of miles away.

He knew where it landed. Turin.

For a moment, the world was beautiful in the moonlight, but as the lightning bolt faded, Conn felt the change. A jolt. A shift in the cosmos that hit him as indisputable power.

The Tipping Point had come.

He breathed the air of this new world, filling his lungs, his blood buzzing, ready to propel him forward.

Conn sent out a whispered prayer to Soren Huxford, the man he'd trusted with the murder of his most hated enemy. "Now, Hux. It is time. Kill him, *mo dheartháir*." Then he raised his gun to the sky and fired a shot that signalled to each of the Soldiers gathered there.

He didn't need to hear the answering shots; he knew his commanders would be firing them in every corner of the world. As if in response to the plan's final, violent consummation, the birds launched into the sky in one movement.

Conn dropped the gun and crouched to the ground, giving himself over to the change. Around him, his men did the same. Low growls gathered in their throats, talons sprouted from their fingers, and eyes turned a deep and deadly red as they transformed.

The Leeches looked around confused, dropping the humans they'd been feeding on, and instinctively backed away.

The Soldiers focused on their scrawny forms and pounced. The howls of their transformation made way for the screams of the victims as the hunt began.

41

VICTORY?

THE MOMENT before the Tipping Point finally hit, Billy wrestled the Advocate to the ground by the mirror, her portal to all the tiny corners of the globe. From there she could see and hear everything, could reach anywhere and anyone.

He could feel the moment getting closer, the impending climax to a plan she'd put into place centuries ago. A plot he knew she had nurtured with every whispered word and manipulative touch, nudging it toward this exact conclusion.

And like the battling Soldiers below, Billy was ready for it.

The fight with the angel had been long, but easy for him. He sported defensive wounds on his hands and arms, and a cut to his cheek. She hadn't come close to his heart, and it occurred to him she must be delaying too. He'd wielded the knife with such ferocity, the angel's flesh lay open in front of him.

Dragging her by one arm to the mirror, he threw her against the rock beside it.

She dropped her knife by her side and smiled up at him. "Tired, Billy?"

He moved back to sit in front of the glass, but kept his own dagger in his hand. The sweat rolled off him, and long black hair flopped over his forehead until he pushed it flat to his head, panting slightly. "In better shape than you, Advocate."

She laughed her acknowledgement. An honest laugh, not the theatric cackle he was used to. Then she gasped, trying to pump the thin, hot oxygen into her lungs while her blood seeped from her. The rip he'd made in her chest revealed the unmistakable gleam of white bone. Yet still she smiled. "True enough."

He could finish her right here, but it was too soon. "You want to die? You don't even want to see the mess you've created?"

"What makes you think you can kill me, pet?" She shrugged and glanced at the wound on her chest. "This is nothing. It won't compare to the pain you'll have when you see what's coming. I can smell it in the air, Billy!" She turned her head to the sky.

"The Tipping Point?"

"Of course. It's inevitable now. No one can stop it. My Stephen will rule this world and the other. The man they would not allow into Heaven. The man they mocked me for loving. A vampire ruling the Earth! And while he rules, I will stand with him, and your little half-breed and my boy will be by my side." She coughed and retched, blood and vomit peppering her dress. "I do regret one thing though, William."

"What's that?"

"Not seeing the look on Ezequiel's face when the world finally burns."

Billy grinned. He'd finally seen the image in the mirror he'd been waiting for. *Time to destroy her.*

He kicked casually at her purple boot, and his grin turned to a sneer. "This may not end the way you think."

Her head jerked up, her smile dropping. "What are you talking about? Stephen will rule as soon as—"

"You really think that little fucker is doing what you want him to, Jegudiel? You think you can trust him? Really?"

"He would not betray me!" But a flicker of doubt flashed in her eyes.

Billy got onto his knees, and crawled to her side, still smirking.

The blood from her chest wound continued to trickle from her, staining his palms and his pants as he settled. He snaked an arm around her back as if they were old friends, but instead of offering comfort, his fingers dug into the back of her skull as he forced her head toward the mirror. "Look, angel, look!"

She turned to face the glass. "What? He loves me..." Her words faded as the mist in the mirror cleared to give a view of the cavern deep under the ground in Turin. The Abbot had just smashed Tazia's head to the stone altar and cut into her neck. "What is he doing? Anastasia is useless to him now!"

Billy's heart leapt as he saw Tazia struggle against her father. *Bastard!* But he couldn't intervene, like them all, there was a role he had to play, and his with here, with her: "Just watch..."

The Advocate's eyes widened as her lover fed from his daughter. She watched as Tazia's skin turned white and waxy, and her eyes rolled back in their sockets. "Will he kill her? But why?"

"Just listen..."

"But, I must go to him."

Jegudiel tried to shuffle toward the mirror and out of Billy's grasp, but he stopped her with a wave of his other hand as he stilled the air. "No, Advocate. You'll stay here and listen..."

The sound of the Abbot's words drifted to them from the mirror.

I wanted to pray Anastasia… to beg forgiveness… to gain the sacrament… cried and begged her to let me go…

The angel squirmed against Billy's arm. "No, Stephen, you believed in my mission—"

But she forbade it. Promised immortality… a place by Satan's side. And in my weakness, my grief… I obeyed. I became a vampire.

The Advocate fought the stasis and leaned forward, raising a hand to the mirror. "No! You wanted it! You wanted me!"

"Doesn't sound like it, Jegudiel." Billy laughed, but his satisfaction was weaker now; a heavy knot had formed in his chest.

So, I did what she wanted. But by then, I could see her for what she was. A harpy. A liar. More evil than even I.

"No! Let me go to him! Please, Billy!"

Billy shook his head. "No, you will listen." He felt the angel's pain, and his chest tightened further.

Jegudiel gave a loud sob as she turned back to the mirror.

So I built a failsafe into her plan. I made the child she wanted—I made you, Anastasia. But I conjured my freedom in your blood. She never knew. I ensured your existence would give me the ability to start over. To be human again.

"No, Stephen, no!" She clutched at Billy's arm, and he found that instead of using his hand to force her to face the mirror, he was squeezing comfort into her shoulder.

When the Tipping Point comes, daughter, your blood will transform me to human. I will live again as a man. I will no longer be owned by her. I will be free… free to lead a good life… and when I die a natural death, I will beg and pray my way to Heaven.

Jegudiel screamed. "He is supposed to lead the demons to victory over this Earth. To rule where God has failed. I was giving him ultimate freedom."

"He never wanted it, love." Billy spoke softly, no longer needing revenge. Justice was moments away.

"He was all I had, Billy. I held my Faith in him." Her tears were falling, but her tone remained proud. Overhead, the lightning bolt slashed the sky. It surged through their land, and onward to the plane below.

"It's here," she said in a tiny voice. "The balance is gone." The silence hovered for a moment between them, and in the distance, they heard the bolt hit the Earth with an ear-splitting crack. "And I have nothing."

42

JUSTICE

SOREN HIT THE CAVERN FLOOR, sliding the last few feet in a spray of gravel, just as lightning tore the darkness apart. Billy's mojo had transported him to the hillside just moments before she'd arrived. The burn from the angel's icy touch on his forehead still smarted.

He'd stayed hidden, crouching behind a large rock outside, watching as Bello's goons escorted Anastasia to the cave, and she'd dropped into the darkness. It was all he could do not to leap to her aid. But Cuinn had been very clear: the Abbot had to be human for their plan to work. Soren had to wait for the transition before he could get her clear and kill him.

So, he'd waited. Long enough to see that crows and jackdaws had gathered above him and were now staring silently down into the cave entrance, tracking Anastasia's steps as surely as he.

Soren recovered from the slide only to be knocked off balance again as lightning cracked through the centre of the cave, and hit both Anastasia and her father.

The energy caught her up in a vicious hum that drowned out her surprised scream as she flew and smashed against the wall to his right, sliding down the scalpel-sharp rocks to the floor.

Scrabbling to her side, Soren put an arm around her to heave her up. "I'm here now."

Eyes wide, she clutched at him. Warm blood soaked through the back of her shirt, slick on his hands as he heaved her up. *Get up,* he urged silently, his own muscles straining. *We have to be ready!*

Whimpering, she pulled his head down and whispered so close her lips brushed his ear, "He'll become human... any time now." She looked from Soren to her father, who had landed twenty feet from her and was just stirring.

She'd fared better. His left arm hung loose, dangling at an odd angle just above the elbow. He dragged the broken limb toward him with his other hand and held it gingerly across his chest. Yet, he didn't cry out. Nor did he acknowledge Soren's presence.

Instead, his expression was rapturous. "It's time, daughter." Still gripping his arm tight, he pushed his shoulder against the wall to lever himself up and headed over to the rock. The blast had created a deep fissure, reopening the passage to Hell below.

As the Abbot approached, a snaking pillar of fire rose from it, swirling and twisting its way through the centre of the cavern and high to the cave entrance.

The heat scorched Soren's throat and his lungs contracted as the flames sucked the oxygen from the air. A sound like a scream erupted from it as it roared upward, and a moment later, the stink of burning feathers drifted down from the entrance above. *The birds.*

While Soren and Anastasia pressed against the rock walls, clutching onto the coolness that remained, the Abbot seemed pulled towards the column of fire.

Already the heat whipped at his clothing and hair, sending

remnants of singed fabric flying upward to the night sky. He put up a hand and dabbed at the whirling haze, groaning ecstatically as the heat itself, not flame, scorched his flesh. The skin on his fingers blackened and bubbled.

"He's going to kill himself." Her voice broke, and she grappled to free herself from Soren, but he held her tight.

"Let him. He will be reborn, and once he's human, I can kill him. Heaven will deal with him. That's Cuinn's plan." Holding her with one arm, he removed the rifle slung over his neck to be ready after the transformation was complete.

"No, you don't understand—" She wrestled against him again, trying to get free.

"You can't save him—"

"I don't want to save him," she hissed. "I want to kill him myself."

Her words pulled him up short.

In all the time she'd suffered at his hands, she'd never once voiced a desire for his death. Even when they had killed him together less than a year ago, it was to enable him to get to Hell. To his freedom. She'd been carrying out his wishes, not her own. Why revenge now?

Besides, Cuinn had trusted him with this job—

I need this from you, man. That bastard needs to die. He killed my family. Take him out, Hux. Kill him, and I'll stand with you if you ever need it. No questions asked. I can't trust anyone else with this.

"Anastasia, listen! If he dies before the transformation, he'll go back to Hell, ready to be fished out by the Advocate or some other entity again. It won't be over—"

"But if he comes back human then we kill him, he'll go to Heaven! That's what he wants Hux—he told me. He'll be a fresh new soul waiting for judgement. They'll free him—an innocent—they'll have to. And then we would give him the exact thing he wants. He'll never suffer, Hux, not the way he made me suffer! I need revenge."

Fire burned in her eyes. Whatever the Abbot had just done, it had pushed her past some ultimate limit—further than a century and a half of cruelty ever had. It had tipped her over the edge.

Soren pulled her closer and shouted in her ear over the roaring of the flames. "It has to be this way. Heaven will not judge him as innocent, Cuinn says it's taken care of. Your father has to be reborn for the Advocate to be destroyed—she has to see it—or she'll live, and the cycle continues. The mission is to kill two enemies, not just one."

"No!" This time, she pulled free of Soren's arms and threw herself at her father. The blistering air blasted against her skin, savage red wheals dancing over her forearms and cheeks until she put up her arms to protect herself and stepped back.

"Goodbye, daughter. I will return to you…" The Abbot called over the roar of the flames and stepped forward, dropping out of sight into the fire.

Soren pulled Anastasia further back from the fire in case, for one stupid moment, she meant to follow her father down into the hole. He stood between it and her, offering protection from the flames.

"Let me go!"

"No."

Even a few months ago, her strength would have sent him stumbling. Now, her fists beat against his chest with desperate, failing force. He absorbed the blows and continued to push her back from the fire's edge.

The heat did more damage than she could do. The skin on his back burned, blisters appearing, bursting, and healing over and over.

He pulled her away urgently, seeking a spot to shield her from the vicious effects of the furnace. As they reached the safety of the wall again though, the fire serpent suddenly withdrew, sucked back down to Hell below. Its job was done.

Transfixed, they watched the place where the Abbot had disappeared. Above them, the storm had gone, the Tipping Point over. Now, the only sound was their laboured breathing.

Within seconds, a pure white hand reached up from out of the fissure, then an arm, then the other hand. Bit by bit, the Abbot pulled himself out of the hole until he stood naked in front of them.

He looked the same age as before, but his hair was now a uniform black, with no grey streaks, and his skin was pristine. Unblemished and unlined, it glowed white and luminous in the moonlight that filtered in from the cave entrance above. His arm was healed. He held it up and stared, examining each part of his body in wonder, his eyes round, a smile dancing on his lips.

"I am human again, Anastasia. Human. The magick I conjured in your blood renewed me. Hell spat me out!" He opened his arms wide to her, grinning stupidly. "Come to me, child. Celebrate with me. We can be a family now. Leave the running of this world to them—the monsters outside. Be humans together."

Impassive, Anastasia turned to Soren and held out her hand. "Give me the rifle. At least let me kill him."

He hesitated. "You deserve justice, Tazia. Justice. Not revenge." He kept the gun lowered at his side. "Believe me, killing him is not the answer."

"Give it to me!" Her eyes flicked wildly to her father again. His lips moved in some quiet prayer, giving thanks for his resurrection, no doubt. "I want to kill him… All the things he's done, Hux. All the pain. All the things he made me do!"

"I know… but—"

"But nothing. Give me this. Give me revenge. He created me just to serve him. I exist for this." She waved an arm at her father. "Only so he can live."

"I know…" He spoke gently to her, "But, he's your father.

Believe me. If you kill him it will stay with you forever. It will scar you—your soul will be lost."

She pulled at the rifle, desperate tears flowing. "Let me do it. Please!"

Still caught in the wonder of his return, the Abbot's prayers echoed around the rock chamber, sounding almost musical.

Anastasia rubbed at her cheeks. She was exhausted. Black shadows darkened her eyes, her cheeks hollowed and bones sharp.

Soren wanted to take the pain from her. "Let me do it. I'll get you justice."

"No!" She tugged at the rifle again.

This time he let her take it. "Can you live with the guilt of this?"

Her face set, lips clamped together. She turned and raised the rifle.

The Abbot stopped praying, confusion clouding his eyes. "Daughter?"

Soren continued, "I haven't been able to live with it…"

She hesitated, gun raised midway to her shoulder. "What?"

"Tazia, I killed my father. In cold blood. I killed him…"

She dropped the nose of the gun a little. "You killed your father?"

Soren nodded, "He murdered my mother, so I killed him to —" he shrugged "—to get my revenge. I was only a boy, but I knew what I was doing. And I killed him. The guilt still eats at me. I get no rest. And you won't either."

Slowly, her arms lowered, and the weapon hung loose between her hands.

"You don't need to be the one to do this, lover." He gave her a half smile. "It won't work, anyway. If you do it, he'll always be in your head. You won't be free." His voice was raw. "That last look he gives you. The last breath you see him take.

It'll be there, every time you close your eyes. He'll always control you with that look. Don't let him win."

She stared again at her father, his fierce eyes holding hers. Her whole body sagged.

The Abbot's joy at his rebirth appeared extinguished now, too. "You will come to me, girl. Obey me. Now! Serve me as you were born to do."

Soren saw a little light spark in her eyes. She winked at him.

Then, turning back to the Abbot, she giggled. The sound circled the cavern, playing with every crevice, every shadow. "You haven't changed one bit, father. As evil now as then, even as a human with a brand new shiny soul. Heaven will not welcome you. And I will not go down with you." She held out the gun to Soren. "Do it!"

"Sure?" He said.

She pushed the rifle further into his hands and raised her voice. "Do it, Hux. Do it for me, do it for Cuinn. Do it for you. Put the monster down."

She gave the order. Casually rubbed the dust from her knees, then walked away to start her ascent up the ramp that would lead her from the darkness into the moonlight.

A thought flashed through his mind. *This is the end.* This moment is what Jacob had foretold: he was here at the start, and now at the finish.

Without ceremony, Soren lifted the gun and fired at his target. The shot pierced precisely the same place as the first had done all those months ago, straight between his eyes.

The Abbot fell to his knees, staring after his daughter's receding form.

Before he hit the ground, a lightning bolt blasted from the clear night sky. It shot through the opening of the cave, hit the walls and bounced to the Abbot's body, burning it to a crisp in an instant.

At the same time, an otherworldly scream sounded in the sky high above them. The note held strong for a painfully long moment, then faded into a low, anguished moan.

As the sound receded, the walls of the cavern cracked, and the precariously balanced rocks began to loosen and fall. The floor under Soren's feet violently vibrated. He spotted Anastasia bounding up the rock ramp, dodging the falling rubble, until his view was lost behind the curtain of debris that tumbled down around him.

He threw himself back against the wall of the cave, hoping for some protection. It seemed this cave was determined to kill him. Dropping to his haunches, he put his arms up over his head, sharp shards of quartz raining down on him—

A hand gripped his wrist.

The little light that still seeped into the cave from the entrance above reflected off the crystalline rock particles that covered Anastasia's body, illuminating her form. *She's here. She's glowing.*

She pulled him up and grinned a dust-covered smile at him. "Come on, lover. Let's get out of this fucking cave."

———

As she watched the Abbot's death through the mirror, the Advocate used the dregs of her strength to scream her pain into the ether. And with the cry, something inside her broke.

Billy felt it—the angelic energy that had fired her for centuries. The remains of what had passed as a twisted Faith, just… gone. Her plan had failed.

Jegudiel moaned her loss, then gasped for breath, forcing oxygen into her lungs as best she could, but there was nothing to hold it there, no hope. The air slipped away again. She looked at Billy. "I'm dying?"

Yes," he whispered. "He betrayed you, Jegudiel. And now he's dead."

That was all it took. He watched the light in her eyes fade, the very essence of her unravelling. It was exactly as Cuinn had said: *Angels are sustained by Faith. It's the engine that drives them—their heart. Sever an angel from the source of their Faith, and you sever them from life.*

A second way to kill an angel. And far crueller than any blade.

She relaxed into him, resting her head on his shoulder, and put a hand in his. He kissed the top of her head and stroked her long red hair. He only hoped to comfort the dying angel who, at one point, had served the same God as he.

Two short breaths later, and she was gone.

He didn't move until her physical body had faded away. Then he was clutching the amber light of her angel self, and still he didn't let go until that too had finally dissipated into the universe drop by drop, and his arms were empty.

He sensed nothing left of her. No consciousness, no memory. Just a quiet return to the Source like a billion specks of starlight into the dawn.

Exhausted, Billy headed out to pass on the news—one of God's angels was no more. But the other angels already knew. Their voices raised around him, sharing his howl of pain.

43

───────────

AFTERMATH

CONN O'CUINN SAT on the battleground surrounded by the corpses of well over a thousand vampires. The rays of morning sun eased over the land, beating the darkness away, and each body in its path smouldered. Soon, the entire field would be lit with the fiery remains of the Leeches.

Tears stung his face. Joyful tears. It's over. *It's fuckin' over.*

He remembered little of the battle. It was almost with regret that he felt the change come over him. Those last moments of his usual self, a demon, yes. An animal, no.

For a little while, he'd been able to stand back and observe, just long enough to see the fear in the eyes of the vampires closest to him as they realized what their fates would be.

Then he looked out through blood-red eyes, and the overwhelming buzzing of bestial energy surged through his body. Suddenly, he couldn't wait for it. Desperation to rip through their flesh and taste their blood. Conn O'Cuinn faded.

He'd dropped his shotgun and fallen to his knees, talons forming on his fingers and sharp fangs in his jaw. The rest of his physical form remained the same, but he wielded it differently.

He held his body like an animal, slashing and biting, jumping through the air, and using his weight to roll his victims to the ground. He'd chewed through their necks or pulled out their hearts with bone-strong claws. No other weapons needed.

How long had it taken to clear the battlefield? Minutes? An hour? More?

The other Soldiers had also transformed. Kevin, by his side as always, had been the first to turn, and bounded off to chase down the vampires that were still harassing the people by the cliff edge.

When all were dead, they had slunk away to revert to their usual forms in private, dragging a body or two with them to consume and replenish their energy after the change.

But he'd stayed, slowly shedding the beast and becoming Conn O'Cuinn again. Alone. Surrounded by the dead.

It was a victory here, but he needed to know more.

Radios buzzed. News reports dripped through. A mud-splattered runner from the battle just five miles away arrived to report their triumph.

It was the same everywhere; the Soldiers had turned against their Leech "comrades" in overwhelming numbers and slain them, each demon following orders perfectly. It didn't matter what brigade or unit they belonged to, just like the Demon War before this, the Soldiers had answered the call.

The pride lumped in his throat, and the tears dried, replaced with a smile. *Family. Feckin' family!*

Most of the humans had escaped, and for that, he was relieved. Some had picked up discarded weapons and used them against the Leeches. Their efforts killed few outright, but slowed them down long enough for the Soldiers to finish the job. Most had clutched their wee ones to them and run for safety.

They would recover soon enough, and the balance would

again fall the other way. The Tipping Point reversed. *The way it should be.*

Still, he sat in the mud and blood. The soft crying of loss around him, the freshening breeze, blue above, and no birds. Already the sky had emptied of them annoying little feckers.

He couldn't leave yet, had to wait for news of the Abbot. He'd seen the second bolt of lightning, heard the scream, but still needed more. Had Hux done the job he'd trusted to him? Was his family's murderer dead?

He'd wait here all day if he had to, surrounded by the stinking smoking corpses of these animals, just waiting for that news.

Without a fanfare to announce his arrival, the air in front of him winnowed and a tall, thin man appeared.

He wore his long dark hair tied back with a black satin ribbon at the nape of his neck, and leather battle armour over a simple white tunic. If Conn had seen sandals on his feet, he thought he might puke, but his footwear was a solid leather boot.

On his shoulder perched a sparrow hawk, its feathers sleek and grey as storm clouds. Conn knew the breed; it was a warrior's bird, much like the one he'd once trained. This one, however, was unnaturally still, its sharp yellow eyes fixed on him with a cold, unwavering intelligence.

The man looked around at the smoking remains of the vampires and nodded, a sedate smile on his face. "You did well."

"It was a feckin' rout, man."

"Yes, I was watching."

"But didn't want to get any blood on yerself?"

"Not this time, Conn O'Cuinn."

Conn shook his head. "For sure you're a sneaky bastard, Ezequiel. Get everyone else to do your dirty-work for you. Always been the same, so you have."

"Didn't you get what you wanted? What we agreed?"

"Depends. Is he dead?"

The angel smiled. "Yes, the Abbot was killed by Soren Huxford. His soul has already taken flight and is awaiting judgement. And your Anastasia is free."

Conn sighed. Years of emotion and frustration eased from his body. The plan—this plan—had taken so long in coming to fruition.

It had been agreed on another battleground, one just like this, when he'd gripped the bodies of his wife and child close to him, that he would have revenge for their murder.

Then, Ezequiel had asked for his help. He'd asked Conn to protect a child—his enemy's child—to be born three centuries later. It was the same deal that he'd presented to Billy: to live his life in ignorance of his promise until the moment when he would be needed.

Tazia would have two guardians: one, an angel, and the other, a demon.

That first time back in Detroit, he'd not recognized her. Sure, he'd felt a connection, even seen it with his Core when it walked inside her, but he'd thought it was his old enemy calling to him.

That still didn't explain the responsibility he felt for her, though. That wasn't revealed until Conn hurtled to Hell at Hux's hand.

The Red River washed away more than his life. It destroyed the angelic magick that had locked away the secret of his agreement with Ezequiel, and finally, his memory cleared.

By pulling him out and setting him on a fresh path, the Abbot inadvertently signed his own death warrant, and Conn would have the revenge he craved.

The plan had been beautiful.

"And did you get what you wanted?" Conn asked him.

The angel nodded. "Jegudiel is gone forever. William did his job well."

"Then our agreement is done, man."

A weak blue light rose around the angel as he faded away, but for a moment he shone strongly once more. "What will you do about the girl?"

"Tazia? Nothin'. She's human now. She should be with a human man, not an old Soldier like me." He smiled. "Besides, if she chooses him, Hux needs her. He has a fair way to come back from."

"And you Conn O'Cuinn. What will you do now?"

"Get the Leeches back where they should be. Drive them all underground again. Then I'll drink a fine bottle of whiskey, find me a nice girl, and sing some of the auld songs!"

He grinned. "I'll be grand. I'm home."

"Good. I will listen for your singing. You are the best of your kind, Conn O'Cuinn. Good luck to you." He faded away, his presence replaced by the roar of flames as the vampire corpses ignited and the battlefield burned.

Conn watched the fires, a wide grin spreading across his face. He was home.

"Sure," he murmured to the rising sun. "I'll be just grand."

———

Soren gazed around the penthouse, finally feeling a little reality creep back into his body. The black leather sofa still squeaked under his weight, the alarming photographic shoe studies still gazed from the walls, and he'd just used an opener in the shape of Dracula's mouth to prise the top from his bottle of Stella. All was good.

Billy had shazamed him and Anastasia back to London, diverting briefly to Las Vegas and Detroit to pick up scattered belongings, including her Bowie and his rifle. Cuinn had stashed them safely in the lockup in the Irish Club. Billy now sat sprawled beside him, while Anastasia occupied one of the chairs, resting her feet on his knees.

"Is *shazamed* your new word?" she asked Billy.

"I'm trying it out. More politically correct than 'mojo'."

Once the news from Ireland was confirmed, they were planning a trip to a Soho club if they could find one open. If not, Thomas had declared he'd "dance in the bloody street." He sat on the back of the sofa, his feet on the cushions on either side of Billy's back, and had already put on some old acid house tracks to get them in the mood.

Like Billy, Soren had dressed in a suit, glad to get out of combats for the first time in weeks, and was enjoying the softness of the fine grey fabric next to his skin. Billy's was blue —upcoming London designer—the cut slim and tight. The material was sharp, some sort of sueded linen by the look of it, and Soren couldn't resist running his hand over Billy's leg to appreciate the quality. It had earned him an appreciative wink from Billy and a raised eyebrow from Thomas.

Anastasia saw the look and spluttered a laugh into her beer.

He grinned at her.

She swam in a tracksuit borrowed from Billy's sports supplies; the waistband rolled and the pant legs turned up, but somehow she made the baggy grey fabric look like couture. They'd shared a shower together when they arrived, a quiet, careful space where they'd washed away the blood and muck for what he hoped would be the last time, making a few decisions of the "let's see how things go" kind.

Afterwards, he'd doused her body in her healing skin oil, carefully rubbing it into the burns and grazes from the cave. Her hair still danced around her head at a crazy angle from the hack job, but when he'd told her it looked cute, she'd beamed. Or maybe, she could wear a sack, and he'd still think she was the most incredible thing he'd ever seen. For now, he had hope to sustain him. That was enough—

"Tom, get your feet off the leather, you peasant," Billy grumbled, but there was no bite in it.

Thomas just laughed and leaned down, wrapping his arms loosely around the angel's neck from behind, resting his cheek on his. For a second, Billy stopped fidgeting. He leaned back into the embrace, his hand coming up to squeeze Thomas's forearm.

Soren watched them for a moment, and found himself smiling. They looked solid. Unbreakable. Whatever happened next, those two had already won.

He risked yet another look at Anastasia.

One day?

The chime from the PC interrupted his thoughts. Joshua's face appeared, looking more frayed than usual.

"Dudes," he said, his voice crackling. The imaged glitched, pixelating for a second. "It's… man, it's done."

Billy jumped up and fiddled with the settings until the image settled, and the sound stopped jumping.

Anastasia straightened up, her face pale. "Cuinn? Is he…?"

"He's fine, Taz. Covered in blood, but little of it his. He's home. Says he's staying in Cork."

Soren felt a knot of tension release in his shoulders. Glad his brother was alive. Sure. But also glad he was staying away. They all needed time. He reached forward and squeezed Anastasia's hand. "And the battle?"

Joshua's face glitched again. He seemed to struggle to process the data. "Total carnage, dude. I… I jumped from body to body just to stay close. The kids… so many little kids. I saw parents… they were jumping. Straight over the cliff. Just to keep the demons from getting them... Soon as the lightning hit, they turned. Those Cores… they're savage. The vamps didn't know what hit them. It was fuckin' destruction, just like Cuinn planned."

He fell silent, and the picture snapped off.

Billy fiddled with the settings again. Looked at the others. "It's not the tech or the signal. His energy. He's overwhelmed. We forget Josh is human."

The mood in the room plummeted. Anastasia's grip tightened on Soren's hand.

The computer pinged again, and the picture flashed back, steady now.

"What about the other cities, Josh?" Billy leaned forward, his expression serious. The others hadn't checked in yet.

"Same everywhere. I jumped to Dublin. Aideen and Jacob held it with some serious heavy-duty glamour spells from the covens there. The Leeches were so confused they were easy pickings when the Soldiers went postal. They're heading to Boston as soon as the airport opens."

"Cork though, dudes…" The image stilled and buffered. "The angel helped, though," Joshua's image cycled again. "Looked like he gave Cuinn serious closure."

They all stared at the screen. The word hung in the air.

"Angel?" Soren asked. His first thought was of Jegudiel. He glanced at Billy. "But the Advocate is dead."

Billy nodded, his eyes narrowed on the screen. "What angel, Josh?"

Joshua approximated a shrug. "Some bloke. Tall, long dark hair. Good-looking dude… showed up right at the end."

"Ezequiel," Billy breathed.

Soren remembered the motel. Cuinn's comment: *Other stuff too, but we'd be here all day.* "I knew he wasn't telling us everything. Did they look like they knew each other?"

"Well, they weren't snogging if that's what you mean?"

Thomas snorted at Billy's shocked expression. "Angels do kiss, babe." He winked.

"Ezequiel doesn't! He's way too… perfect!" He turned back to the computer. "Seriously, Josh…?"

"They looked… familiar."

The room was quiet for a moment.

"Anyway, I can't see Cuinn leaving Ireland for some time. He's doing the whole St. Paddy thing with the snakes and shit."

They all looked at him in confusion until he added. "You know… only not snakes… Leeches. Chasing them from the country. Christ, you don't know your mythology?"

"Not well enough, obviously." Billy glanced up at the King James Bible gathering dust on the shelf. He looked back at the others and shrugged. "Present from Julie. I guess I should read it at some point."

"That's probably the most ironic thing I've ever heard." Anastasia got up from the sofa and went to the fridge to get more beers. She set to pulling off the tops, then passed them around. She raised her own. "To Cuinn."

Solemnly, they all repeated the tribute and slurped from the bottles.

"So, where do you two want to go after clubbing? I'll shazam you anywhere." Billy grinned at them.

"Turin?" Soren asked her.

"Yes, please. I want my purple chairs and my flowery wallpaper."

Soren groaned. "But after more beer. I need a bigger buzz."

"That was the last." She indicated his bottle.

"Beer run?" He pulled Anastasia up from the couch to leave. "Is it legal to shazam drunk?" he asked Billy.

"Always with the humour, Hux."

"I'm funny. You just miss it." Soren brushed a kiss on Anastasia's lips. Still holding her hand, they started for the door.

"Bruv, your jacket." Billy picked up the suit jacket Soren

had left on the sofa and threw it over to him. He caught it deftly, folded it up, and draped it over his arm. As he did so, a crumpled business card flew out of his pocket and fell to the ground.

Anastasia released his hand to pick it up. She read it, then glared at him. "Who the fuck is Sowilo Skye?"

———

The End

AUTHOR'S NOTE

The *Dark Urban Rising* trilogy was my first published work in 2017, then slightly updated in 2019. I had several novels hidden in desk drawers (or more accurately, stashed on old laptops) but had never felt my stories were ready for an audience until *Fighting Spirit* was born.

In 2025 I decided to review and improve the trilogy. My writing skills had improved and I felt that finally I could represent the stories in the way I first envisaged. The rewrites were an act of indulgence, but I'm glad I took the time. I hope you are too.

—S M Henley, January 2026

Here is the original Author's Note from 2017:

Thank you for reading *Raw Deal*. I hope you enjoyed it. And I hope you enjoyed the whole trilogy.

So what did I learn with this novel?

This was like bringing up that third child, you let them have a lot more freedom. The other two had proven that despite my worst fears, they didn't run into the first moving vehicle, or tumble from the tree, so I let it evolve a lot more naturally.

The opening to this novel is my favourite of the three. I think I managed to get a bit of a classic noir feel to it in places, too, which was very exciting for me.

And then there's Soren Huxford.

Like Billy, I've always had a bit of a thing about "a cross between a denim-clad cowboy and a tall Viking warrior." Unfortunately, I never met one in real life, so ta-da, I made one up!

I just loved writing Soren, though I did put him through hell, at times it was almost too painful to watch. I've got a feeling he may have another appearance at some point. So if you loved him as much as me, watch this space.

It was also great to get Conn O'Cuinn back in the mix. I missed him.

When he left the story at the end of Book 1, I got my first hate mail from beta readers! Bringing him back was an act of self-preservation as much as it was because he still had story to tell. Though, the Ezequiel twist at the end was one I didn't plan out, so hey, more surprises.

So we move to the adventures of Ms. Sowilo Skye in the next series. I'm really looking forward to writing her. There will be five books, and then we shall see where she goes from there. There are a lot of stories she could tell but five will complete the first arc.

If you want to find out when *Dead Playboy* will hit the shops, keep up to date on https://darkishfiction.com/, or sign up on the website for news as and when it happens. But it you'd like a sneak preview just turn that page!

Always in darkishness,

S M Henley

PS We haven't quite finished with any of the characters from the *Dark Urban Rising* trilogy. Tazia, Billy, Conn, and Soren, are all getting the prequel treatment with their own standalone novellas. Some key Easter eggs will be explained! Watch the website for news.

And—should I tell you? Well, okay. You twisted my arm…

Joshua may just have a role in a future series. But he will look *very* different.

EXCERPT FROM DEAD PLAYBOY
1. ONE LAST FISH BREATH

Triple espressos are hazardous at any time of day, but knocking one back late on a Tuesday night in a sleazy Vegas cafe, full of juiced-up bankers and plastic sex workers, has a certain foolish bravado. The danger isn't in the locale or the patrons. It's in the way the bitter liquid strips your tongue dry and peppers the back of your gullet like bullets from an AK-47. But in the words of the great John Lennon: "Whatever gets you through the night."

Swallowing the last drop, I drummed perfect scarlet fingernails on the side of the cup and waited for the pain. It was preferable to staring at the bent head of the young man sitting opposite me, waiting for a reply to the question I'd asked five minutes ago—

Oh yeah, there it was: a blast of sweet caffeine blistering at my temples. Alive and kicking, for sure. After a thousand-some years on this planet, I tended to wonder.

While the bitter heat flooded my system, and the kid fiddled with his tsunami-proof dive watch—it had probably cost the same as my Merc—I squinted around the place. The harsh lights above the table were more blinding than even the multi-coloured neon that spilled in from the Strip outside.

Why the hell had I agreed to meet in this dive? It wasn't my usual style. Not a glittering chandelier in sight. No sign of the sweet rum cocktail that permanently hummed my tune, and no guy in a tux tinkling on a lounge piano. This place had fluorescent lights, terrible coffee, and an emo kid painted in full make-up and dressed in a long black trench coat, singing an a cappella version of "White Christmas" in the corner. Not only the spring heat made *that* weird.

The one thing to recommend Red's Bean Shack (yes, that's really its name) was that the off-duty police officers hunched over the tables seemed uninterested in the dodgy deals being struck all around them. They sat in silence, in twos and threes. When not gazing into their own versions of life-giving brew, they constructed little sugar-packet pyramids. If a miniature toppled over, a sigh rippled through them all, leaping from cop to cop, table to table, in some sort of sweet psychic connection.

The recent demon risings had taken it out of our brave law enforcement community. Last winter's human victory saw their ranks drastically thinned. Demons viewed police souls as tasty entrées.

Despite their disregard, these guys made me jumpy. Potion-infused id badges swung from their necks, making them immune to my multiple charms, magick or otherwise. That left me on the back foot. Not to mention the police-issue revolvers that come out to play far too often for my liking. Guns make me tetchy.

My companion risked a look at me, then zipped his eyes back to his watch. (I swear he'd only ever worn it in the shower.) He was testing my patience.

Entertaining this boy was a favour to his father. He'd insisted: "The kid needs some confidence, Sowilo. Make him feel special. But he's got to learn—don't make it too easy!"

He hadn't told me his son had the attention span of a goldfish.

Stifling a sigh, I twisted my coffee cup in its saucer to check what shade of lipstick stained the chunky white porcelain: Crimson Harlot. Each night it started as the colour of my profession. As I zeroed in on my client's requirements, it transformed. Tonight, the familiar colour comforted me: I half expected Black Cherry Death Kiss to match my mood.

My impatience bubbled over, and I snapped the question a second time. "So, do you understand how this works?"

"Erm…"

He didn't even look up.

"Justin!"

He jerked his head up to face me, wide-eyed. "Can you, erm, explain it again, please ma'am?"

Ma'am? Seriously.

Once again, I launched into the spiel I gave all the men looking for the same thing: love, companionship, titillation occasionally a step over legal.

He listened intently. Grinned. Dropped the smile when I frowned. Then, nodded seriously, before ruining his composure by giggling.

This time I did sigh. The boy was exhausting.

It's fair to say my clients were usually a little more experienced in the ways of the world. They understood the hustle of a negotiation, certainly knew the value of my shapely behind, and could definitely grow more than bum fluff. "How old are you again?"

"Twenty-one…"

"Really?"

"Erm." He squirmed in his seat. "In a few weeks, " he said, and blushed almost purple.

At twenty-one—sorry, twenty—he was still a little gawky. He shifted his shoulders within the confines of the Cucinelli suit, which looked just like daddy's, and attempted to pull down the cuffs to disguise the sweat glistening on his palms. The cracks in his ego leaked a stench of too much cologne and a private school education. While the fragility of his young soul sang a warning lullaby. With one wrong word, it would split and cascade at my feet.

On the instructions of his father, I hadn't deviated from my usual pantomime. I'd singled him out at the nightclub a couple of nights ago, smiled and flirted, before dropping my business card in his jacket pocket while the rest of his baby-faced entourage looked on in stunned silence.

It was a full twenty-four hours before he'd called and stammered his suggestion we meet here. He believed this was a date, bless him!

"Okay, I'll go over it again." I said and started the explanation from the beginning.

When I got to the end, he still had a look of screwed up anguish about his features.

"Maybe, I'll just show you," I said.

"Okay." He glanced at the exit.

Would I have a runner? That hadn't happened since seventy-three. Eighteen seventy-three.

"Give me your hand." I stretched my own toward him, and managed a half-smile, tempered with a touch of sternness.

By now his eyes roved my face, trying to probe behind my disapproval. I could feel his mind ticking over, reaching for the course of action that would please me—probably a technique he'd perfected for his mother. It was working, too: wide-eyed innocence sucking me in. I'm not a total robot.

He put a nervous hand into mine.

Good job, kid! Now we're getting somewhere.

Despite impatience raising my blood-pressure faster than the mercury in the hundred-degree heat, I couldn't help liking the kid, so I rewarded his bravery with a proper smile.

He stopped giggling and returned one with a touch of promise to it. Stirrings of the man he would become. As usual, it was my job to get him there.

At his touch, the energy shifted between us; his soul quietened, and his heart sang. Just a Joni Mitchell sort of whine at first. Then, gathering confidence, he smiled again, and Joni turned into Alanis's little sister.

"Do you feel it?" I asked.

He gripped my hand more tightly and flicked his head with sudden street confidence. He said, "Yes, ma'am. I believe so." But his attitude was like: "Yeah, bitch. I got you down!"

It was all I could do not to smirk in his face.

But whatever the flavour of this energy, it did the trick. He'd made the connection work and now images brewed between us.

Using my charms is not a slick magic trick. There's no sleight of hand or distraction, no reading of expressions or hand gestures. It's about stretching my awareness toward my target. We make contact, and the charm is released with my energy: the heat of my skin, the look in my eyes, or the feel of my lips on theirs. They are left helpless. Their hearts open, their desires are revealed to me, needs sometimes hidden from even themselves.

I sifted through the images I received from the boy. His heart's desire swam into view: a girl, brunette, super cute. But I needed more, so I floated a gentle breath toward him, sweet and invisible—a ruffle in the air—yet he felt its caress and shivered.

His excitement intensified just enough, and the picture got clearer.

The girl danced in a nightclub with her friends, the music pounding, lights illuminating her curly chestnut hair with strobes of blue and pink. Compared to the others, her clothing was demure: a dark blue dress with a flared skirt that grazed her knee, like something out of a fifties movie. I liked her style. The wide boat neckline balanced precariously on her shoulders, revealing smooth skin over delicate bones.

And then it hit me. The thing that got him excited. Why she was so special. She was just a promise. More than sweet and sexy. Her innocence marked her just out of his reach. And, oh God, how that made him want her more!

I needed to adjust. My smile was too sinful: red lips too slick in the heat of the overhead lights. I felt them dull to Sweet Virgin Rose. He saw it, too, and his eyes widened.

The hook was baited.

"You don't have to tell me what you want, Justin. I can already taste it." I would usually run the tip of my tongue over the edges of my teeth, but for him that would be too much. Even licking my lips would have been too... foxy. Instead, I gave him a shy smile. "I can see your longing as clearly as the cup you're gripping onto."

The boy squirmed and let out a little ragged breath before replacing the cup he'd been white knuckling on the table. A few more beads of sweat popped on his forehead, but he didn't take his eyes off me.

Time to reel him in.

For another few minutes, I talked, keeping my voice low, not wanting to spook him. "That girl in the nightclub last year. She still keeps you up at night, doesn't she? Was it her hair? Those curls had a life of their own!"

I let my smile morph into a replica of the one the girl had given him that night, and sensed my long red hair bounce up into darkening ringlets. A deception. An enchantment.

"Wow! Your... your... hair, and your... smile! They're changing!"

"To your eyes only. That's how it works. I know what you want, and so I give it to you. You don't even have to ask."

I traced a finger with now muted rose-painted nails down

the side of his cheek, tickling. The magick strengthened and a wave of Taylor Swift's latest fragrance rose from me. It caught thick in my throat. So wrong for the girl. But as her scent hit him square in the face, his eyes closed a little, and he sighed.

He was mine now.

"So, Justin. Do you want to come with me?"

He nodded—mouth dropping open and gasping one last fish breath.

I stood up. "Okay, let's grab an Uber. We can talk money on the way." All business again, I picked up my phone and flicked to the app.

"Anything... I'll give you... anything." He pushed himself to his feet, wobbling slightly.

"Just what a girl likes to hear!"

And he would, too. Give me anything I asked for—they always did. Shame this one was at a discount. I'd already agreed on money with his father. I liked to keep the good Doctor sweet; he had a certain *Goodfellas* way with the Vegas PD that kept them off my back.

As I finished ordering the car, and before I could put it away, my phone rang. "Hold up, Justin." I put a gentle hand on the kid's shoulder to stop him wandering off down the street, still lost in a love-sick daze, and checked the caller.

The screen declared, Mr Fabulous, and a picture of a grinning young man in aviator shades and razor thin cheekbones flashed underneath.

I held it to my ear. "Freddy?"

Freddy's voice whispered, "Sowilo... Help me... I'm... burn..."

Justin was lost in a daze of curls and sweet perfume.

I wasn't.

All I heard was the roar of a fire.

Freddy's whisper.

And then the scream.

THE SPOIL HEAP

The Spoil Heap is not a newsletter. It's an introduction to the things you missed. A round-up of what I've already dragged to the surface of **The Midden**, along with a look at what's still buried.

It's there for those with the sense to ask. Just give me an email worth using.

—Digger

https://darkishfiction.com/sign-up

New subscribers receive *Bleeding Ebony* by return. Consider it a first round, on me.

ACKNOWLEDGEMENTS

My gratitude goes to:

My editor, Mary Matthews, for her commitment to pickiness and sheer force of will; to Kieran Clynes for his ongoing support, and for living with the characters this long; to derangeddoctordesign.com for a kickarse cover; and, finally, to Rick Gualtieri for his words of blurb.

And, of course, to you wonderful readers for giving a new author a chance!

ABOUT THE AUTHOR

S M Henley was brought up in an English seaside town singing to Echo and the Bunnymen and worshipping Siouxsie Sioux. She now lives in rural Alberta, Canada, with more pets than people, where everyone is friendly, winters are long, cheese is bright orange, and the occasional moose wanders through her yard.

Her writing spans Urban Fantasy through Horror. The UF is darker than average. It dips a toe into Dystopia and splashes blood freely. The Horror is a little darker and is written under the pen name, Ellis Marsh. Still paranormally themed, characters run from flawed to freaky, blood is optional.

ABOUT DIGGER

Digger introduced himself after the first trilogy was written. He now tends bar and watches the signs.

He knows more than the Author, but not too much more. He writes **The Midden** and curates **The Spoil Heap**.

Learn about the author and Digger on the website: https:// darkishfiction.com

ALSO BY S M HENLEY

Available now in digital and paperback versions, the complete *Dark Urban Rising* trilogy:

Book 1 - Fighting Spirit

Book 2 - Hero Worship

Book 3 - Raw Deal

The Dark Urban Rising Box Set (the Complete Trilogy) (ebook only)

And the prequel novella (ebook): *Bleeding Ebony*. The story of Tazia's time at Her Majesty's Pleasure in 1995. Only available with newsletter sign up.

———

And from the continuation series set in the *Dark Urban Rising* world just after the Tipping Point, *Skye Quest*:

Skye Wolf (a prequel novella) (ebook only)

Book 1 - Dead Playboy (coming soon in ebook and paperback)

———

For synopses and purchasing information and to keep track of new releases, visit: https://darkishfiction.com